P9-DWS-214

THE ROSE THRONE

THE ROSE THRONE

BY

METTE IVIE HARRISON

EGMONT
USA
NEW YORK

EGMONT

We bring stories to life

First published by Egmont USA, 2013
443 Park Avenue South, Suite 806
New York, NY 10016

1 3 5 7 9 8 6 4 2

www.egmontusa.com
www.metteivieharrison.com

Library of Congress Cataloging-in-Publication Data

Harrison, Mette Ivie, 1970-
The rose throne / Mette Ivie Harrison.
p. cm.
Summary: An ancient prophecy hints that the kingdoms of two princesses
from rival lands, one with magic and one without, will be united under one rule—
and one rule only.
ISBN 978-1-60684-365-9 (hardcover) -- ISBN 978-1-60684-366-6 (electronic book)
[1. Magic--Fiction. 2. Princesses—Fiction. 3. Fantasy.] I. Title.
PZ7.H25612Ros 2013
[Fic]--dc23
2012024692

Printed in the United States of America

Book design by ARLENE SCHLEIFER GOLDBERG

FOR CANDICE

Chapter One
Ailsbet

"PRINCESS AILSBET, your father demands your attendance at court this morning," said Duke Kellin of Falcorn, bowing. He was King Haikor's new favorite, looked hardly older than Ailsbet, and was dark-haired, tall, broad-shouldered, and handsome in a dark sable cloak over a silver-embroidered tunic.

"You will give me a few minutes to prepare myself," said Ailsbet. It was a request, though she spoke it as a command.

At sixteen, Ailsbet was of marriageable age, and it was time for her to build an alliance that would be of use to her father. Since she had shown no neweyr, the magic of life that bound women to the earth, and was past the age of developing it, she was now considered unweyr. The well-born unweyr were occasionally used as ambassadors to the continent, where others would suffer deeply without weyr, but that was unlikely in Ailsbet's case. Her father would want to use her marriage to strengthen his own seat on the throne, as well as her younger brother Edik's claim to it in time.

"Your father is anxious to see you. It would be wise for you to avoid his displeasure," said Kellin in the careful accent of the palace itself, more southern than northern, the harsher consonants smoothed out. What his true accent was, Ailsbet could not tell.

Was there true concern for her in his eyes? If so, he was the first of King Haikor's noblemen to see her as anything other than an oddity. Ailsbet knew she was no beauty, for she looked too much like her father. His red hair was fading now, and his skin had grown coarse, but Ailsbet still had the bright flame of color around her face, and her fair skin was dotted with freckles. She had the king's arresting nose and nearly his height, taller than every other woman at court by at least half a head.

"And do you think I am wise?" asked Ailsbet. The

duke could not possibly be as bland as he seemed, always agreeing with her father, wearing somber clothing in comparison to King Haikor's elaborate court costumes. She wanted to know who he was, behind his pointed chin and correct demeanor.

"Wise? Your Highness, I think you are your father's daughter in every way," said Kellin.

"In every way?"

"Your Highness, I serve your father," said Kellin.

"Only my father?" asked Ailsbet.

"In truth, I serve the kingdom of Rurik," said Kellin, his eyes distant, as if he saw something far off in his mind, something bright and perfect. "I serve an ideal, of safety and protection to all the people within the borders of our land. I serve the king, who has done much to ensure that security. But more than that, I serve the future of our kingdom."

"And does my father not call me to him now because he believes I will help secure the future of Rurik?" Ailsbet asked. She often watched with detached bemusement as her father's lords jostled for position. In recent months, some had dared to hint at an offer of marriage for Ailsbet despite her oddity; others mentioned a sister or daughter who might be a bride for Edik. But soon there would come a time when it would no longer be a game, and a choice would have to be made by the king. Was today that day?

"Your brother, Edik, is the one who will secure Rurik's future as heir to the throne," said Kellin. Edik was twelve years old and had already shown a small measure of taweyr, the magic of death and war, which male animals and humans shared with the forces of the world itself. Since men developed their weyr later than women, Edik would have until he was eighteen to prove himself fully capable of taking his place in taweyr, and then he would be named the official heir to the throne.

Ailsbet felt a fierce, burning surge of anger at Kellin's dismissal of her place in the kingdom. She turned away from him, not wanting to show her feelings.

"I require a moment to myself," she said.

"Your Highness—" Kellin said, and then stopped.

Ailsbet itched for her flute. When she was angry or agitated, her music could bleed the feelings from her. She closed her eyes and thought of an old, familiar lullaby about a child and a bluebird.

"Princess?" Kellin said.

"What is it now?" she asked, opening her eyes.

"Your Highness, your brother—" said Kellin.

"I know my brother is the one who matters, not I,"

said Ailsbet. All her life, Ailsbet had been told that her father had sacrificed for the kingdom, that her mother did, that she must.

"Perhaps not now," said Kellin.

He said no more, though Ailsbet waited to hear him elaborate on that comment. Perhaps he meant she must in time produce an extra heir, in case Edik's children were not sufficient?

"Give me a moment," said Ailsbet again, and retreated to her inner chambers to examine herself in the mirror.

There were spots of red standing out on her cheeks, as if she had a fever. She dipped a cloth in cool water and pressed it to her face. What man would want a woman who was so tall and strongly featured? Who did not have the neweyr to speed the growth of plants or enhance the birth of animals? Who was not as his mother and sisters were, and could have only a distant conversation with other women about such things?

Only a nobleman who planned to spend his life at court, where the neweyr did not matter at all, would value a marriage with her. Only a nobleman who would never care for her personally, but for what she brought him in political connections.

Ailsbet had known all her life that her father

would choose her husband for his own reasons, and she would be yoked to a man who did not love her. She would bear it, not for the sake of the kingdom, but for her own dignity. It would be foolish for her to imagine that she would find happiness in her marriage.

She turned away from her reflection and reached onto her shelf for the carved wooden case of her flute. She wished she had time to play it now. Few people with the weyr seemed to appreciate music, but it was the one thing she did well. She meant to bring it to court to remind her father of her rare gift.

Holding the flute in its case, Ailsbet left the inner chamber and walked with Kellin down the steps of the Queen's House, where all the women of the court lived. They passed through the muddy court-yard, where guards practiced with their taweyr and swords. Ailsbet could smell the anger and sweat in the air, and the sound of the swords rang in her ears like badly played music.

The courtyard was empty of greenery, the mud a dull-grayish black. Small stones were thrown down every few weeks to give some traction, but they quickly disappeared into the mud. In the distance was the river Weyr, and Ailsbet could hear the ships coming into port from the continent, the groan of the timbers and the shouts of the men. She could see the tops of buildings not far from the palace, though none was higher than the King's House, which was built from fine black stone and red oak brought all the way from the northern end of the Weyr, nearly at the land bridge to the other island.

At the entrance to the King's House, Ailsbet and Kellin stopped in front of the guards. They stood in front of the enormous, strikingly white door, twice as tall as any man, carved with the face of King Haikor himself as well as the stag that represented the kingdom of Rurik. The guards nodded as Ailsbet announced herself, then allowed her and Kellin inside.

The Throne Room had a high ceiling and red-and-black stained-glass windows looking out onto the Tower Green. Her father had had the windows made at the same time that he had replaced the old wooden and dirt floors of the palace with marble. On the walls, there were still a few ancient wool tapestries showing the kingdom's history, but more often the wall hangings were the colorful, new silk imports from Caracassa, a kingdom many days' journey to the east across the ocean. Her father's heavy taxes in weyr and gold ensured that his nobles were limited to the less expensive trade from kingdoms on the continent to the west of Rurik, a few short miles across the water.

The throne was the only object in the room that was original to the King's House. Too large to move very far, it was made of ash and carved all over with intricate roses. It was the same throne that King Haikor's father had sat on, and his father, back generations until the beginning of the kingdom of Rurik nearly one thousand years in the past. The legend was that the wood itself had come from a tree that had stood at the juncture between the two islands, and had been the last place where the two weyrs had been held together before the islands split apart. Ailsbet thought that was fanciful, but the throne was certainly impressive. The seat was as high as most men's shoulders, and upon it, her father towered like a giant over anyone else at court.

Ailsbet approached the throne a step behind Duke Kellin.

"Duke Kellin, my thanks," said King Haikor as Kellin knelt before him. The king wore a grand black leather robe over top of his elaborately slashed coat. His thin legs, clad in hose, seemed incongruous compared to the rest of him.

Every time Ailsbet saw King Haikor these days, it seemed his girth had increased. He wore the gold crown of Rurik, with the great black sapphire in the front, surrounded on all sides with rubies, and by diamonds around the back. Underneath, his thinning hair was turning gray.

Her mother, Queen Aske, sat at the side of the king on her own throne, smaller and less impressive than her husband's. It was carved of white birch, with delicate, spindly legs. She wore a gown of faded red, and while it might once have been beautiful, it was now out of date and stiff at the seams. The queen held her head erect and her back straight. Everything about her posture was perfect, and in her bones there remained the lines of beauty that had been present when she had been crowned queen. She often excused herself from court, but the fact that she was here today seemed to lend credence to Ailsbet's assumption that she would hear from her father that she was to be betrothed. Edik was too young to be forced to court when there was no need for him there.

"Princess Ailsbet, greetings and welcome to court on this auspicious occasion," said King Haikor formally.

Ailsbet curtsied, focusing on keeping herself calm. A betrothal would change many things, but it would not change everything. She would still be princess, and still her father's daughter.

King Haikor gestured to Earl Deiderik of Wilfors, a young nobleman who stood at his side.

The earl was ambitious, thought Ailsbet. He was blond and handsome, with a strong chin and fine eyes. His teeth were straight. But there was nothing else about the man that she found attractive. Whenever Ailsbet had spoken to him in the past, he had always seemed to be hinting at some coarse joke. He was also a man who was known to be continually in debt, and therefore not the first man she would have thought her father would choose for her. King Haikor's lavish style of living had caused the crown to fall deeper into debt over the last few years, and the king had mentioned several times that a noble-man's wealth might make him a better candidate for Ailsbet's husband.

The earl of Wilfors grinned at Ailsbet, leering crudely.

Ailsbet cringed, but her father either did not see it or did not care.

King Haikor nodded, and the earl went down on one knee before him.

"You willingly offer a double tax of the taweyr?" asked King Haikor.

Ailsbet heard an audible murmur throughout the court as Deiderik nodded his assent, and she herself was shocked speechless. A double tax of taweyr was the stuff of legends, given by the old heroes in the time just after the two weyrs were split, but it had never happened in living memory.

King Haikor officially collected taxes twice a year, in both coin and taweyr. The neweyr could not be gathered in the same way, and he would not have done it in any case. As for coin, tax collectors went about to each district in the kingdom, but the taweyr had to be paid personally by each nobleman. Ailsbet had never seen a man die from the tax, but she had seen men faint and have to be carried from the room.

In this way, King Haikor made sure that his lords were not strong enough to rebel against him, as they had against his father, who had taxed taweyr only once a year. King Haikor's father had put down three bloody rebellions in his lifetime, each of which had nearly destroyed the kingdom. Haikor had not had the same difficulties, because he had proved himself far more ruthless than his father, and at an early age.

The king leaned down and put his hands squarely on Wilfors's shoulders. The man jerked suddenly and then let out a slow hiss. The air in the Throne Room grew warm as a bit of taweyr leaked out from the exchange. Ailsbet could see some of the nobles moving closer.

Vultures, she thought. She felt no particular sympathy for Wilfors, who must have thought her father would reward him for his sacrifice with his daughter's hand in marriage and a close relationship with the crown. Ailsbet knew her father better than Wilfors did, it seemed. The young nobleman would be dead soon, and then what? She would go back to waiting for her father to decide her future, knowing that at least one man had died for her sake.

King Haikor threw back his head. He looked as if he were in ecstasy.

Ailsbet glanced at her mother. Queen Aske was turned away from the king, as if embarrassed.

Wilfors began to rock back and forth. There was a smell like burned hair that filled the room.

Suddenly, the king pulled his hands away and Wilfors fell to the floor. Ailsbet was surprised to see that he was still alive. He opened his eyes and glanced at her, lips twitching as if to speak. Did he think he had triumphed?

"He overreached himself," said King Haikor. "And he has his reward. Is there anyone else here who dares to put himself forward to take my daughter in marriage and challenge my son for his place as heir?"

The Throne Room was dead silent. No one breathed or moved.

King Haikor clapped his hands to call for his servants. "Take him away," he said. "Throw him into the river."

The tidal river would take away the rest of Earl Wilfors's taweyr. If by some miracle he survived, he would surely know better than to come back to the court. But looking at his lax body and rolling eyes, Ailsbet did not think he would last a moment.

"Now, onto the true business of the kingdom," King Haikor said. "Princess Ailsbet."

Ailsbet stepped forward and met her father's eyes directly. He liked that in her, though few others in his court could get away with the same.

"I am here at your command, Your Majesty," said Ailsbet. "But first, if it pleases you, I would like to play my flute for you. I have been working on a new piece, which Master Lukacs left for me before he returned to Aristonne. It was written four hundred years ago on the continent."

That should prick her father's pride. When young King Haikor was newly come to the crown, Prince Albert of Aristonne had crossed the ocean to challenge him. With a force of ten thousand men and the claim that the islands had always belonged to

Aristonne, the prince had nearly taken the palace. But King Haikor had used the taweyr against him and the Aristonnians had no magic of their own, though they believed their superior numbers would be sufficient to conquer the taweyr. Twenty years later, King Haikor still delighted in proving that Aristonne was the inferior of Rurik in every way.

"Four hundred years ago?" said the king. "Then I shall hear it. Do you play it well?"

"Listen and you will be the judge," said Ailsbet. "If it is not well played, you may send me away and tell me never to bring the flute into your presence again." She thought her father might admire her for daring to suggest this. This was her own game now, and she hoped she played it better than the earl of Wilfors.

"A wager is it, then?" said King Haikor, raising his eyebrows.

"A wager," said Ailsbet. She knew her father loved to gamble.

"Then play," said King Haikor.

"If you do not mind postponing the reason you have for requesting my presence in your court," said Ailsbet daringly.

"Let us see how well pleased I am with your

playing," said King Haikor. "Though all shall happen according to my own plan, as I am king of Rurik." Of course, he could not be seen to capitulate to his daughter in matters of state.

Ailsbet opened the wooden case and took out her flute. She closed her eyes. She had practiced this piece a hundred times perfectly, and yet each time brought a new twist. There were many people in this room, and that would change the sound, as would her own fears, which she could not completely hide.

There was no chance for her to warm up. The piece was nearly thirty minutes long, and she could also not afford for a single person in the court to become distracted or bored. It had to be surprising, delightful—perfection itself—to people who cared not a whit for music.

She began, softly, the first note rising slowly like the whispered flight of an owl in the night. From there, she lost all her self-consciousness. The anger she had felt before, with Kellin, slipped away, and she felt only the music. She became sure of herself, her hands moving gracefully, strong and delicate at once.

She let the music lift her, winging her way on the wind, over treetops, over freshwater, looking down on the world of cities and palaces. If the neweyr was like this, she could understand what it meant to those women who had it in abundance and could feel connections to plants, animals, and other women hundreds of miles away.

She could almost imagine that she could reach all the way to Aristonne, to Master Lukacs, who had been the anchor of her childhood until he had left four years ago. He had been stern with her, had loved her and complimented, chastised, and disciplined her as her parents had not bothered to do. She missed him desperately sometimes, and never more than when she played her flute. Yet she always felt happier when she had the instrument in her hand.

Suddenly, she was at the end of the song, the final delicate notes that had to be played with a haunting quality that would make them ring for days afterward in the minds of those who had heard them. She finished them and held tightly to the flute, her whole body spent and exhausted, her head bowed.

Then she heard one set of hands clapping. She lifted her head just enough to stare into her father's eyes. He was pleased indeed.

She knew then that it did not matter that the others in the court had not applauded. His reaction was enough. A moment later, the rest of the court joined in, as if they had intended to do so all along.

As Ailsbet curtsied to accept the applause, she saw

Kellin staring at her in surprised pleasure, the first real emotion she had ever seen on his face.

"So, Princess Ailsbet, high musician of the court of Rurik, you shall have your reward," said King Haikor. "What is it to be?"

Ailsbet bowed. "I thank you, Father. If you do not mind, I should like to spend a few weeks alone this summer, in peace." A last summer of freedom before she was betrothed.

"Where?"

"Wherever you should choose to send me," said Ailsbet. She had not gotten that far in her thinking. It only needed to be away from here, from him, and from the thought of marriage.

"Then I shall choose, and you will be informed in the morning," said King Haikor. A small revenge, this not telling her.

Ailsbet did not care. She nodded.

"Your mother will go with you, with the women she chooses," said King Haikor.

"Of course," said Ailsbet, who did not wish the queen and her ladies to go with her at all.

Ailsbet shifted her gaze to her mother. It was not that she disliked Queen Aske as much as she feared she would become like her, insignificant and power-less.

"And as for Duke Kellin, I have a special errand for you in the north," King Haikor added.

Kellin glanced up at the king. "Of course, Your Majesty. I am eager to serve you, as always."

"Come to me this evening, in my private chamber, and I shall tell you the details," said King Haikor.

Ailsbet, as well as the rest of the court, were left to guess at what this errand might be. Something to do with the land bridge? Or with Weirland itself?

Chapter Two
Ailsbet

*I*N THE MORNING, King Haikor sent a message to Ailsbet announcing that she would go to the south for the summer to visit Baron Bartel of Terrik on the coast of Hewell as her reward for her performance on the flute. Terrik was a nobleman not well known at court, and Ailsbet could not tell if her father meant to burden him with the support of the princess, the queen, and their entourage, or if the man was deserving of some honor that the king did not want to bother with in another, more expensive way.

In any case, three days later, Princess Ailsbet and

Queen Aske rode from the palace in separate litters, through the capital city of Skorosa, to the south of the kingdom. Ailsbet wished she could simply ride one of the horses that would be coming with them, but it was not considered appropriate for noblewomen to be seen riding in public, except on the rare occasions when they joined the hunt, so she was forced to travel by litter.

She could hear the sounds of wagons all around her, the natural music of voices in different accents from all the travelers who converged in Skorosa. The road was not quite wide enough for wagons passing abreast, and so they constantly had to stop and start as horses were maneuvered on and off the road. Were the king traveling himself, he would have demanded the road cleared for the entire day, ending any hope of commerce. But for the queen and the princess, such extreme measures were unnecessary. Ailsbet peeked out once to see a merchant beating a horse with taweyr as the animal whinnied its distress. She turned aside, sick at the noise and at her own interest in it.

This was the main road that led south from Skorosa, and it was far better, from what Ailsbet had heard, than the web of roads that went north in the kingdom to the land bridge and to Weirland. It took all of the morning and into the heat of the afternoon to get through Skorosa. In the later afternoon, the road grew quieter.

Ailsbet wondered if her mother would lean out and ask for a stop to rest, but she did not. Hot and bruised from the bumpy road, Ailsbet looked forward to seeing an abundance of neweyr at work in the countryside. She had seen paintings of what the south had looked like in her grandfather's time, and even generations before that, when the two islands were newly separated from each other. She had expected to see fields golden with wheat, to hear songbirds overhead. She had wanted to see the neat lines of cultivation, the deep, reddish brown of fertile fields, the green and white and yellow of growing crops.

The palace itself was so filled with taweyr that there was little greenery there. There were only patches of neweyr in the city, where women looked after small gardens. Most of the food for the populace and for the palace came from surrounding lands. But in the summer heat, as they went deeper into the countryside, Ailsbet saw men and women side by side, kneeling and tending crops by hand in dull black dirt that did not look rich or fertile. Ailsbet recognized wheat and barley but few of the other plants, and she was embarrassed at the ignorance this revealed.

Her mother ought to be touring the kingdom regularly to add her own neweyr to the fields or leading the ancient neweyr rites in spring and harvest season. But the queen had never been strong in the women's magic, and since King Haikor saw little use for it, she had done even less than she might. Beyond the crops, Ailsbet could see the trees drooping, bark shedding from their trunks. The animals looked wild and hard-eyed, some of them staring at Ailsbet as she passed, not tame, but uncaring.

Ailsbet wondered what sort of princess she was, that she could do nothing to help her kingdom. But because she was unweyr, the only thing she could do for her kingdom was to marry and produce heirs. It was a somber thought. She felt vaguely guilty that she had never even thought of coming this far from the palace before now. Her father took the court into the countryside on occasion, but she had not been invited with them and had always enjoyed the quiet time in the palace when they were gone.

At the end of the journey, late at night, Baron Bartel came out to greet the travelers and the queen with his pregnant wife and his five daughters. He had no son. As his wife greeted her royal guests, it was clear she was ready for sleep herself, so Ailsbet allowed herself to be shown to her room. The house had only two wings, and it was obvious that the guests had been given the larger wing, which meant that the baron and his family must be sleeping in the servants' quarters. Still, Ailsbet suspected that her own servants in the palace had sturdier walls than these and that their floors were not of dirt. She looked at the rushes that had been laid on the bed and could see ticks and other creatures moving around them. She shuddered and contemplated sleeping on the floor, but told herself that the creatures would be just as plentiful there.

Her mother knocked on her door, and Ailsbet was glad of the interruption. The queen looked old and tired, Ailsbet thought. The wrinkles around her eyes and mouth were deep and shadowed, and there was no ease in her movement.

"You think to escape your duty to marry," Queen Aske said. She was dressed for bed in a yellowed nightgown with elaborate lace and gathers on the sleeves and the high waist. It made her look bloated.

"No, Mother. At least, only for a little while."

"You are a woman. Unweyr or not, you must do what is necessary to keep your father strong," her mother said.

"Is my father so weak, then?" asked Ailsbet.

"He needs you, Bez," the queen said, using the diminutive that had been part of Ailsbet's childhood.

"I have said I shall do my duty," Ailsbet said.

"And after that?" her mother pressed. "Will you love him still?"

To have both love and obedience demanded of her seemed too much. "I am tired, Mother." She yawned deliberately.

"And so am I," said her mother. "More tired than you know."

The queen left Ailsbet alone then, to toss and turn through the night. She dreamed she was dressed in her mother's nightgown, walking the halls of the palace in Skorosa, but she must have been a ghost because no one heard her or paid any attention to her.

She woke early the next morning, relieved to find herself in her own undergarments. She put on an everyday gown of dark, serviceable cotton and, with the household asleep behind her, went to the stables for a horse to ride. As long as she was near the shore, she was determined to see the ocean. The southern portion of the river Weyr was tidal. The effect of its salt water on the weyrs was similar to that of the ocean, and those effects grew as the river cut through the last section of land to the coast. Ailsbet had heard of men being burned by a mere splash from the ocean, of women becoming barren after they had fallen into the salty sea. She knew of the way the ocean's storms tore at the weyr of any man or woman close at hand. For Ailsbet, of course, there was no danger in the ocean. It was the one advantage she knew of to being unweyr.

As soon as her horse was past the gates of the estate and onto the dirt road that led east toward the ocean, Ailsbet could taste the salt in the air. To her surprise, even before she saw the great blue horizon that stretched over the coast of Hewell, she could feel pressure, a darkness clouding over her. Her heart began to beat faster. Even from a distance, she could tell there was something malevolent in the ocean, something toothful and grimacing. She could hear it as a voice in her mind, taunting her.

But at the same time, Ailsbet could feel something pulling her closer. This was a different force, one that was like a song. It drew Ailsbet in with a beat of its own, slow and steady. It reminded her of the way Master Lukacs would play the first few measures of a piece of music for her to learn, before letting her hear how it resolved. She would beg him for the rest, but he would shake his head sternly. Only when she had played each section well enough would he play another few bars, and then another, until she finally knew the piece all the way to the end.

The dark gray ocean taunted her in the same way. Ailsbet dismounted from her horse and stood on the very edge of the red cliffs, looking down at the waves on the rocky beach below. As unweyr, Ailsbet had thought she would feel nothing in the presence of the ocean. Instead, it called to her and made promises of what it could give her if only she was willing to give up her home, her place, her very name. If she was no longer Princess Ailsbet, nor even Ailsbet the daughter of King Haikor, she could be—what?

Dead, for one thing, for she could not swim all the way to Aristonne. And even if she found a boat to take her, what then? On the continent, she would be hated for her father's sake. Even if they did not know she was princess of Rurik, people who knew where she came from would likely be terrified that she would use her weyr on them, whether she could do so or not. There were not many who had left Rurik to live across the sea in Aristonne or in the Three Kingdoms, but on the whole they did not prosper.

She almost fell to her knees from the pull of the ocean. Trembling, she did the only thing she could think of to restore herself. She put a hand into her pocket and drew out her flute, and played, harmonizing with the salt water.

It was a disjointed tune at first, for the ocean seemed angry with her, and it resisted her, singing anger when her flute sang peace, calling out hope when she played despair. But then she began to see the rhythm, and she could play with it. Sometimes she enjoyed the dissonance of playing opposite the ocean. Other times she turned around and caught it, like a parent snatching up a mischievous, flee-ing child. It was draining and exhilarating, and like nothing else she had ever done in her life.

She could hear the muffled sounds of her horse behind her. She had climbed off without tying it up, and it did not like the ocean. It had shied away but was afraid to go too far, and it paced back and forth, whining for her.

Suddenly, Ailsbet caught sight of a boat moving closer to the beach. It was too small to have crossed the ocean from the continent. It must belong to a larger ship that she could not see or to some unweyr trader who used it to move goods along the shore.

Ailsbet stepped back from the edge of the cliff, her hands on the flute going slack. She watched as a white-haired man stepped out of the boat and pulled it toward the beach with a rope. Another smaller, wiry man waited within the boat.

The white-haired man cried out suddenly and

began waving. Ailsbet followed the direction of his wave and saw a third taller and broad-shouldered man, and a young girl of perhaps ten years of age, hurrying down toward the boat from the other side of the red cliffs.

At first glance, Ailsbet assumed the two to be father and daughter, but as she looked more closely, Ailsbet recognized the man by his pointed chin and his long, forceful stride. It was her father's favorite, Kellin, the duke of Falcorn. He was not dressed in court clothes, but rather in the coarsely woven, dark-stained linen of the peasant class. And why was he here in the south, when he was supposed to be traveling north on a secret errand for her father?

Who was the girl with him?

Ailsbet slid to the ground so as not to be seen, but kept an eye on Kellin.

The girl stopped close to the ocean, moving stiffly, as if in pain. Kellin encouraged the girl to move forward, until at last she reached the boat and was hauled aboard. To the man on the shore, Kellin held out a bag that Ailsbet could see was full of coins, for it glinted in the early morning sun. Then Kellin turned and looked up at the cliffs. She lay flat against the ground until at last he headed back along the coast from where he had come.

Certain the man's attention was elsewhere, Ailsbet stood and turned back to the anxious horse. She felt cold, but she did not think she had been seen. She grasped the reins and wound them around her hand. But before she could mount, she heard the sound of barking.

She turned to see a pack of large black hounds running along the gentle hills of the south, and behind them a half dozen men in black cloaks whom she recognized as her father's ekhono hunters, closing on her.

Now suddenly the scene below her made terrifying sense. The girl must be ekhono, one of those who had been born with the wrong weyr. Because she had taweyr, not neweyr, the hunters were after her. But why had Duke Kellin risked his own life to save the girl? And why had he come so far out of his way to do so?

She thought quickly and realized that her father's ekhono hunters must be frequently on the roads toward the north, where the ekhono fled, and if the girl was from the south herself, it might have been faster and safer for her to take a boat directly from here to Weirland. Not safer for Kellin, however. As her father's favorite, Kellin was the last person she would have suspected of helping the ekhono. King

Haikor hated them and claimed that they were able to do terrible things to those with the proper weyr. If he ever found out the truth, Kellin would face a death sentence.

Ailsbet turned to the men on horseback, the ekhono hunters.

One of them, a man with a hulking upper body, strode toward Ailsbet. "You there!" he called out. Clearly, he did not recognize her as Princess Ailsbet, daughter of King Haikor of Rurik, his master. She had dressed hastily this morning and at first glance must seem more servant than lady.

"What is it?" she asked.

"How long have you been here? Have you seen anyone hurrying by? A man and a girl, perhaps?"

"No one," Ailsbet said.

The man threw back his hood and she saw that his head was shaved and covered with scars. Burns, presumably, from the many fires he had set to burn the ekhono, in accordance with her father's laws.

"I saw no one," she repeated.

He came closer to her. "Do not lie to me, girl. Tell me where this man went. He is a sympathizer of the ekhono and will be burned with the girl. If either of them should escape Rurik, the king will be very angry."

"I think you are trying to make me do your job for you," Ailsbet said angrily. "I told you I saw no man. If you know where he went, why do you not follow him? Perhaps I should be the one to send a message to the king, telling him that you expect women to hunt for you," she finished.

With a closer look at her face and gown, the hunter seemed to reappraise his initial assessment of her. He bowed and spoke more gently. "If you please, then, good lady. Have you seen anyone? A man and a girl, perhaps? Who might have looked suspicious?"

Ailsbet glanced over the heads of the hunters and saw a fox scurry by on the road behind. The creature stopped for a moment and glanced at her. It was as if she could hear its thoughts, not in words, but in feelings, fear and anger and hatred toward the hunters. And the lust it felt for life, for the females of its own kind, for the taste of fresh food in its mouth.

The anger Ailsbet had felt toward the ekhono hunters suddenly surged away from her, like an extra limb, growing and extending. She could feel it lurch toward the fox, but she could not stop it. Like a flame drawn by the wind, the heat of her anger encompassed the fox, which gave a cry of pain and fell dead on the ground.

Ailsbet felt a moment of cool relief, her anger

gone. Then her heart sped up in her chest. She felt a rush of sound in her ears, and she nearly fainted.

The lead ekhono hunter turned and saw the dead fox, then gave a whoop of excitement. "She must be nearby!" he shouted to his men. "This is her taweyr, surely. It is newly come to her, and she cannot control it. Spread out and find her!" Ignoring Ailsbet, he leaped onto his horse and led his men away.

Ailsbet was left with the sick realization that she, and not the young girl, had killed the fox. Which meant she was the one who could not control her taweyr.

The anger that she had felt so many times over the last few years, the same hot anger that had led to the fox's death—it had not been anger at all. It was the taweyr. It had always been the taweyr.

She was not unweyr. She was ekhono.

She had felt the fury of the ocean because it had tried to pull her taweyr from her.

But when had it come to her? Her mother had tried to teach her neweyr when she was twelve, to no avail. But many girls developed their neweyr later than that. Ailsbet had held out hope that she had neweyr until she turned sixteen, when even late-blooming girls would have shown their magic. But it seemed that she had followed the path of men, who came into their taweyr later than women came into their neweyr.

She felt a rush of sympathy for the ekhono, who were forced to flee Rurik for Weirland when they could no longer hide what they were. In Weirland, the ekhono were accepted, or at least tolerated. And before King Haikor came to power, the ekhono were part of Rurik, as well. They had been seen as different, but as useful, men who could speak to other men about the female magic, and women who could be warriors. There had been no need to burn their bodies to keep their taint from spreading, and no public burnings of those ekhono who were unfortunate enough to be captured alive.

Oh, there had always been stories about the evil that the ekhono could do, stealing weyr from others, tainting it. Ekhono women who killed their husbands on their wedding nights to feast on their magic. Ekhono men who disguised themselves in the clothes of the other sex so they could work in a noble household and take advantage of the women there. Ridiculous stories that Ailsbet had never believed, not even as a child. She thought them as likely as stories about the continentals who could fly through the air while singing and attack her father's men in the battle with Aristonne.

Even before her father's laws against them, the ekhono in the far reaches of the kingdom were sometimes killed by angry mobs, blamed for plague or illness, blamed for wives who had been unfaithful, for falling stars, for wishes gone awry, and even for disobedient children. But as far as Ailsbet could tell, throughout the history of Rurik, the ekhono had been law-abiding citizens, contributing to their communities in the same ways that those with the more common weyr did.

Now Ailsbet wished desperately she had learned more stories of the ekhono, true or not. She certainly could not dare to ask for them now, when even the slightest hint of the truth could end her life. As someone who helped the ekhono, Duke Kellin had a deadly secret, and that gave her power over him. But her own secret was far worse. If she were found out, her father would have no mercy. He would gladly stand and watch while she burned.

And after she was dead, he would do worse to her memory. Her name would never be spoken. Her mother and Prince Edik might be implicated in her disgrace. Her servants might be killed for helping her hide the truth, whether or not there was any proof of their guilt. The whole palace would be turned upside down as her father searched for other hidden ekhono.

Ailsbet mounted the horse and rode it back to Baron Bartel's estate. She returned to her bedroom, where she was lectured by Queen Aske about her responsibilities as a princess, and how she had worried everyone by leaving without a word. On a horse, the queen added, which might have thrown her and left her lying dead in a ditch somewhere in the vast countryside.

Ailsbet listened and said nothing, neither agreeing nor disagreeing. The queen might be stupid not to see the truth, but some part of her must know that there was something truly wrong with Ailsbet, even if she did not name it. For once in her life, Ailsbet was glad that her mother was not given to seeking the truth or to speaking it aloud.

At last, the queen left and Ailsbet turned to her flute for solace. But even music did not soothe her now. It could not change the truth of what she was, and the danger that would lurk at every turn, as long as she lived.

Chapter Three

Issa

*P*RINCESS MARLISSA OF WEIRLAND stood on the ramparts above the castle at noon, looking out on the craggy hills that surrounded her in all directions. Summer was waning, and soon Issa would use her part of the neweyr to bank the growth and fertility of the season, so that next year would be even more abundant than this one. But now, the neweyr of summer and life was at its height, and there was nothing in Issa's mind as beautiful as the land. She could feel the harvest plants growing fat and heavy, the warmth of the air settling deep into the black soil. It was as delicious to her as any taste on her tongue, as sweet as any imagined kiss.

"Issa, there is an emissary come from Rurik, waiting to speak to you in the Throne Room," said her father, King Jaap, coming up behind her.

"I am sure he would rather speak to you than me, Father," said Issa. Since her mother's death, she had taken the queen's place in guarding the neweyr. But she had not yet decided if she would encourage the distant cousin who was her father's heir to propose marriage to her. She had once considered marrying Lord Umber, whose lands were near the land bridge, but he had disappeared only a few weeks ago and was suspected of going to Rurik to give information to King Haikor. Whether he expected coins or new lands or a title for this betrayal, no one knew.

"His name is Duke Kellin of Falcorn. He is one of King Haikor's court favorites. He has come to offer a betrothal."

"A betrothal?" said Issa. Well, this would be interesting, at least. A duke of Rurik had never been to the kingdom before. In fact, Issa could not remember any official emissary ever coming from Rurik, only spies. She might have fun with this.

Issa climbed down and made her way to the Throne Room in the other wing of the castle. Before she entered, her father touched her arm and she turned back to him.

"I have sheltered you," the king said. "Kept you from your responsibilities as princess."

"I have been guiding the neweyr in my mother's place since I was eleven years old," Issa protested. "How is that sheltering me from my responsibilities?"

"Not the responsibilities of the neweyr, but the responsibilities of the throne. You are a princess, Issa, and it is time that you were used as one."

Issa still did not understand what her father meant, but she puzzled over it as he led her into the Throne Room. A man stood when they entered. He was tall, with broad shoulders and long legs. He was dressed in a long, thick, wool cloak that was adorned with pearls along the edge, and he seemed utterly untouched by the wear of the weeks of travel he would have endured on the journey here. It made Issa more conscious of her own worn tweed gown, the edges of her sleeves dirty from her work in the garden early that morning, the skirt with a tear to one side.

Issa glanced back up and saw Duke Kellin observing her every movement. There was a kind of arrogance in the set of his mouth and in the point of his chin. He seemed to Issa everything that she would have expected from a nobleman of King Haikor's court. He was younger than she had expected, but perhaps King Haikor had run out of older, more experienced men. It was said that his favorites died with a frightening regularity.

"King Jaap," said Kellin with a formal bow. Then he turned to her. "Princess Marlissa." He bowed again, and held out his hand.

Issa gave him her own hand. When he kissed it, the sensation was strangely cold. Did he think she would marry him because he was handsome and powerful in King Haikor's court?

"I come to you with gifts from King Haikor." The duke offered Issa a small velvet bag. "To match the shine of your eyes," he added.

Inside the bag was an emerald the size of a hummingbird's egg. Issa had never seen anything so valuable. Despite herself, she was impressed with the gift. King Haikor must truly value Duke Kellin, if he was willing to send such a gift to the woman Kellin hoped to marry.

Issa could have used her neweyr to reach inside the faint veins of life inside of the emerald and expand the flaws that lay deep within. It would crumble to dust in her hands if she wished it. But she resisted the impulse and instead glanced at her father to see if she should accept it.

King Jaap nodded, so Issa held the emerald in the palm of her hand, moving it this way and that to see the facets shimmer. It was beautiful indeed, and it was worth half the castle, she had no doubt. Kellin was handsome, to be sure, but she did not know if she liked the brooding look of his.

"And this," Kellin said, "to bring you the sweetest smell of summer even in the dark of winter." He handed her a tiny box, which, when opened, let out a strong scent of lavender. It was not soap, but a candle.

A gift from a man who knew nothing of the neweyr, she thought. If she wished to have the scent of any summer flower in winter, she could bring it up from the banked neweyr in the earth herself. She set the candle gently on the table.

"Finally, a gift from Prince Edik himself," said Duke Kellin, holding out a tiny metal figure.

From Prince Edik? Issa took the gift at her father's nod and held it up to the light. It was a female figure, dressed in a simple shift, holding a peace lantern. The details were exquisite.

"I thank you," said Issa politely. "I shall keep these gifts close to my heart." Though she did not understand why Duke Kellin had brought a gift from the king, as well as the young prince. Why would Kellin not bring something from his own estate, if he wished to offer her a personal touch?

"Perhaps you should begin at the beginning, Duke Kellin," King Jaap suggested. He took this all more seriously than Issa did, it seemed. "The princess would like to tend to all of the details of the betrothal."

Duke Kellin glanced at Issa. "Of course," he said. "I have come to offer a betrothal between you and young Prince Edik of Rurik, Your Highness."

And suddenly, Issa was no longer amused or puzzled. A betrothal with Prince Edik of Rurik? Her father might have warned her. She glanced at him and saw a hint of apology in his eyes. But it was her fault, for not thinking more carefully. Her father had been all seriousness. This was not a betrothal she could simply refuse out of hand. She dared not insult King Haikor, who had threatened before this to come across the land bridge and, with his superior army and taweyr, take Weirland for himself.

"Prince Edik is a child," Issa said, struggling to keep her voice calm. She knew that much of the ruling family of Rurik.

"He is twelve years old and will soon be thirteen," Duke Kellin answered. "He has already begun to show the wealth of taweyr that is his inheritance as the son of King Haikor, and his father believes that he is ready to be betrothed. Of course, the wedding will not take place until he is of age, at eighteen."

"Of course," echoed Issa. Though there had been stranger marriages than this one in the history of the two kingdoms.

"Your father has a portrait of the prince, which King Haikor also sent to you," added Duke Kellin.

At this, Issa looked up, and King Jaap passed her a miniature portrait, small enough to hold in the palm of her hand, the decorative wooden frame around it dwarfing the subject.

Issa saw a boy with dark hair and small features. She hoped that the grim expression was the painter's attempt to make him look martial, for it did not seem to fit the rest of the figure at all.

"He is every inch his father's son," said Duke Kellin, as if that were something that would sway Issa in the boy's favor.

In her own mind, Issa was glad to see that Prince Edik looked little like the descriptions of King Haikor she had heard. The king was supposed to be an enormous man, in height and girth, known in his youth for his red hair, though now it was streaked with gray. It was said that he was capricious, ruthless, very canny, and had not an ounce of loyalty to anyone but himself. How could she marry the son of that man, however unlike him? How could her father expect that of her?

She looked at King Jaap, but his expression told her nothing. "What else can you tell me of the prince?" Issa asked, turning to Duke Kellin.

"He is well mannered, a little shy of court as yet, though he is still young and will grow into his place. He reads widely and has a good hand. I'm sure you will see that when you receive his letters. He has already learned the elements of combining sword-play with taweyr and practices daily with the king's guard."

All these were things that Issa would expect the emissary to say about the prince and future king of Rurik. Duke Kellin could hardly say anything other than what would be complimentary, whether or not it was true.

"When would the betrothal take place?" asked Issa.

"On the first day of autumn in the new year," said Kellin. "That would give enough time for the preparations to take place, and for the negotiations to be complete."

In little more than a year's time, she would be betrothed to a thirteen-year-old boy? Issa could not imagine it. "And it will be in Rurik? Not in Weirland?" said Issa.

"Yes, of course."

Of course, because Rurik was the more powerful kingdom and because King Haikor would not allow anything to happen to his son that was not in his direct control.

"So I shall be coming to Rurik before the betrothal?" asked Issa.

"You will come next summer, so that you and Prince Edik will have a few months to become acquainted with each other."

Though by then the arrangements for the betrothal would be done. There would be no chance for either of them to change his or her mind.

No, this was the moment of decision. Once Issa gave Duke Kellin her agreement, there would be no turning back, no matter how she found the prince in person. If he was disgusting or mute or an idiot, he would be her husband even so. Because she was the princess, and in the end, she must do what her father asked her to do.

This is what he meant when he had told her he had sheltered her from responsibilities. Since her mother had died when she was eleven and Issa had come into her own neweyr, she had done everything she could to fulfill the responsibilities of the queen with regard to the neweyr. But Issa had always believed she might marry for love, as her father and mother had. Her father had hinted at the changes in Weirland's position as King Haikor grew more powerful and wealthier in his trade with the continent. He had allowed her to hear stories of the king's spies sent to Weirland to discover its weaknesses. But he had not come out and told her that she would be sacrificed to protect Weirland. He had waited until Duke Kellin had come to bring the difficult news to her, and she had no time to prepare herself for this.

"Will my father not come with me?" asked Issa.

Duke Kellin's eyes flickered toward her father. "King Haikor believes your father would prefer to stay in his own kingdom, to keep it safe."

Of course, King Haikor did not want King Jaap in Rurik. The betrothal and the wedding were to be all in his control, and King Jaap was not to be seen as a different sort of king to the example King Haikor himself presented.

"If you agree to this, Princess Marlissa, I can tell you of all the details at some length."

Issa nodded. It was not Kellin's fault that her father had not told her of the news he'd brought. "Thank you. I shall think on the betrothal and give you an answer on the morrow."

Duke Kellin bowed and departed.

Now Issa was alone with her father. "How long have you known?" she asked.

"King Haikor sent an official letter early in the spring," King Jaap admitted.

"Lord Umber?"

Her father shook his head. "He did not know if it."

"I suppose he will have plans of his own in Rurik. And I must accept the offer," said Issa. Did she want her father to treat her as a child again, tell her a comfortable lie instead of the real truth?

"There would be consequences if you insulted King Haikor," said King Jaap.

"Perhaps that is what he truly wants, to be given an excuse to invade us and take Weirland for his own."

Her father shook his head. "If he wanted to have an excuse to invade, there are easier ways of arranging it. No, I think he has decided that this is the easiest way to get Weirland. No more need for spies, no need to expend either armies or taweyr. Only his son."

"And your daughter," Issa put in.

"You cannot be king, Issa, but you can serve Weirland this way."

"You will make Edik your heir, then? He will be king of Weirland and Rurik?" The distant cousin who was currently her father's heir would be disappointed, but he had been waiting for years for King Jaap to remarry and have another child. He would not suffer from shock.

"He has the taweyr, and you do not," her father reminded her. "The throne needs to be held by both weyrs, you know that. Only one, and there would be an imbalance."

"That does not seem to bother King Haikor, who refuses to allow the neweyr to be used anywhere in his palace. Though his queen is not much bothered by the rule, since she has nearly as little neweyr as her daughter, so we hear." They were sharp words, and out of character for Issa, but she felt she deserved to be out of character just now.

"And that is another reason for you to accept the offer," said her father. "You can help restore the balance of the weyrs in Rurik, before the effects there are too strong to reverse, and before they touch Weirland, as well."

Yes, this was what she had been born for. It was all laid out for her now. Should she blame her father that she had not seen what was so obvious? He had encouraged her blindness, but she had been willfully blind. Perhaps that was the effect of her immersion in neweyr. She had spent all her life trying to see the connections between all living things. She could look out at the pink flowers that grew on the hillside and sense the sweet nectar that waited for the bees. She could sense the field mice quivering in the shadows of the castle, fearful of the hawk circling above. But she had not thought of what the kingdom itself needed, the balance of the weyrs.

"And then there is the prophecy to consider," said King Jaap.

Issa knew the prophecy. She had learned it as a child.

> One child will hold two weyrs.
> One child will hold two thrones.
> Two islands will be one.
> Or the sea will swallow all.

The prophecy was said to have been spoken by King Arhort on his deathbed, his vision of the future that would heal the breech of the two islands he had himself divided in his great grief after his wife's death. Issa did not know what kind of power would have allowed him to tear two landmasses apart, leaving only a small land bridge between them, but legend said this was also what separated the two weyrs. King Arhort had taken the magic of death and anger for himself, leaving the magic of life and growth to women.

"But it's just a rhyme," said Issa. "It's an old story, a myth." That was what most people even in Weirland believed now, though the prophecy had a stronger tradition here than in Rurik. Issa could not understand how it was possible that the weyrs could ever be combined or how the two islands, so long separated, could be literally joined again.

"It is real," said King Jaap. "And this may well be the chance to make it come true. A child of yours and Edik's would sit on both thrones. Perhaps that child would also have both weyrs, and would bring the islands together literally, as well as in name.

"Edik is young enough that he may still be molded," the king added. "Perhaps you may be able to do a little of that yourself. You may write to him over the winter if the betrothal is agreed upon. I imagine that will give him even more reason to be swayed by you."

"I always thought that I would remain here in Weirland all my life, as you have," said Issa. If she went to Rurik in the following summer, would she ever return home? She might for a short time, but she would only be a visitor then.

"When you arrive in Rurik, you must learn quickly the ways of Haikor's court. Women have power there, though it is not the power that you are used to."

She would have to begin all over again, making friends and allies. And it would be in a new court where she would be seen as the interloper. She would have to give up all thoughts of love. Because her kingdom needed her to do so and because she was a princess and had been born to be sacrificed for her kingdom and her people from the first. Her father had never forgotten that, even if she had.

CHAPTER FOUR
Issa

HE NEXT DAY, with a clear head, Issa could see the advantages of the betrothal. It would end the threats of war with Rurik and the constant fear of spies from King Haikor. The stress in her people's hearts would be decreased, and the neweyr would benefit, as well, since it could unfold more freely in the south, without the threat of invasion.

And even if the two islands were not magically combined as the prophecy promised, they would still be politically united. Weirland had suffered for years from the tariffs that the Rurese charged when goods were transported north. Because ships from the continent could more easily cross the ocean to the southern island of Rurik, the Rurese had almost complete control of continental trade that was shipped north over the land bridge. But all that would be ended if the two kingdoms were one.

Telling herself that she had not yet given up her place in Weirland, Issa went out to the tangled Queen's Garden, which lay in a far and private courtyard of the palace. She could always feel the neweyr strongest here, since both she and her mother had left paths of it in past years. This was where she had gone the day her mother had died, just before she had come into her own neweyr, when only the earth itself seemed able to comfort her.

Issa fingered a wilting pansy. She could withdraw the neweyr from it, letting it wither quickly and sink back into the earth, but she felt that it had beauty even at the end of its life, and so she let it be. She noticed the ivy growing near her window, and with a wave of her hand, directed it to remain at a height that would keep it from pulling down the white stones of the castle.

Putting a hand on the ground, she let her sense of neweyr sink down into the lower level of the dirt, beneath the upper layer of soil, below the bedrock on which the castle's foundation had been built. Each part had its own distinct taste of neweyr, the oldest parts darker and colder, the newer parts richer and fuller. Guiding the neweyr, Issa brought water up from an underground stream to saturate the dirt. Coming from this depth, the water was cold, which would stimulate the plants to prepare for winter. She enjoyed the smell of the decaying leaves, the neweyr floating off of them into the air to share with all the surrounding life.

When she looked up into the sky again, she realized she had spent too long in the garden. She had to prepare for her meeting with Duke Kellin. She hurried inside to dress.

Issa's maid used neweyr to coax her thick, curly dark hair into a single plait that sat low on her back. The braid was traditional in Weirland, the sign that a woman had come fully into her neweyr. Only a girl without neweyr wore her hair unbraided. But there were some women who wore many bunches of small braids, who looped their braids into elaborate coifs to mimic the court style of Rurik. For today, Issa would wear the simple style to show Duke Kellin that whatever happened with the betrothal, she would always be a princess of Weirland.

She wore her best short-sleeved damask gown, but added a shawl over it, for the castle could be cool even in late summer. The shawl had been knitted with neweyr in an elaborate pattern that echoed the braids the women wore. Issa had designed it herself, and she was proud of her work.

She went downstairs and found her father on his throne. It was made from a single piece of white sea-stone, shot through with threads of black and silver. They formed patterns that Issa had once believed would show her the answer to the prophecy, if only she looked hard enough.

Duke Kellin and her father were already there, waiting for her. Their silence was not a comfortable one.

"I am sorry to be late, Father," said Issa, head bowed.

"I shall explain any necessary details to you later, Issa, when Duke Kellin has gone," said King Jaap. "There is no need for him to waste his time with repeating what he has already said."

"My time is not wasted when I am serving you in any capacity, Your Majesty," said Kellin. "Though perhaps your daughter does not know how valuable the time of her father the king is."

"She is my only child, and the image of her dead mother. I have indulged her too much," said King Jaap.

Issa flushed, embarrassed that her father was forced to lower himself in the eyes of another kingdom's emissary. "I apologize to you, as well, Duke Kellin," she said.

"Clearly. I should ask King Haikor to send someone else to speak to you on this matter, someone whose company you would find less loathsome," said Kellin. "It would take some weeks for the journey back to Rurik and here again, but it could be done. King Haikor would want to ensure that you had no grudge against the man with whom you will hold such a deep obligation."

"No! I did not mean that at all," said Issa. "It was nothing personal. I was late because I was distracted with the neweyr in the Queen's Garden." She hated to admit a true weakness, but she had no choice.

"Yes? And does this happen often?" asked Kellin.

"I shall work hard to ensure that it does not happen when I am in Rurik," said Issa. To herself she wondered if there was enough neweyr there for anyone to be distracted by it, either in King Haikor's court or out.

"You will work hard?" said Kellin.

"She will make sure of it," King Jaap said.

"My own subjects appreciate my abilities with the neweyr," Issa said stiffly. How dare this duke of

Rurik come here, demand she marry the puny prince of his kingdom, and then tell her that she was not good enough as a princess?

"But Rurik is different than Weirland, as perhaps you might have heard if you had been here while I spoke to your father."

"I have said I am sorry and I have promised it will not happen again," said Issa.

Kellin took a deep breath. "Quite right," he said, and the tension seemed to melt out of him.

There was a silence and Issa knew that it was her place to break it.

"I shall agree to the betrothal," she said, and found herself looking for her father's smile and slight nod of approval.

"That is good to hear," said Kellin. "Well, then the official ceremony will be scheduled for the first day of autumn in the new year. I shall remain for a few days here in Weirland until I know all your father's needs with regard to the official documents," said Kellin. "King Haikor instructed me to tell you to bring a retinue of up to twenty women to the palace, as well as twice that many guards."

"I do not know how many guards my father will wish to accompany me." Twenty guards was more than he had for himself, even when he left the castle.

But Weirland was not Rurik. "I shall not need so many women, however. Perhaps five." It would be difficult for her to find that many, in fact.

Kellin's eyebrows rose. "Five for the princess of Weirland and the future queen of Rurik? Well, it is to be your choice."

The future queen of Rurik and Weirland, Issa thought to herself.

Kellin turned to her father. "Then we are finished, King Jaap."

"Wait," said Issa. "I had a question to ask you regarding Prince Edik. What does he love best? If I were to bring a gift for him, what should I bring?"

"I am sure that he would like anything that you would like to bring him, in honor of your own kingdom and yourself," said Kellin.

But she did not mean that kind of gift. Of course, she would bring official gifts from her kingdom. She meant a personal gift. "A metal soldier?" she hazarded.

There was a momentary twitch in Kellin's face. "He has a fondness for metal soldiers," he admitted, but it seemed it was with reluctance. He had brought a metal figure as a gift for Issa to Weirland. In Rurik, however, her presentation of Edik's gift would be public. It would be very different and the boy would not wish to be seen as a child.

"I might bring instead something that he will remember me by. A book of poems that I loved as a child?" said Issa.

"Yes," said Kellin politely. "I'm sure that he would like that." His eyes seemed distant.

Not a book of poems, then. "Or a hound that I have raised myself?" Issa asked. Must she continue to guess at what the prince would like?

"You raise hounds?" asked Kellin with surprise.

"With the help of my servants," said Issa.

"Well, then, a hound would be a perfect gift. Edik loves the king's hounds. I am sure he would like to have one of his own," said Kellin.

"Ah," said Issa. "Thank you!" Some truly personal information about the young prince at last.

Duke Kellin bowed and excused himself, leaving Issa once more alone with her father.

"I am sorry," she said again. All this time, her father had put up with her. She had not seen herself as petted and spoiled until now. "I did not mean to embarrass you in front of that man." She shivered, though she knew she would have to get used to him, and more than that, to King Haikor himself.

Her father put a hand on her shoulder. "You are

doing well, Issa. You have always made me proud of you, and I expect no less this time. You may even enjoy the court of Rurik. You have a bright mind. There will be so many things for you to learn there that I could never offer you here."

"I'd rather not learn them, then," said Issa. It was true, even if it was petulant.

"King Haikor is not the only man in his court," said her father. "There will be others who are as interesting as Duke Kellin is."

Issa did not like Kellin at all. He was arrogant, presumptuous, and he could only see the bad in things. Or at least the bad in her. "If by interesting you mean disagreeable," she said.

Her father laughed. "My only worry is that Duke Kellin is too honest and faithful a man to last long with King Haikor."

"He seems intelligent," Issa allowed. "But that does not excuse his arrogance."

"And so you would not mind seeing him die at King Haikor's hands, his heart stopped with taweyr on the Tower Green?" asked her father.

The thought made Issa feel ill. "Of course, I would mind that," she said. "I would not wish to see anyone face that fate, especially undeserving."

"Well, Issa, try your best to see that he is not

deserving of it. He may be your one ally when you arrive there."

Issa did not understand what her father meant. If she was sure of one thing, it was that Kellin was not to be her ally, here or in Rurik.

CHAPTER FIVE

Issa

THE NEXT DAY, Issa went to visit the ekhono, refugees who had come to Weirland from Rurik. They were housed past the courtyard, beneath the guardhouse beside the castle pastures, underground. Once, Issa had asked her father why he kept them hidden. He had told her that the purpose was to keep those who had newly arrived from Rurik safe. Otherwise, King Haikor's spies might find them and do them harm, even in Weirland.

It was cool and dark inside the ekhono refuge, with a deeply peaceful quiet that was one of the things that drew her back there often. Her father knew of her trips there and did not disapprove, and Issa liked it that the ekhono from Rurik did not treat her with the same caution and formality that her own people did.

The damp smell grew more intense once Issa entered the elaborate underground courtyard. Here, heavy sunflowers, black currant bushes, and creeping moss grew with neweyr drawn from underneath the ground. Light came in from openings cut into the dirt ceiling and candles placed at regular intervals along the walls. Within the refuge were nearly a hundred ekhono from Rurik. They typically stayed for a year or more. Once they could prove that they could use their weyr well, they were placed in homes around Weirland where there were those willing to protect the ekhono. Some married and had children, but most lived rather solitary lives and were unable to inherit property or to run a business without help.

In the courtyard, both men and women were sewing and knitting, cleaning skins and making boots. There were a few young mothers who had brought their children with them out of Rurik, playing and cooking food over a large hearth that vented upwards through a chimney. But mostly, the ekhono were youths and a little older, those who had come to Weirland to be able to show their weyrs freely. They were all familiar to Issa from her previous visits, except a man standing by Kedor, a bright youth whom Issa had met two years ago. She moved toward the man, thinking that he must have come recently to the refuge.

But when he turned, Issa realized it was Duke Kellin. He looked up at the same moment and seemed startled.

"Princess Marlissa," he said.

Issa glanced back and forth between Kedor and Kellin. She had not noticed the similarity between them earlier, but now that he was standing next to Kedor, she could see that they had the same dark coloring, the same pointed chin and sharp eyes. They were quite obviously brothers.

It seemed that there was more than one reason for Duke Kellin's journey to Weirland. Had he come before? If so, she had not seen him.

"Kedor," said Issa. She did not know what else to say.

"Good to see you again, Princess Marlissa. And this is—" Kedor began.

"She knows very well who I am," said Kellin, his chin lifted. "And now that you know the truth about my brother, what will you do with that information?"

"You may count on my discretion," she said,

determined to give a better impression than earlier in the Throne Room.

"Oh?" Kellin seemed dubious.

"I swear to you, I shall tell no one."

"Not even your father, who could use the information to force me to give him more favorable conditions for the betrothal?" asked Kellin.

Issa paused a moment, thinking how difficult it would be for Kellin to explain to King Haikor how King Jaap had managed that. "Not even him," she said. Why did Kellin have to think the worst of her at every step? She had not come here to embarrass him. She only meant to help the ekhono.

"Thank you." Kellin nodded.

"Your father says that it won't be long before I leave here," said Kedor, sounding happy. "I'm almost fully trained in the use of neweyr."

"Would you like me to show you the sunflower again?" asked Issa. She had done several lessons with Kedor, trying to get him to use the proper amount of neweyr for flowers, so they did not grow too large and rip their stalks out of the ground. It was one of the reasons there were so many sunflowers here, for their neweyr was tricky and hard to handle.

"That would be very kind of you," said Kedor.

"Do you know how many years he has been

waiting here?" asked Kellin, a sour look on his face. He did not wait for her to answer. "Nearly three, and there is still no place for him? It is hardly better than Rurik for the ekhono here in Weirland."

"In Rurik, your brother would be dead, would he not?" said Issa. "That is why you brought him here. And that is why you are able to come visit him."

"I visit him in this prison," said Kellin angrily.

"My father has his reasons for what he does. I'm sure if you asked him—" said Issa.

"You promised you would not speak to him of this. I am here as Duke Kellin of Rurik, the right-hand man of King Haikor. I cannot be known to have any connections to the ekhono."

Issa put up a hand. "I only meant that my father has reasons for what he does here in the underground. He wants to protect the ekhono, from their own untrained weyrs if necessary, but also from the people of Weirland who are unsure of them. There are far more ekhono in Weirland now than there were in previous years, and some are uneasy about it."

"Kellin, whatever you think of the king, I have heard many speak of the kindness of Princess Marlissa," Kedor interrupted.

Issa blushed at this compliment and turned to the young man. He would be very handsome in a few years, perhaps even more so than his brother. "You are so sweet," she said. "Thank you." She leaned over and kissed him on the cheek.

Kedor turned bright red. "Thank you, Princess Marlissa," he said. "I hope that you will rule many years after your father."

There was a silence and Duke Kellin began to laugh. "Kedor, think about what you say first."

Kedor looked at Issa, confused. "Did I offend you?" he asked.

"No, of course not," said Issa. "It is only—there might be more than one way to interpret what you said."

"I don't—" said Kedor, and then he went white. "I meant, when your father has ruled many more years," he added haltingly. "I do not look forward to his death, of course. I only meant that you will be a fine queen. Not that he is not a fine king. Nor that your mother was not a fine queen. Though I never met her, but I hear from others that she was much beloved. As I know you will be. Not that you are not loved right now."

"I cannot rule as queen alone," said Issa. It was apparent Kellin had not told his brother his true reason for being here, about her betrothal or about Prince Edik. "If I married my cousin who is in line for the throne, I might be queen. But it does not look likely now."

"I can't see why. Any man who met you would fall in love with you immediately," said Kedor. "I'm sure you must have lines of men waiting to ask for your hand in marriage."

Duke Kellin shook his head. "Enough, Kedor," he said.

The young man stopped. Issa could see a pinched expression appear on Kedor's face and she felt sorry for him.

"It is time for me to leave now," she said, suddenly aware that she did not belong here, that she was intruding.

"Please come back to visit again soon, Your Highness," said Kedor shyly. "For my sake, if not for my brother's. I think he spends so much time being agreeable to King Haikor that he has to save up his rudeness and expend it here."

Issa wondered how often Kellin had come to visit his brother, since Kedor had come to live here. How often could he make an excuse to get away from King Haikor's court?

"My brother is indeed the better of the two of us,"

said Duke Kellin. "He has always had an open heart and an open countenance."

"But I have not had your difficulties, Kellin," said Kedor. "You know that you would not have become like this except that you were trying to save me."

"Would I not?" said Duke Kellin. "It is impossible to know. But I don't think I was ever quite like you, Kedor."

"You are the survivor," said Kedor. "I would never have managed in your place."

"Oh? You might be surprised to discover how one can change, when one must. Your life was at stake, and the lives of all our people," Duke Kellin replied.

"The duke of Falcorn is not known to have a brother," said Issa, thinking aloud.

"I died," said Kedor, winking at her. "Three years ago."

"You look very well for being dead so long," said Issa.

"Thank you. I feel well for being dead so long."

Duke Kellin said, "He had an accident. On a horse."

"I was never much good on a horse," added Kedor.

"Then it is well that my father did not ask you to be a stable boy," said Issa.

Kedor smirked.

"You are not what I expected you to be, Princess Marlissa," said Kellin.

"Issa," she corrected. "And what did you expect? Claws and horns?"

"Quite the opposite. Clouds and sunshine. A girl who had never seen sadness and would be blown away by the first hint of a cold wind."

That was how he had treated her, and perhaps what she had deserved. She had acted like a spoiled princess. "I have faced winds," said Issa. Her mother's death, for one. And now, this betrothal with Prince Edik.

"I suppose you have. It is too bad for you and Kedor, though. He is already in love with you, I fear. You should have stayed away, and kept him safe from a broken heart."

"You are cruel, Kellin," Kedor complained. "You make me glad to be away from you for so much time."

It was not true, Issa thought. He obviously adored his older brother.

"Well, then perhaps I shall not come back," said Kellin.

"And perhaps I shall not miss you," said Kedor.

The two laughed together.

"He knows I would never leave him alone," said Kellin, turning to Issa.

"You could stay in Weirland, then," Issa offered suddenly. "And you would not have to be away from him at all." Her father would offer Duke Kellin refuge, surely, if he offered it to the ekhono. Or was she being the spoiled, naïve princess again to think this was possible?

"Rurik is my kingdom and I am bound to it, to King Haikor, and to Prince Edik," said Kellin.

"There are others who could take your place, surely," said Issa.

"There are not, Princess Marlissa," said Kellin coolly, moving away from her.

Issa left the courtyard moments afterward, conscious of the fact that in Rurik, she would not be able to express any concern for the ekhono, that they would not be visible at all if they were to survive there. In fact, her own life would soon be so changed she did not know if she would recognize herself.

Chapter Six
Ailsbet

AILSBET AND HER MOTHER had returned after six weeks in the south to find that the weather in the capital city had completely changed. It was chilly, often overcast, and autumn was well underway. For Ailsbet, all the pleasure she had imagined finding away from court was now eaten up in constant vigilance. She could not allow anyone to guess she had the taweyr, not even that she had a secret worth discovering. All her life, she had been skilled at putting on a mask, but now her skills were tested as never before. Perhaps it was good practice, she told herself. She did not speak often to the other ladies, and she knew they considered her arrogant and unapproachable.

While she was away, she had soon tired of watching Baron Bartel's wife and daughters and even her mother's ladies using their magic to brighten rooms with flowers or make elaborate hairstyles or braid weeds into rugs for the winter. They were quaint arts, and though the ladies lamented Ailsbet's inability to join in, she found herself bored and not at all unhappy that she did not have the neweyr.

Except for the fact that the taweyr was so dangerous, she found it far more interesting. She wondered, if she were not the princess, if she would have had a little time alone somewhere in the woods to play with the full glory of the taweyr. The ekhono hunters might truly come after her then, but it could be worth it.

Ailsbet did not see her father for a full week after her return, and she was left to wonder what his plans for her were. At last, on a gloomy autumn day when the clouds threatened to hold the sun captive forever, King Haikor commanded Ailsbet's attendance upon him in the Great Hall, the larger and more public room used for dancing and entertaining of guests.

She was so bored with her time inside that Ailsbet

was eager to go to her father, even if it required going through the courtyard into the driving rain. Once inside, she shook herself off, and patted at her hair. Then she entered the Great Hall and curtsied to her father, but not with the full formality that would be required in the smaller and more ornate, gold-toned Throne Room.

With a gesture, King Haikor bid her rise. As she looked up, Ailsbet took in the frieze on the farthest wall, the one that depicted King Haikor's final battle against Aristonne. It was one of the first pieces of art her father had commissioned after assuming the throne and proving himself capable of defending the kingdom against foreign attackers. There was Prince Albert of Aristonne on his side, wounded, and standing over him, the young King Haikor with a sword in his hand and no mercy on his face. The prince had died on the field of battle, and though his armor and sword were sent home, his body had been torn apart by animals, called by her father's taweyr and scattered to the corners of the island of Rurik. Such was the fate of those who stood against King Haikor. Ailsbet had never felt the message as powerfully as she did now.

Ailsbet took in the sight of the court around her father, which was the largest audience she had seen in at least a year. There had to be nearly a hundred courtiers here, including those who normally pled illness, and those who were old and infirm. Taking in the whole of them, Ailsbet felt her stomach clench. She turned to see the queen standing at the side of the king, dressed in a gown of organza and pearls that she did not recognize until she realized that her mother must have had it made from pieces of other gowns for precisely this occasion. The queen looked triumphantly at Ailsbet.

So, it was time. She had delayed as much as possible. She must be prepared for marriage now, to a man who would suit her father and her position as princess. Ailsbet's first concern must be making sure that her future husband did not guess she was ekhono, no matter how much time she spent with him nor how closely they were bound together.

"My beloved Ailsbet," said King Haikor. "You are welcome on this special occasion."

"Ailsbet, you will be a true princess of Rurik today," said her mother.

Ailsbet offered a strained smile and breathed deeply. She focused her mind on her flute, on the beginner's songs that Master Lukacs had taught her when she was very young, simple and repetitious. Above all, she must not get angry. Anger was her father's favorite way of concentrating his taweyr, but to give in to it would be fatal for Ailsbet.

"Sir Jarl," said King Haikor, turning to the high-collared, conservatively dressed nobleman at his side. "Is not this occasion a special one?"

Ailsbet had seen Sir Jarl before, though he had not seemed of any particular interest to her. The only thing remarkable about the man was the size of his nose. She wondered briefly if he would take Duke Kellin's place as her father's favorite. Kellin had been gone for weeks now, and there was no hint that he would return anytime soon. Perhaps Kellin had been sent north on an errand because he was in disgrace. Perhaps he would never return.

"Indeed, Your Majesty. Any occasion in which you are present is special," said Sir Jarl, staring at Ailsbet. She stared back at him, not allowing herself to be cowed by him—or by any man. That had always been true, and her father admired her for it. To behave differently now would only make the king suspicious.

Had her mother approved Sir Jarl as her affianced? Queen Aske seemed more interested in the court proceedings today than she normally was. After a moment, Ailsbet remembered Sir Jarl was the queen's second cousin, once removed. A distant relation, Ailsbet thought. No wonder her mother was pleased with the choice.

"Sir Jarl, you have often gone with me on the hunt, have you not?" asked Haikor.

"I have indeed," said Sir Jarl, smiling at the queen.

"And you are often in the fray, though I do not think you have ever struck the final blow."

"No, Your Majesty," said Sir Jarl. "I have held myself back from that final glory. It is yours alone, I believe."

"You have not yet given me your tax of taweyr this year," said King Haikor. "In the spring, you offered me a kingly sum in gold instead. You pleaded illness, if I recall correctly. And my queen pled your case for you." He turned to Queen Aske, who now wore the carefully blank expression that she seemed to have perfected after years with her husband.

Sir Jarl went pale.

Ailsbet watched him carefully. She thought this was supposed to be about a betrothal. Why would her father want him to pay his taweyr first?

"If I might have a few more weeks, Your Majesty," Sir Jarl said, glancing at Queen Aske.

"Some weeks, yes, if I were to do it on schedule. But my queen has spoken so highly of you, I thought you would be eager to give it to me early."

So was he not the man she was to marry? Ailsbet suddenly felt sick.

"Perhaps we can come to another agreement on the subject of gold," said Sir Jarl. "My county has done very well this year, and we could pay more in those taxes."

"I think not," said King Haikor flatly. He held out his hand and waited for Sir Jarl to kneel before him.

Sir Jarl's voice trembled. "Your Majesty, please, I have not prepared for this. I have used up too much of my taweyr just last night."

"Oh? What have you used your taweyr on, Sir Jarl? For I have had you watched every moment of the last month, and my men tell me that you have not used your taweyr once in that time. Very strange for a man at court, would you not say?" said King Haikor.

"I—I am unweyr, Your Majesty," stuttered Sir Jarl. "I admit it. I am ashamed of it. It reflects badly on my father, who is dead now, and indeed on my whole family." He glanced at the queen again, and then at Ailsbet, who felt her heart begin to beat like a drum.

Sir Jarl turned back to the king, a bead of sweat dripping from his long nose. "I can still serve you, Your Majesty. As an ambassador to Aristonne, perhaps. Or to the Three Kingdoms. Or here in Rurik, working with the continental traders. Or on a ship that carries your own goods." These were all the traditional jobs for the unweyr, jobs that Ailsbet herself could not dare to do, for fear of revealing herself.

"You are not unweyr," said King Haikor softly. "Or anything like."

There was utter silence in the Great Hall. Ailsbet trembled, remembering a hundred tiny things she might have done that would have revealed herself as ekhono rather than unweyr.

"I am—I swear to you," said Sir Jarl. He was sweating profusely.

"You are ekhono," said King Haikor. "You have been tainting all the weyr in my court for the last year. I suspected that there was some hidden ekhono in the palace last summer at the hunt. But I did not know who it was until my queen brought you to my attention."

"No, Your Majesty," said Sir Jarl. "It is not so."

Ailsbet wished she could sense some connection in him with life and growth rather than war and death. But Sir Jarl seemed exactly as any other man in the court. What if it was her fault that he was being accused, her fault that the king had detected an ekhono tainting the weyr? What if the king had sensed that the ekhono was Ailsbet?

She should step forward and reveal herself, she supposed. Save Jarl's life in exchange for her own. That would be the way a character in a story would do it. A hero.

But Ailsbet was no hero.

And she did not believe that Sir Jarl could be saved by any confession on her part. If Sir Jarl was ekhono, he probably had very little of the women's magic, but that did not mean he was safe from her father.

"I have done nothing wrong!" shouted Sir Jarl as the king's guard approached him, swords raised all together as if they had practiced this. "If I do not have taweyr, then that is no crime. I see no reason that I should be punished for it. Surely, it leaves more taweyr for the rest of you. It does not take from you."

It was a valiant argument, but it would not work. He knew it, too, thought Ailsbet. He was making a show of defiance, and her father had always liked a show.

"Do not touch him if you can avoid it," King Haikor advised his guards. "Use your swords to prod him forward. If he tries to escape, run him through."

Sir Jarl looked wildly about the hall. "If I am ekhono, what then? You should be afraid of me. I shall make you all regret this. I shall shower out my neweyr on this place, and the taweyr will be ruined. Isn't that what you are most afraid of?" he said, but his manner made it clear that he was grasping at anything. He had no real belief in his own power.

King Haikor nodded to his guards, who began to use their swords to push Jarl out of the hall. They did not use the taweyr on him, only their own strength and the weapons of steel. To touch an ekhono man with taweyr would run the risk of taint.

"Let me live and I shall leave Rurik!" Sir Jarl pleaded. "I shall freely give you all my lands, all my gold. I shall ask for no recompense but my life. I shall serve you all my days, on the continent."

How King Haikor would be able to hold him to such a promise Ailsbet could not understand. But the man was mad with fear, and he would have promised anything in the moment.

Because he would not move as the guards demanded, Jarl's mouth and tongue were pierced with a sword, and he did not speak after that.

Ailsbet could see the rest of the court moving to the windows to look out on the Tower Green. In a few minutes, Sir Jarl emerged. The guards forced him to kneel, and he was stabbed over and over again. Since they did not use taweyr, it was a slow and painful death. His body would be burned on the Tower

Green once he was dead, to keep the taint of the ekhono away from the court.

Would her own death be like that? Ailsbet wondered, feeling cold at the thought. Sir Jarl should have kept far away from her father to avoid scrutiny and she should do the same. Whomever she married, she should make an excuse to keep away from court and have a quiet life. She had once wondered if she would help Edik when he took the throne, whisper to him when he needed advice, become the power behind him. But now that seemed too dangerous.

The silence ended, and the court began to murmur again. Ailsbet struggled with anger that Sir Jarl's life should so easily be dismissed as unimportant. Then King Haikor clapped his hands, and Ailsbet immediately jerked to attention. "But that is not the special occasion that I spoke of. There are happier things for us to celebrate this day. Princess Ailsbet, I present to you Lord Umber of Weirland," he said, nodding to a man at the far side of the Great Hall, who strode forward.

He was tall and thin, and he dressed very well. He wore a black wool robe with silver embroidery along the edges, and his eyes sparkled when he looked at her. His face was young and striking, with wide cheekbones and thick brows over deep, brown eyes.

He would look handsome when he was an old man, Ailsbet thought. His face had good bones, and he moved with grace.

Ailsbet glanced at her mother's face and thought she saw a rare hint of anger there. She was surprised; surely her mother was used to her father doing whatever he pleased by now, even where her own kinsmen were concerned.

"Lord Umber of Weirland, Her Highness Princess Ailsbet of Rurik," said the king, completing the introduction.

Ailsbet curtsied to Lord Umber, remembering now that he had fled Weirland and come to Rurik to ally himself with King Haikor. He had information to offer, though he had given up his title and his land.

In return, Lord Umber bowed deeply to Ailsbet. "I am honored to meet you at last. You are even more beautiful than your father promised me."

"And I am honored to meet you," she replied with a smile. But she felt nothing at all, not fear, nor happiness, nor despair. Was the taweyr interfering with her ability to think?

Suddenly, Queen Aske stood up and left the Great Hall without a word. The whole court stared after her. But King Haikor said nothing, turning back to

Ailsbet and Lord Umber as if the queen had never been there.

"Princess Ailsbet, Lord Umber has just now agreed to the terms of your betrothal," said the king. "There will be an official betrothal on the first day of the new year, and you will marry on the first day of spring."

Betrothed in three months and married not three months after that? "Is there some reason for haste?" Ailsbet asked her father.

Lord Umber answered gallantly, "Your beauty and my undying love for you are reason enough for me."

He almost made her believe it, his words were so smooth. But Ailsbet was no romantic. Marriage to Lord Umber would make an invasion of the other kingdom easier for King Haikor. Did her father expect Ailsbet to thank him because the man was also young and handsome and well spoken? At best, she could hope for Lord Umber to treat her kindly for the sake of her father and her title. Now and again, he might even be enjoyable company. She had to admit it could have been much worse.

Ailsbet looked up and found that Lord Umber was looking back at her with eyebrows raised, waiting. "I thank you, Father," said Ailsbet, then turned to Lord Umber. "I am eager for our betrothal and marriage, milord." The words tasted like large, whole eggs in her mouth. She was afraid of cracking them and spilling the yolk down the sides of her face.

"Pleased? It sounds as if you are speaking of a pair of boots, rather than a living, breathing, hopeful nobleman," said Lord Umber.

Ailsbet forced down anger at his flippant tone.

Then King Haikor began to laugh out loud, and Ailsbet found she could not help herself. She joined in, and so did the rest of the court. When King Haikor laughed, they all laughed.

"I am very fond of a good pair of boots," Ailsbet said to Lord Umber.

"That I believe," said Lord Umber, and he smiled at her with what seemed genuine pleasure. "Perhaps once you have broken me in, I shall live up to your expectations."

"We shall see," said Ailsbet. "You are an interesting man, Lord Umber," she added.

"Interesting? I shall consider that high praise from King Haikor's daughter, who is so often bored by everyone and everything she sees."

"Is that what they say of me?" said Ailsbet. "I have never heard it."

"Well, of course, they could not say it to your face. It would only bore you more."

"Indeed," said Ailsbet. "Nothing is so boring as being told about being bored." Suddenly, she was aware of the eyes of the whole court on her and Lord Umber.

For a moment, it had felt as though they were having an intimate conversation, but that was an illusion, a dangerous one. She might enjoy this man's wit, but she must not forget herself and her place.

"Umber's father was the son of the sister of King Jaap's grandfather," said King Haikor.

A complicated relationship. Ailsbet tried to remember exactly what his place had been, in line to the Weirese throne. Fourth? Fifth? Had he decided he was tired of waiting for others to die and come to Rurik to increase his chances?

"I have given up my title and my lands in Weirland to serve your father in Rurik. And he has been so gracious as to honor me with your hand," said Lord Umber.

And had he also promised to lead the king's armies to victory in Weirland, if there was an invasion? At the thought, Ailsbet's head sang with death and triumph. She realized she would enjoy going to war. She knew that she could not tell anyone this, Lord Umber least of all. But she liked the looks of him, and she thought he would make a good warrior. That, more than anything, made her decide that she would marry him willingly.

"And now, Princess Ailsbet, I have a gift for you," said Lord Umber. He clapped his hands, and a servant brought him an ornately carved, white, wooden case. He opened it for her, and inside lay a flute plated in gold.

Ailsbet could feel a roar of taweyr in her ears as she stared at the beautiful instrument. She knew that the man meant well. He had doubtless been prompted in this gift by her father. But a flute made with the wrong material, however beautiful, would have no proper sound. Anyone else in the court would think it was a fine gift for a musician, for none of them understood music as she did.

"Thank you," said Ailsbet, feeling the gold warm under her fingertips.

"Play it," her father commanded.

Ailsbet put the flute to her lips and attempted to play. The sound was weak and strained to her ears. But no one else seemed to notice, and Lord Umber looked very pleased with himself.

CHAPTER SEVEN
Ailsbet

KING HAIKOR USED AILSBET'S betrothal as an excuse to have a celebration of some kind every night that autumn, with feasting and dancing and laughter. Already two weeks had passed, and the official betrothal ceremony would take place on the first night of the new year. Her father had sent the royal seamstress to Ailsbet, and she had been fitted for several new gowns, one of them heavy red damask decorated with jewels. Ailsbet hated the color, and thought it did nothing to compliment her pale skin and flaming hair. But she had no choice in the matter, just as she had no choice in when or where she would be betrothed. Her father had decided on the Throne Room, and he also had chosen all the celebratory dishes to be served afterward in the Great Hall.

Despite the fact that the official betrothal had not yet occurred, the king still referred to Lord Umber as her betrothed. The other ladies of the court teased Ailsbet, and she couldn't ignore them, as she had in the past. One lady gave her advice on how to kiss Lord Umber properly; another told her to withhold her kisses to make him want her more. Still another told her to kiss him gently and shyly, and let him believe he must teach her passion. Ailsbet nodded and smiled to all of them. She did not know if she wanted Lord Umber to feel anything for her but what she felt for him—a cool and rational hope that they would get along.

They were spending so much time together Ailsbet felt sometimes as if she could not breathe without him watching her do it. Lord Umber sat next to her at dinner and went on chaperoned walks with her around the palace.

"You do not like the golden flute?" said Lord Umber one dry, cold day when the sky looked like iron. Umber himself wore a bright red cloak, and Ailsbet, who wore the same color, wondered if he had bribed her maid to tell him what she would wear so he could match it.

"It is beautiful to look at," said Ailsbet.

They were outside, and Lord Umber had drawn her aside for a private moment away from her chaperones.

Ailsbet could see the river Weyr just below, winding its way through the city, down to the ocean in the south and north to the center of Rurik, where it began. It was a faint green color, and the light glinted off its depths. The Weyr was wide and deep, and Ailsbet had distinct memories of once riding in a boat to see the whole of the city. She had begun by counting the roofs of the grand estates near the palace, but there were soon too many roofs to count. She remembered the thick, rotting smell of refuse thrown into the river and the smell of roasting meat.

"Beautiful," said Lord Umber. "As you are. With a hint of danger beneath."

Ailsbet turned back to him, preferring to speak of the flute. "It was a fine gift."

"You have an interesting way of speaking the truth," said Lord Umber.

"Are you saying that I am a liar?" asked Ailsbet, smiling in spite of herself.

"Not at all. You are very careful in your truths. You simply choose to tell the ones that suit you."

"And that bothers you?" asked Ailsbet.

"I hope that in time you will feel comfortable enough with me to tell me even truths you think I would not like to hear."

"And what would be the point of that?"

"Truth itself?"

Ailsbet smiled again. "You wish me to believe that you value truth for its own sake?"

"I am from Weirland. We value the truth there," he said.

"I find it difficult to imagine what it would be like to live in a place like that," said Ailsbet.

"And yet I think it would suit you, strangely. I cannot think of anyone else in your father's court of whom that could be said," said Umber. "Certainly not your father himself."

"But he covets Weirland."

"Yes. He would enjoy knowing it belonged to him, though he would not visit it often, I think. It is too wild a place, too uncivilized and uncultivated. The wonders of the neweyr in the country-side would not suit your father. There are no cities there, and few buildings with the comforts your father would expect. Even the castle in Weirland is as small as a minor noble's estate in Rurik, I think."

Was this a hint as to why Umber had given up his title and lands? Ailsbet thought over the implications of the fact that her father had taken in a traitor. Was it desperation or merely another part of his game? King Haikor was growing older, but she had not seen him begin to weaken.

"I could guess at why this flute is not fit for a musician. It is not suited to your hands. It is too heavy. It is not the instrument that you have grown to love. But only you can tell me the truth of it," said Lord Umber, drawing her back to the conversation.

Ailsbet hesitated. "It has a shallow sound," she said at last.

Lord Umber put a hand to her chin.

Ailsbet flinched. She was not often touched. It was against the law for any to touch the king without his permission, and the same austerity was extended informally to the rest of the royal family.

"Do I look angry to you?" asked Lord Umber.

Ailsbet stared into his eyes. "Yes," she said. "You keep it veiled, but it is there."

He laughed, his face coloring to match his cloak. "Angry at myself, then, not at you. I wanted to please you with that gift."

"I am sure it sounds well enough for most ears," she said stiffly.

"But you have a finer ear," said Lord Umber.

Ailsbet sighed.

Umber smiled. "Clearly, I thought too well of my first instincts. I assure you, the next time I bring you a gift, I shall make sure it is one that you will treasure. Will you trust me on that?"

"Of course," Ailsbet said. "What woman would say no to a man offering gifts?"

"That is not what I meant," said Lord Umber.

Ailsbet hesitated, wanting to trust him. "Music is what I am," she said at last.

"But not all of what you are," said Lord Umber. "You are your father's daughter, as well, intelligent and witty and strong."

She was uncomfortable with his compliments, though they seemed sincere enough. It sometimes felt as if he must be speaking to someone else who looked like her, but was not her. To the princess, but not Ailsbet.

If she had been born in Aristonne, Ailsbet sometimes imagined, how different she might have turned out to be. Her musical talent would have been praised and encouraged from the first, and she might have been able to spend all her life making music. Instead, in Rurik, she had to act the part of a princess. She had to worry about her gowns and her speech and every detail of courtly manners.

"And yet you live among others who do not understand your music in the least, yes?" said Lord Umber, persisting.

Ailsbet nodded.

"Do you know, I think you and I have something in common."

"What is that?" It was obviously not music, Ailsbet thought.

"We both want one thing very much, to the exclusion of everything else. And we can help each other get it," said Lord Umber.

"And what is it you want?" asked Ailsbet.

Lord Umber put his hands to his head as if laying a crown there.

Ailsbet went cold for a moment. He wanted her father's throne and his crown? But how did he think he would get them? This was not about an invasion of Weirland, not to him. Lord Umber was thinking beyond this year, beyond her father's lifetime. Married to her, Lord Umber would have a good chance of holding both thrones. If her father died before Edik was fully grown, Lord Umber would be the more experienced man, in politics and the taweyr. But even if her father lived many more years, he might have a chance to take the throne. He had qualities that Edik did not.

"You are very quick to see the truth. That is what I admire in you," said Lord Umber into her ear.

She stared up at him. "If you think I wish to be queen of both islands," she said softly, "you are wrong."

"Oh, no. I know you better than that. Do you think I have not heard a word you have said? You want music, Princess Ailsbet, and I can give that to you, when I have power of my own." Umber gestured toward the river Weyr, which led south to the Channel of Arhort. In that direction lay Aristonne itself, the seat of all music, the place where Master Lukacs had been born, and to which he had returned. Where he lived now and where Ailsbet might go—if she were no longer tied to the crown.

Umber was ambitious, Ailsbet knew, as well as sly and smart. Perhaps she was wrong to let herself feel something for him, but for the first time, Ailsbet thought that she actually liked Lord Umber.

Chapter Eight

Ailsbet

As the weeks before the formal betrothal ceremony passed, Lord Umber began to tease Ailsbet with a wicked sense of humor so dark that she found it irresistible. Many at court tried to compliment Ailsbet on her delicate hands or her graceful dancing, things she did not care in the least about. But Lord Umber would whisper under his breath some truer compliment, like "what sharp eyes you have, like knives cutting through fat" and "what strong legs you have, to run away from those who become too obsequious."

"You have the sparkling wit of your father," said

a foul-smelling older nobleman one night.

Lord Umber motioned to her and spoke so softly only she could hear. "Your father's wit is fading like his hair. But your wit—it will remain strong long after you are old."

"An old woman's wit, that is what I have?" asked Ailsbet.

"Like my own nanny," said Lord Umber.

The following day, King Haikor announced that there was to be an autumn hunt, and all the nobles of the court were to attend him.

"My father used to let me hunt with him, when I was younger," said Ailsbet privately to Lord Umber. She thought she would like to go this time, and she was considering asking her father before the entire court.

"When he could pretend that you were a son and not a daughter, perhaps," said Lord Umber.

Ailsbet stared at him. Had he guessed the truth about her? She had not thought about what it would be like to be married to a man who also had taweyr. A married husband and wife normally had separate spheres of influence, he with his taweyr and she with her neweyr. Ailsbet had not thought how it would work when she believed she was unweyr, but it was more complicated now. Could she keep it secret from Lord Umber that she was ekhono, or would it have to come out? And what would she do then? Would he decide that it was to his advantage to keep her secret? Or would he betray her?

"Which he clearly cannot do any longer, however strong and tall you are," Umber added with a sly glance at her bodice.

It took Ailsbet a moment to understand what he was saying, and then she felt a flood of relief. He meant her father's hunt.

"But there are many noblewomen who love to hunt," Ailsbet said. "The outdoor air is pleasant and the thrill of the chase exhilarating."

Umber shrugged. "Of course. But since your father has grown less nimble and has increased his girth," he said, "he has become more cautious about showing himself to those he wishes to impress."

"I am not one of the ladies of the court, surely," said Ailsbet, "for my father to worry over his appearance."

"You are exactly that," said Lord Umber. "How can you forget that you are a lady of the court? I never do." And again, his sparkling eyes took in her figure, now clothed in a fine silk gown of ochre, cut low over her breasts and clinging tightly to her arms.

It was strange, thought Ailsbet, how at times when

she was with him she could almost forget that she was a woman.

⚘   ⚘

On the following day, Ailsbet dared to stand before her father in the Great Hall with Lord Umber at her side. "Is there any reason why the ladies of the court must not attend the hunt, as they have done in past years?" she asked. "There are some who would not wish to come, but for those who do, surely horses enough can be found for them, and the hunt itself would be enlivened, would it not, by extra company?"

The answer was immediately apparent in the king's dark expression, though he did not reply himself, but turned to one of his ministers.

"A princess is far too delicate to risk on an autumn hunt, when the male animals are at their peak of taweyr before the winter waning," said that minister, a Lord Maukrin. "You must see this as your father's demonstration of love for you, that he keeps the other ladies of the court away when he cannot give you permission to come, as well."

"Am I to receive no reply from the king himself?" Ailsbet asked. "I am a princess, and his daughter, yes?"

"You are what your father wishes you to be," said King Haikor softly. "And for now, he commands you to remain at the palace, where you belong."

Ailsbet turned away, struggling with anger and taweyr once more.

Lord Umber, dressed in a matching deep indigo waistcoat, caught up to her and whispered, "He is afraid that you will ride ahead of him," he suggested. "With your youth and health, he does not wish you to best him."

Ailsbet realized in that moment that Umber had somehow seen her impulse more clearly than she had. She did wish to best her father, for she had no outlet for her taweyr. She was not allowed in the battle courtyard with her father's guard, as Edik was. If she were, it would be the end of her. And even if she were allowed on the hunt, she must be careful. She might reveal herself as ekhono.

For a moment, Ailsbet wondered what it would be like if a man knew that she was ekhono and loved her still. What if he let her compete with him, or even loved her more because she was like he was and could talk to her about his taweyr as he could any man?

But that would never happen in Rurik, at least not while her father ruled. She had thought she was better off spending more time with Lord Umber and the other men of the court, but now she saw the danger in it. She must keep Lord Umber at a distance, making sure he never saw her anger nor recognized it, nor felt her use taweyr near him.

The king and his nobles went on their autumn hunt alone and Ailsbet stayed at court and thought about the truth. When they returned late in the evening, Ailsbet excused herself. Afterward, Ailsbet was quiet for days on end, answering with as little speech as she could manage. Lord Umber responded by becoming more outrageous in his mocking of her father.

Oh, when the king was before him, Lord Umber was nothing but a flatterer. He told King Haikor that any of the ladies at court would love to have the king's wandering eye on them. He told King Haikor that he was in his prime still, that his eyes were as fine as a scholar's, and that he ate his meat with a man's strength, tearing it with his teeth.

But as soon as they were out of earshot, he told Ailsbet, "Ah, how well he thinks of himself, your father. I need not make up my own compliments, for he tells them to us all."

Ailsbet smiled despite herself. She did enjoy Lord Umber's company. She thought of the night before, when the king had proclaimed that he must buy a new robe because his old one would not sufficiently cover his manly girth.

"He blows wind and his teeth rot, but if only we could sell his perfume, think what a fortune we would make," Lord Umber continued, "beyond what the whole kingdom is worth. How many men on the continent would wish to give off the scent of an old bull as your father does if it would give them his power?" He waved his fingers above his head like horns.

Ailsbet had to cover her mouth and pretend she was coughing to hide her laughter.

"And now, look, see how he dances, like one who is being fattened for the slaughter. But he does not know he is the pig. He does not see his butchers all around him."

Ailsbet made a motion like a scythe cutting a throat, and only Lord Umber understood what it meant.

"Ah, there is your brother, Edik," said Lord Umber a moment later. "He walks like a rabbit, sniffing about him, always expecting an attack."

Ailsbet loved Edik, but he was like a rabbit, hesitating, turning this way and that. He knew the names and faces of the courtiers, but he did not understand the hidden meaning in their words or actions. He had grown several inches recently and his voice had begun to change, squeaking at inopportune times and making him even more quiet at court than usual. He moved gawkily and often banged into people and walls, unused to his new size. His face had changed, as well, growing wider and becoming spotted.

Lord Umber wisely changed the subject. "See Lady Maj? She must have found a tentmaker to sew that gown for her. She moves like a teamster with a wagon, looking back before she nudges the horses forward."

Lady Maj's gowns were indeed of an old-fashioned style, with sleeves so long and belled her hands were hidden, and she wore her hair in an elaborate coif and then covered it with a gable hood that was as drab as her gown. She had a way of speaking about everything that made it clear how unhappy she was, how the world had been better in her youth.

There was no cruelty in her, and she was loyal to the queen, with whom she shared the same birth year, but she was ridiculous.

"And there, look at Lady Pippa," said Lord Umber. "She leans toward your father, do you see that? Making sure that he has a good view down her bodice. She might as well be offering him two ripe melons. And will he refuse her? Though your father pretends to power in his own court, who is it who rules here now?"

Lord Umber offered Ailsbet an arm and led her to the dance floor. He leaned in and whispered to her, "If you step on my toes, I shall take it as license for me to hold you in my arms and lift you above my feet. It will be a signal between us. Do you understand?"

"And what if I step on your feet because I am a bad dancer?" asked Ailsbet.

"Then you will have to bear my touch as your punishment."

Ailsbet had tried to avoid dancing with Lord Umber, but it was inevitable. The danger was that to feel the beat of another heart, to be warmed by the breath of another in her ear, stirred her taweyr. She felt dangerously breathless around him. Yet she worked hard to keep herself guarded.

Lord Umber leaned into her hair, which had been curled into two big bows in front and left loose in the back. "Your own perfume is the scent of strength and youth and the dark forest, all combined. Did you know that?"

"I think you exaggerate," said Ailsbet, fearing he was coming too close to the truth yet again.

"And why would I do that? What benefit for me

in flattering you? I should apply myself to your father instead."

"Or to anyone else in the court. But you do not. I can only think it is because you have very poor taste."

"Poor taste? You wound me. But in what other way would you prove that I have shown this terrible flaw? In my clothing? Perhaps my vest is too tight."

"No," she said, and felt her heart leap into her throat.

"Then my hose. They are too loose," he suggested.

Ailsbet looked down at his strong legs. "No," she said.

"My dancing? My strategy at court? My whispering to your father?"

"In me," said Ailsbet, staring at him.

"And what is poor in my taste for you?" demanded Lord Umber. "You are everything that is spice and danger."

"Everything?" said Ailsbet.

"Coriander, and turmeric and black pepper, cumin, and bay leaves and cloves, nutmeg and cardamom, and cinnamon," said Lord Umber.

"Not cinnamon," said Ailsbet. She thought it too sweet and too feminine.

"Not cinnamon, then," said Lord Umber.

As for Lord Umber, Ailsbet thought he must be

more smelling salts than spice. With him next to her, she was always alert, always attentive. She could not nod off with boredom nor be content with what had always been. She wanted more, as dangerous as that was. If she was to be in Rurik, surrounded by taweyr, she wanted to feel Umber's taweyr and to show her own.

CHAPTER NINE

Issa

KELLIN REMAINED IN THE PALACE for more than a week after the betrothal had been agreed upon. It was early autumn, and as yet there had been no snow to block the roads south as there sometimes could be in Weirland, but Issa wondered how long Kellin would put off his return to Rurik. It would be a long journey home for him, and surely King Haikor was anxious for both his return and his news. And yet, Issa knew how much Kedor enjoyed his brother's company, so she hated to bring up the topic of Kellin leaving with her father, fearing that would hasten the departure.

Furthermore, Kellin's questions about the underground ekhono refuge had made Issa reconsider the simple answers her father had given her in the past. One morning, she asked King Jaap, "Why must the ekhono refugees from Rurik remain here so long? Why are they not immediately accepted into the larger kingdom?"

"Over the years, they have come in increasing numbers, and I have not found places for them all. There is nothing sinister in it," said King Jaap.

"But they come here for freedom. Why must they be hidden underground? In Weirland, we know that the stories about ekhono tainting the two weyrs or stealing power are false."

"Do we?" said King Jaap. He stopped and turned to her.

"Issa, you have lived in the castle all your life. You have been protected from the baser instincts of the people you are meant to rule over. Fear of the ekhono is deep-seated and part of the islands themselves, possibly as deep as the two weyrs. Those who are different are always a target of fear."

Issa winced at the proof that she was as naïve as Duke Kellin had suggested. "But our own ekhono—" she started to say.

Her father shook his head. "When something goes

wrong, it is always the ones who are different who are blamed. And the ekhono from Rurik are doubly different here, foreigners as well as born with the wrong weyr. Some have been accused of being spies, others of ruining the weyrs of Weirland, as they have ruined Rurik."

"Who would say such things?" Issa asked.

King Jaap shook his head. "The stories that are told in Rurik are told in Weirland as well, and they always have been. Fear of the ekhono crosses the border as often as the ekhono themselves. This very month, an ekhono woman whom I had placed five years ago with a smithy in the north was found dead, drowned in a small cavern. It was carefully done, well planned, and no one in the county will give a single name. They will not turn against one another, only against her."

Issa held her breath. She had not imagined this, when she had asked her father to tell her the truth. "I am sorry," she said at last. How horrible, to know such a thing, and to have to share it.

Her father continued, "I shall tell you another story, about a family who came from Rurik with two children, both ekhono. They were wheelwrights and lived not ten miles from here.

"Their house was burned, and their shop ruined

only this year," said the king. "It seems that a group of local boys were angry that the girl was as strong in the taweyr as they were. They began to whisper that she had stolen their taweyr because she was ekhono."

"What did you do?" asked Issa.

The king said, "I asked the boys' parents to pay recompense as they could. They agreed to the plan, but I could not demand more than that or I would be in danger of a rebellion the like of which we have never seen in Weirland. It is King Haikor's uniting of his people's anger against the ekhono that has protected him from the rebellions his father faced. That and the way he taxes his lords in taweyr."

Issa knew her father was right, but she did not like it. "And so the ekhono must stay here in the underground courtyard for years on end?" she asked.

"Only until I can find places for them that I trust."

"How can you ever trust that there is safety again?" Issa asked.

"I must trust, both in myself and in my people. And I hope that when you are queen, you will find better solutions than I have."

"This is why you look to the prophecy for a better future?" said Issa. "So that the weyrs are no longer separate and there are no ekhono, because both men and women will have both magics?"

Her father nodded. "If the weyrs are drawn back together, then there can be no more divisions between the properly weyred and the ekhono. But perhaps it is a foolish dream."

"Why is it the ekhono and not the unweyr who are attacked?" asked Issa.

Her father sighed. "Because there are so many ekhono here now in comparison to the unweyr. The unweyr do not challenge our assumptions of which magic should go to which person. And they are useful in trade with the continent."

Issa had nothing more to say, and excused herself. Even if she did not believe in the prophecy, it seemed that marrying Edik was vital. What better way to help the ekhono and preserve peace than by going to Rurik?

Later that afternoon, Issa reached the Throne Room just as Duke Kellin was leaving it. He was dressed more ruggedly than yesterday, with long boots to the knee and a cloak made from the coarse wool of Weirland rather than the finer fabrics of the Rurese court.

"Your father has agreed already to my request to go out into the countryside with some of the members of the court," he said. He paused. "I would be pleased if you accompanied us, as well. I feel that I would be able to give Prince Edik a better picture of your kingdom if you were there to help me see it as you do."

"I would love to accompany you," said Issa eagerly. Then she reconsidered. "If my father agrees, of course."

"You will be perfectly safe. I shall bring my own guards as well as your father's, and it should be a large party of courtiers."

"I was not worried about safety," said Issa. "My own people are no threat to me." What would it be like to live in a kingdom where the king himself had to bring guards to visit his own people, his own countryside?

"I would especially like to hear what you have to say about the neweyr here. I do not know much of it."

"Because King Haikor has no interest in neweyr," Issa said sharply.

"Yes, that is true. But it is Kedor's magic, and I would like to know more of it. I cannot ask openly about it in Rurik."

At that, Issa was embarrassed. She should have guessed what he meant. "I thank you for the chance. The weather has given us a mild autumn, and I would like very much to see the countryside with you." As soon as she said it, she wondered if he might think she was speaking out of turn. "I mean with Prince Edik's emissary, not you personally—"

He held up a hand. "I know what you mean. It is quite clear how you feel about me. I should apologize for speaking so honestly to a princess. I would never have dared to do it in Rurik."

"I do not mind honesty," said Issa. "Why should you think that?"

"You enjoy being insulted, then?" said Kellin. "Being told that you are spoiled and ignorant?"

Issa looked away. "No, not that."

"No, like any woman, you expect compliments."

"I do not expect anything," said Issa. "Least of all from you."

She was about to stalk away when Kellin said, "I apologize. It is difficult for me to play two roles here. I am Kedor's brother and protector on the one hand and Edik's eyes and ears on the other."

"I see," said Issa. She did not know if she could believe the apology or not.

"Please tell me you will come with us to see the countryside," said Kellin.

"It is my countryside," said Issa, and went on her way.

She asked her father his opinion.

"Are you sure you wish to go? I had thought to keep you away from him. You do not seem to like him much."

"It is my duty," said Issa. "Is that not what you would tell me?"

"Your duty is to marry Edik, but you do not have to make friends with Duke Kellin."

"Do I not? You said I must have allies in the court when I arrive next summer."

"That is true," said her father. "Then go with him and make him see Weirland as you see it. Make him understand why it is that you love your kingdom and will not give it up wholly when you are queen of Rurik."

Issa nodded to him and went back to her own rooms, wondering why it was that Duke Kellin's disapproval bothered her so much, and what it was she hoped to gain in showing him around her countryside.

※　※

The next morning, Issa dressed in her best riding gown, the blue cotton one that Lady Neca had said brought out the color in her cheeks. She put her hair in several braids and looped them around her ears, then stared at her reflection in the mirror. Her maid came in and clucked at her, undoing the braids and plaiting her hair in one large piece down her back, as before.

"You look beautiful, Your Majesty, as you always do," said the maid as Issa stared at herself critically in the mirror. How did she look to a man like Duke Kellin, who spent all his time in King Haikor's court, with the wealth of the world at his feet and another princess at his side?

Lady Neca met Issa at the stables. "I did not know you were coming, Your Majesty. But I am very glad for your company. You do look a little flushed, though. Are you ill?"

"No!" said Issa quickly. "No, I am well. I am only warm with the thought of the exercise to come."

Lady Neca nodded. "Of course. If you say so."

Issa was helped to mount her horse by one of the servants, and then Duke Kellin led them out of the castle gates with Lady Neca by Issa's side. She loved the smell of a bright autumn day. The sun rose late at this time of year, but when the sky was clear and blue, she could feel the neweyr deep below the earth, sleeping and becoming stronger with the rest. The hills were mostly gray, but there were occasional spots of yellow and blue from the fall flowers that grew by the streams.

"You have a fine seat," said a voice next to her. It was Kellin.

She glanced about and realized that she had gone too far ahead and that the rest of the company was behind her. "Oh, I am sorry," she said. Now it was her turn to apologize.

"I worried that you might be headed to the land bridge on your own, too impatient to wait for next summer," said Kellin, smiling.

If this was his attempt at teasing, it felt awkward and forced.

The land bridge was a half-day's journey from the castle of Weirland. The farther north in Weirland, the colder and more difficult the terrain, even with the help of the neweyr. Both island capitals were nearly at the southern end of their kingdoms.

"I thought we would go north," said Issa. "To see as much as possible that is different from Rurik's landscape." The hills here were rocky and black, not covered in green, and the trees were smaller and already bare of leaves.

"Would you like to lead?" asked Kellin.

"If you are not afraid of where I shall take you?"

said Issa. Without another word to Kellin, Issa kicked her horse to a gallop and took them north to the line where only pine trees grew. The line had been pushed back year by year by the neweyr and had in former years been much closer to the castle. Here were real mountains, not just the hills around the castle, and there were deep black scars where nothing grew at all, places some said had still not recovered from King Arhort's grief and rage a thousand years before.

Issa could feel the neweyr even here, though it was a starker, quieter kind than she felt at home. She reined in the horse and felt at peace.

"You are trying to show how good a horsewoman you are," said Kellin, breathing hard as he came up to her side once more. "So that I can warn Prince Edik never to challenge you."

"I only wanted to be sure that you saw this part of Weirland." She gestured to the mountains. "Rugged, scarred, even barren in looks. But deep within, there is life."

"I see," said Kellin.

She turned away. "But we had better start back if we are to reach the castle by nightfall."

They turned back and met up with the others, where they ate a hurried picnic. It was then that a fierce autumn storm silvered the sky and cut through the air with sharp needles of rain. The party tried to continue onward, but they had not gone far before the guards insisted that they could not see their footing and it was too dangerous to go on. Issa could have trusted her neweyr to guide her, but not all the ladies had as much as she did, and there were the men. It seemed rude to leave them behind. So they found a small woods and sheltered there for the night.

Kellin had seemed distracted and moody that evening, as if angry with her for the storm. She kept away from him, but she did not sleep well. In the middle of the night, she woke to a sound outside the makeshift tent the guards had erected for her and Lady Neca.

She stood up and saw a figure in the distance moving furtively away from the campsite. She followed out of curiosity. The storm had blown over, and in a few minutes she recognized Kellin in the moonlight, leading his horse. What was he doing out in the countryside of Weirland without an escort to guide him?

At the edge of the woods, he mounted his horse. Using her neweyr, Issa called for her own horse and was able to keep Kellin in sight while staying far enough back to avoid his notice. He seemed to have a very good idea of where he was going.

Hours later, near dawn, when they arrived at the shore, Issa could hear the waves slapping against the mossy rocks. Her neweyr senses did not reach out to the water, but she was sure there was a ship there as the moon came out from behind the clouds of the storm.

Kellin hurried toward the group on foot, his horse trailing after him. Three adults were helping along several children. Kellin spoke to them and seemed to be giving directions.

Ekhono refugees, Issa thought. Kellin must have promised he would come to help them. Issa turned back to the woods on her horse and crawled back into her tent before the guards awoke.

When she emerged from her tent in the morning, Kellin was there. "Did you have a good sleep, Your Highness?" he asked.

"Yes, and you?" she asked.

"Like a baby," he said.

Did he know that she had followed him? She did not think he did, but she did not know what to make of the man. Knowing he had an ekhono brother was one thing, but he continued to help the ekhono even while he was in King Haikor's court and surely in terrible danger if the least hint of his true motives was discovered.

The company made their way back to the castle, and Issa did not say a word to anyone about what she had seen.

CHAPTER TEN

Issa

THREE DAYS AFTER the countryside visit with Kellin, Issa went to her father's library. She had always found books to be the best way of seeing the world anew, and she needed clarity now more than ever. Her life would change dramatically soon, but she would still have to remember who she was and to whom she owed her duty. She stared at the rows of books in the circular shelves all around her, as high as she could see, up to the stained-glass ceiling overhead that bathed the room in a blue-and-green tinged light. Her parents had designed this library, and it was one place that had nothing to do with neweyr or taweyr; it was about knowledge that could be written down and shared with anyone, weyred or unweyr.

But the library was not as comforting as she had hoped, and she was just leaving to go back to her own rooms when she saw Kellin.

"Princess Marlissa," he said. "I was looking for you."

"And why is that? Have you come to shout at me again? To tell me how fortunate I am and how easy my life is?"

"It is easy, compared to many others. You have privilege and wealth many others can only imagine." He nodded at the books.

"You think I know nothing of hurt and darkness and sorrow?" said Issa, wishing again she did not argue with him every time she met him.

"You have lived your whole life protected by your father, by your servants, by people who love you," said Kellin. "You are a princess who will spend her days with nothing more on her mind than what jewels and gowns will suit her best. Your greatest fear will be boredom, or perhaps an occasional cruel word."

Issa gaped at him. "That is truly what you think of me?"

"And why should I not?" said Kellin.

"My life is not an easy one," she said.

"No?"

"Do you think you are the only one who has faced loss? My mother died when I was only eleven years old, when I was just coming into my neweyr. The whole kingdom was looking at me to take her place, and I had no one to guide me. I was a child, a little girl who wanted to weep for her mother.

"Instead, I had to be a grown woman, with all the burdens and none of the friendships. When other girls were using their neweyr for fun, to connect with one another, I had to use it for the kingdom. Every breath I take, every moment of every day, even my dreams at night, they are for my kingdom."

"And you think that is pain?" said Kellin. "Shall I tell you about when I discovered that Kedor was ekhono?"

"Yes," said Issa. She could not believe his life was so much worse than her own.

"My father told me that it was up to me what to do. I could choose to reveal the truth and get the reward when Kedor was publically burned. It would be good for the estate to have the king's favor. Or I could choose to take my brother to Weirland. We had to make the journey on our own, however. My father would allow me to take nothing from the estate, in case we were captured.

"When I returned home, my father simply handed me a list of tasks. He never spoke of my brother again. It was only about using my taweyr, always using my taweyr, and making sure it was seen clearly by all around."

"Kellin, I am so sorry," said Issa, putting a hand out to touch him. All her anger had melted away.

But he jerked away from her. "That is not what I came here to say," he said.

Issa was confused. Did he despise her? Why would he tell her something so personal if he thought so badly of her? "Then what did you come to say?" she asked.

"I came to speak to you about Prince Edik," he said.

Issa stiffened. That was the last name she had wanted to hear at this moment. Perhaps she was being childish, but she wanted to put off thinking of her dutiful future for just a little while longer.

"He must have a chance," said Kellin.

"Edik?"

Kellin nodded. "To be other than his father is. To be better. I think you may be his chance."

"When I am married to him," murmured Issa.

"You must give him no reason to be jealous," said Kellin. "If he suspects for a moment that you—feel anything for another—he will tell his father."

"Ah," said Issa. She stared into Kellin's eyes, but he would not look back at her.

"King Haikor needs only an excuse for war. And perhaps not even that," said Kellin.

"You think he would win, then?" Issa asked. She realized she would rather talk to him about this than have him leave her.

"Your kingdom does not have the strength to withstand him. Your focus has been on the neweyr here. In Rurik, it is the opposite: the neweyr has been sacrificed for the taweyr. And the more time passes, the more urgent it becomes for the kingdom of Rurik to be bolstered in neweyr."

"You mean when Edik is king and I am queen," said Issa.

There was a long pause. "Edik will need you," said Kellin, his voice strained. "Do you understand what I am saying?"

Issa nodded. She understood perfectly. Edik needed her and Kellin did not. When she went to Rurik, she must not allow herself to think of Kellin as anything other than a servant of King Haikor, whatever she felt for him. And certainly she could not imagine that he felt anything for her.

"Good. Because all that I do is for my kingdom, for the thing that is greater than I am and will stand long after I am gone."

Of course. Even his helping the ekhono, Issa thought. He did it for his kingdom. He knew the risks and he did not care about them.

"When you come to Rurik for the betrothal, you cannot sit back and think that the court in Rurik will be like this one. You cannot be sure that the best of intentions will rule."

Perhaps he was trying to be kind, to offer her advice, but to Issa it felt only like criticism and it stung. "So you know what it is that I must become? You would shape the queen I shall be?" said Issa.

"I see the beginnings of strength in you. But you must become harder and more suspicious. You must see conspiracies before they come at you. You must hold the throne."

"You want me to be like Haikor? Is that not what he has done?"

"Yes, he has."

"With strength and steel?" said Issa. "With blood and death?"

"That is not what I mean," said Kellin.

"No? But I should be flattered, I suppose, that you think so well of me. That you think I am worthy to be queen of your Edik."

"I was trying to help," said Kellin.

Was he?

Kellin bowed his head. "I must go."

Coward, thought Issa as she watched him leave the library. But she knew that the word applied equally well to herself.

CHAPTER ELEVEN
Ailsbet

IN EARLY WINTER, Duke Kellin arrived home from his secret errand in the north and was closeted with the king for a full day. When the king returned to court again, he announced that the betrothal ceremony between Ailsbet and Lord Umber was to be postponed until spring, and he said nothing about the wedding itself. He did not say why, and though Ailsbet received many pitying glances, she felt relieved. Nor could she see that Lord Umber was concerned about the change. When she asked him, he told her that it was obvious to him that the king had his mind on other matters.

He meant her father's new infatuation with Lady Pippa. King Haikor had fallen in love with a dozen different noble ladies in Ailsbet's memory, always ending with a profusion of gifts and the king's interest in a new lady. Her mother endured it because she had to, though this was one of the reasons she did not often come to court. Now Lady Pippa had taken the queen's place at the king's side while the court dined. While the queen must be content with ancient gowns from her early years as queen, Lady Pippa had new gowns of leather and velvet, with pearls or diamonds sewn on to the bodice. Her sleeves were sable and ermine, and her skirts were wide.

Ailsbet had never been close to Queen Aske, but she resented the way that her father had neglected her mother. The king ignored the queen even when they met in the corridors of the castle. He spoke rudely to her and returned unopened the notes she sent to him.

In particular, Ailsbet worried about Edik, who was learning all the wrong things from his father's example. Though he was not unintelligent, he spent most of his time and energy in court considering how to eat or belch or fart more than the nobles who sat at the table with him. She had fond memories of Edik as a young boy, playing with his metal soldiers and his stuffed animals on the fine Caracassan rugs on the floor of his chambers, but now she rarely had a chance to be alone with him, and they never spoke outside of court.

King Haikor seemed more prone than ever to fits of temper these days, and even his old friends were afraid of him. There were regular executions on the Tower Green, most by taweyr, of those who looked at him wrong, who spoke the wrong word to him, or who had land or titles he wished to give to Lady Pippa. Only Duke Kellin seemed above suspicion because of his canny ability to hold himself humbly, almost invisibly in the court. Whenever he did speak, he seemed to know just what to say to reassure the king. Ailsbet could not tell what this cost him, or if he was truly the sycophant that he seemed.

In addition to the problems inside the court, there were rumors of growing unrest among the peasants, who had suffered from a series of bad harvests. Some said that entire towns were empty of life in the north of the kingdom. Of course, food was still plentiful in the palace, but even the nobles were worried for those who remained at home on their estates.

Each time Lady Pippa appeared in court wearing a new bracelet, smoothing her hands over the imported ribbons that flowed from her waist when she walked, Ailsbet cringed. She could not speak to the woman civilly. She could hardly even look at her.

Lord Umber found it all amusing. He joked that Lady Pippa would soon be forced to hire a litter to carry her about the palace, for she would not have the strength to hold up the weight of her jewels. Sometimes he would put his head to one side, in imitation of her. "King Haikor has given me another gift. Is it not lovely? Am I not the picture of woman-liness?" he would ask in a strangled tone.

Ailsbet laughed, glad that Umber was there to keep her sane. But she discovered soon that he was not entirely to be counted on. One night, he was called to dance with Lady Pippa, because King Haikor was tired and wished to see others enjoying the sport when he could not. Lord Umber seemed to enjoy the dance immensely, laughing, whispering in her ear, gazing down her low-cut bodice.

Ailsbet had danced with him earlier in the evening, but being so close to him made her taweyr rise. She claimed exhaustion, but the truth was, she could not stop herself from wishing that there were true music for dancing that might calm her taweyr instead.

Afterward, Lord Umber returned to her side, out of breath and dripping with sweat. He nudged her when she turned away from him. "Come, now. Are you angry with me? The king commanded me to dance with her. You cannot think I prefer her company to yours? She is a half-wit, with only her face and figure to recommend her. But with you, I am never bored and do not have to retreat from your company to prevent myself from falling asleep standing up."

It was not as convincing as Ailsbet wished. And her doubts continued to grow, day by day, although Lord Umber stayed at Ailsbet's side in court until the king commanded him to dance with another woman. Often it was Lady Pippa, but not always. He seemed to enjoy them all equally, though he always returned to Ailsbet's side.

"A man cannot help but be distracted by a pretty woman," he explained. "But it is only a distraction. You are the honey that feeds my hive." He made a buzzing sound and held out his finger as a stinger, circling Ailsbet's neck until he touched her ear.

But Ailsbet noticed that he did not nuzzle her in private or try to kiss her. He enjoyed their conversation and he appreciated her wit, but sometimes it seemed to her that he thought her another man and not a woman at all. She did not know what she should do to change this. She was afraid of what taweyr she might reveal if she became too intimate with him.

To celebrate the coming of winter, King Haikor invited entertainers to court. There were fireworks, which King Haikor said were to repay all the people of Rurik who paid taxes to the crown.

Ailsbet thought wryly that only those who lived very near the palace could enjoy the fireworks, which could not be seen more than a few miles away. She sat at Lord Umber's right hand as the entertainers set up elaborate scenery with painted trees and streams and animals, dressed in costumes in the black and red of Rurik and the yellow of Aristonne, and used taweyr to enact mock battles. One of them was a reenactment of her father's battle with Prince Albert of Aristonne himself.

"I do not believe that I have ever heard Prince Albert was quite so small as that," Lord Umber said, leaning over and whispering into Ailsbet's ear.

The actor playing Prince Albert was not full grown, but a boy of perhaps ten or eleven years of age, younger than Prince Edik. He was dressed in a yellow nightgown rather than the uniform of the other Aristonnian soldiers. He could hardly hold a sword and when struck, he cried out in a high-pitched voice that made the king and the court roar with laughter.

"It makes it considerably less of a tale that my father defeated him so easily, does it not?" said Ailsbet.

"Next he will be a babe in arms, and your father has only to hold his hand over his mouth for him to choke to death."

"And my father will howl with pleasure because he takes delight in killing anyone who opposes him, no matter how defenseless," said Ailsbet. She did not at first realize how bitter she sounded.

Umber eyed her carefully. "There is the truth from you again," he said, shaking a finger. "I thought you said you had no taste for it? I am afraid that I am a bad influence on you. Soon you will tell your father that your lack of neweyr is his own fault."

Ailsbet held herself very still.

"Ah, I see I am right," said Umber. "You think that if he allowed neweyr in his court, you would have found it. And now it is too late. You blame him, do you not?"

Ailsbet let out a breath of relief, then nodded

vigorously. "You know me too well, Lord Umber," she said. "Entirely too well."

That night, after the fireworks, the entertainers turned bawdy indeed. Now the actors who played women wore huge gowns, with false glass jewels in their hair and pasted onto their skirts. The men wore padded shoulders and fake red wigs to imitate the king, as he was twenty years earlier. Ailsbet tried to leave several times, but her father would not let her, and Lord Umber coaxed her into smiling at his jokes.

When the king stood up, hours later, staggering in a drunken stupor, Ailsbet thought that he was ready at last for bed, and that she could leave and return to her own chambers. But it was not to be so. He began to raise his glass and tell jokes about each member of the court, drinking heartily after each and watching to see that all joined with him. Ailsbet pressed a glass to her lips but drank as little as she could.

At last, the king turned to Ailsbet and raised his rose-crystal goblet. "To my daughter, the ugliest woman yet born and the sharpest-tongued. She is so fearsome that even the women's magic does not dare to enter her. May she forever frighten men in my court into worrying that I might marry her to one of them."

The king lifted his goblet, and the rest of the court did the same.

But Ailsbet threw her goblet to the marble floor, where it shattered. She could feel the heat in her face. She felt a terrible temptation to show her father what sort of woman she was, and what she had in place of neweyr. She could throw him off his feet, perhaps knock him unconscious. And when he woke, what then? He would send her to the Tower, for being ekhono and for being a traitor.

But then Lord Umber threw his goblet down, as well. Not only did the glass shatter, but the red wine splattered onto the king's face.

King Haikor spluttered for a moment, until a servant discreetly offered him a cloth.

Ailsbet was holding her breath. She had not meant to put Lord Umber in danger. "Please," she said to him. "Do not throw yourself into the fire for my sake."

"Ah, but if you are in the fire, where else would I wish to be? You will make me laugh as I roast," said Lord Umber. "At the smell of my own cooking juices, no doubt."

It was crass, but it was exactly what Ailsbet needed to hear. The taweyr inside her damped down as she laughed, as well as if she had her flute.

She turned to see what her father's punishment would be, but the king seemed amused. It worried her. Why was he not angry?

"A brave man," he said, and raised his glass again. The court drank with him, and Ailsbet was left to stare at Lord Umber and wonder what it all meant.

Chapter Twelve
Ailsbet

A WEEK LATER, Lord Umber came to Ailsbet's own chamber after dinner, something he had never done before. She invited him in, though she had no seat to offer him. Her own chambers were not meant for company. She had never had to worry about it much before.

Ailsbet turned her back to him, unsure of what to say, and stared out her small window overlooking the inner courtyard, watching the rise of the gibbous moon over the city. Her taweyr had been particularly difficult that day, and she had had to focus on controlling it while showing no sign of the strain. She wished she had more time to play her flute, for that seemed to help. But she was so often required to be at court all day and into the night.

"You are annoyed with me," said Lord Umber, looking uncomfortable. "Tell me why, and I can beg your forgiveness."

"No, it is not you. You have done nothing wrong," said Ailsbet.

Lord Umber sighed. "I do not believe it. There is something troubling you. Is it your flute? Did I interrupt you? Have you been wishing to play your instrument more?"

She did want to play it, but she was too tired now, and it would only make her more frustrated that she could not do it properly. She moved to the side, inviting Lord Umber to gaze out the window with her. "I am only looking out at the city," she said. "And thinking how wonderful it is."

"It is the essence of Rurik itself," said Umber.

"Is it so different than Weirland, then?" asked Ailsbet.

"Very different," said Lord Umber. "There is nowhere in the north that has so many people living together like this. I daresay there are more people in this city than in all of Weirland put together. More taweyr here, as well. Which is why I came here, with the hope of what I can become here in Rurik, which I could not become in Weirland."

"And is there any beauty in Rurik for you?" she asked.

"Beauty?" Umber said. "The city is very colorful, very busy," he said.

Ailsbet smiled. "Like the court."

"Yes," said Umber. There was a pause. "Perhaps you wish to be alone. I shall be off, then. I shall speak to you some other time," he said.

"Wait," said Ailsbet. "I am sure you came for a reason. Tell me what it is."

"You command me now? Your voice is very like your father's," said Lord Umber.

"You said that you wanted truth from me. But you do not offer it in return?"

He stared at her for a moment. "Very well, then. I came to ask you about Lady Pippa," he said at last.

"What of her?" said Ailsbet.

"She seems entirely foolish and vacuous. I wondered if you had any experience with her to hint at something more than that."

"No," said Ailsbet. "She is of a good family."

"And are they ambitious?" asked Umber.

"There is no one in my father's court who is not ambitious," Ailsbet replied.

Lord Umber tapped a finger on the windowsill.

"What is it?" asked Ailsbet. "You look concerned. Do you think there is a rebellion underfoot?" She smiled.

Lord Umber shook his head. "No, not at all. The opposite, in fact."

"The opposite?" asked Ailsbet.

"Not taking power from your father, but shoring it up for him. Through Lady Pippa," said Lord Umber.

Ailsbet stared at him in incomprehension. And then it came to her in a flash. Lady Pippa, if made queen, could give King Haikor more heirs. Daughters who had the neweyr, perhaps. Sons besides Edik, who did not yet—if ever—show the king's gift for power.

"You see? I do not need to spell it out for you."

Ailsbet could not speak. She felt the roar of taweyr inside of her chest once more. She focused on it and tried to damp it, but it did not work. Moving desperately away from the window, she stumbled, nearly falling, and Lord Umber caught her.

She was in his arms, her taweyr rage hot, and she could feel his body hard on hers. She wanted to strike him, to tear at his eyes, to kick at his legs and feel his flesh weaken under her onslaught. She wanted to make him fall in front of her and never get up.

But she held back her impulses and breathed shallowly, counting each breath. "My flute," she got out at last, waving at its place on the shelf above his head.

"Oh. Here you are," said Lord Umber. When he handed it to her, she snatched it from him and began to play. At first, there was nothing but ragged notes patched together. She hated the strained sound, but gradually, the tune grew more melodic, more practiced, and she felt as if she were coming back to herself.

She played a song she had composed years before, when Master Lukacs left to return to Aristonne. She had packed all of her love for her master and his music into this one song. There was nothing soft or lingering in it; it was all power and dynamics and emotion.

She could feel again the swirl of triumph tinged with regret that she had felt at seeing the pleasure on the music master's face. She had needed no more compliment from him than that.

"I did not know that music could be like that," said Lord Umber in a hushed tone when she was finished.

Relieved that the surge of taweyr had subsided, Ailsbet nodded. "No one knows, here on the islands. We know nothing of music."

"But do you play like that every time? Surely, your

father would want you to do it more often. I have been here some months, and he has never—"

"My father enjoys my music, but not everyone here does. And in any case, my father thinks the music must take second place to my position as princess." She looked at Lord Umber, oddly stirred by his reaction to her playing.

"I did not understand before how you could leave the islands and the weyrs. Even if you are unweyr," said Umber. "But this music of yours is its own kind of magic."

Ailsbet nodded. "And there is so much more that I do not understand," she said. "So many instruments, so many other masters I might meet, so much music to learn and create." The thought of it made Ailsbet shake with need, almost as if she were filled with the taweyr again. But it was a different sensation, a different heat.

"You are very passionate about it," said Umber.

"I am," said Ailsbet. She could feel Umber near her. When it had been her taweyr against his, she had wanted to fight him. Now, she felt curious. She put a daring hand up to his shoulder. He might be the only man who would ever understand her need for music.

He stepped closer and put an arm around her waist. There were only inches between them.

He brushed a finger along her lower lip.

Ailsbet trembled.

Umber leaned in inch by inch. He let her feel his breath on her face first, and then slowly his lips drew closer and closer, until she could feel the faintest sensation of his lips on hers.

She was enjoying herself until Umber pressed harder against her. His arms seemed all over her now, on her back, around her shoulder. Ailsbet felt trapped. Terrified that her taweyr would take control, she bit Umber's lip, then thrust him away with all her strength.

He stumbled backward, surprised, and let out an oath. His eyes flashed.

Ailsbet saw the blood on his face. She had cut him badly.

"We will be married soon enough," said Lord Umber, wiping at his face and straightening his tunic. "There is nothing wrong in this. You know that your father would not see anything wrong in it. Not with what he does in his turn."

"Leave me," she said.

"Leave you? Is this another command?" he asked, eyes wide.

She knew she should soothe his hurt feelings and make everything well between them again. Instead, she found herself unable to say the courtly words she had practiced all her life.

Lord Umber stared at her. "You choose to be alone now as ever," he said. "But there are consequences for a princess who has no allies." He bowed stiffly and left her.

Staring after him, Ailsbet considered what she had just done. She would still be forced to marry Umber, but now he would be angry with her and there would be no hope for real connection between them. Why had she sabotaged what might have been a real chance at happiness in marriage?

Chapter Thirteen
Ailsbet

As winter deepened, things did not improve between Ailsbet and Lord Umber. Even his teasing while they were in court together seemed at an end, and he hardly looked at her if he could avoid it. He certainly did not come to her chambers again, and Ailsbet wished that she knew what to do to heal things between them. But there was her taweyr to be concerned about, so she had to keep her distance from him. Meanwhile, since Duke Kellin had returned from the north, the king's court seemed much as it was before.

One early morning, not long after it had grown

light, Lady Maj came to see Ailsbet in her chambers, wearing a puce gown with matching ribbons in her elaborate wig. "Your mother wishes to see you," she said.

Ailsbet was annoyed. She was busy with her flute, and her mother inevitably made her wait, or when she did speak, nattered on about her duties as a princess. "Tell her I shall come tomorrow," said Ailsbet.

Lady Maj shook her head, her wig shifting from side to side. She must have been in a hurry this morning, and she had not secured it well. Ailsbet could see the pain on her face, and the difficulty with which she walked.

Why had her mother sent this woman, of all of her ladies in waiting? She had to be the oldest of them all, and she was the least capable. But she was also the most loyal.

"It must be today, Princess Ailsbet. Right now, this moment. Tonight might be too late." She looked paler than usual, and there was a beaded line of sweat along her forehead.

"Is my mother ill?" Ailsbet asked. Perhaps if she got permission from King Haikor, she might call for a woman healer who was strong in neweyr, though they were usually banned from the palace.

"No," said Lady Maj. Her eyes flickered around the sparsely furnished room.

"What then?" Ailsbet was impatient.

"She is dying," said Lady Maj.

"She has been saying she is dying for years," said Ailsbet.

Lady Maj said nothing.

Ailsbet saw the woman's trembling hands. She was fairly certain that Lady Maj would have preferred not to speak to her at all. Ailsbet was not anything like what Lady Maj would have wanted for the queen's daughter.

"I shall come," said Ailsbet.

In the queen's large and normally cold outer chambers, Ailsbet felt heat pouring from the fireplace. Lady Maj beckoned her to the inner chamber, but Ailsbet hesitated at the door, afraid of what she would find within. She could not recall ever being in her mother's inner chamber before. The queen liked to keep her privacy, and of her ladies, only Lady Maj served her there.

With a gulp of air to sustain her, she stepped inside, with Lady Maj beind her.

Her mother lay in her bed on the other side of the large room, a sour smell in the air. Her hair had been swept off her face so that her bones seemed to shine through her paper-thin skin. Veins stood out clearly as paint, and her eyes were sunken. Her hands were white on the embroidered coverlet.

"Is that Ailsbet?" the queen whispered.

"It is Ailsbet, my queen," said Lady Maj.

Queen Aske lifted a hand. "Alone," she said.

Ailsbet could feel Lady Maj departing, and then the door was closed behind her. Ailsbet gave a small curtsy and then stepped back, her head bowed, but her mother beckoned her forward. Her mother had always seemed so out of place in her father's court, but she had still been queen. Here, in her own chambers, she seemed so shrunken.

"Poison," said Queen Aske, and as she understood, Ailsbet felt sick.

Her father could have killed her mother in easier ways, but King Haikor was known for poisoning his most hated enemies.

"Are you sure?" Ailsbet asked. And then the face of Lady Pippa flashed into her mind.

Queen Aske took a shallow breath, and for a moment, Ailsbet thought she would not breathe again.

But then she said, "Only one who truly has no neweyr could ask such a thing."

Ailsbet flushed. She had not come to be chastised by her mother for her lack of neweyr.

"There was a time when he was happy with me, and with Edik as his heir. But now all that is over," the queen got out.

Ailsbet should say something, should declare vengeance against her father. But she did not.

Queen Aske shook her head slightly. "I knew I would not live to see Edik crowned. I am glad I lived to see you grow up."

Ailsbet was surprised at this. The queen had never shown much interest in her daughter. She suddenly wondered if it was her mother's influence that had brought Master Lukacs from the continent, and not her father's, as she had always assumed before.

"Ailsbet, you must—" The queen coughed and could not stop. Blood began to drip from her nose.

Ailsbet stepped forward and held her mother. It was all she could think to do, though it felt strange to touch her when she had kept herself apart from the queen for so long.

After some minutes, her mother seemed able to breathe again freely, and Ailsbet pulled back.

"He has already told the court that I am dead," the queen said, nodding at the door. "That is why I am left alone, with only Lady Maj to see me to the end. But it is just as well, for I do not want them to know what I have to say to you, Ailsbet. They see you as even less important than I, but it is not true." She drew a shaky breath.

Ailsbet put her hand on her mother's frigid skin.

"You must stay here. The prophecy," Queen Aske said.

"What prophecy?" said Ailsbet.

"The two islands. They must come together," said the queen. "It is a prophecy from Weirland, but I believe it is true. Ailsbet, you must help your brother come to the throne and make sure that he marries the princess from Weirland."

Of course, it must be Edik and never Ailsbet who mattered. She had been called to her mother's death-bed to help her brother, not herself. "What do you want me to do?" asked Ailsbet.

"Refuse to marry Umber, for that will make him a rival for your brother. Help ensure that the other princess takes the throne with Edik, and that they have the full support of all the nobles in Rurik. Marlissa has the neweyr that you do not," gasped the queen. "With her neweyr and Edik's taweyr, the weyrs may be combined again, and so may the king-doms."

And in the end, Ailsbet was useless, ekhono.

"If you can, keep your father from marrying— her," the queen went on.

Her, meaning Lady Pippa, no doubt.

"Or if he marries her, make sure that she does not have his children."

How was Ailsbet to do that? She could poison them, she supposed. But surely, her mother did not mean that.

"Ailsbet, I know—" the queen began coughing violently.

Ailsbet held her mother again, and when she seemed calm, she said, "Mother—"

But Queen Aske's eyes had closed and her lips were tinged blue, her face gray.

Ailsbet let out a long, low cry. She had not been close to her mother in life, but now, suddenly, she felt her loss keenly. She also felt the weight of the burden she had been given. Was it Princess Marlissa who would fulfill this Weirese prophecy with Edik?

Thoughts swirled around her like a storm. She had not heard of a betrothal between Edik and Princess Marlissa of Weirland before now, but of course now she could see that must have been why Duke Kellin had been sent north. And what of her own betrothal to Lord Umber? Now that Princess Marlissa had accepted Edik's hand, was Umber in danger? Was she?

At last, Ailsbet went to the door and opened it.

"She is dead?" Lady Maj asked, risingly slowly to her feet.

Ailsbet nodded.

"I shall see to her."

"Wait." Ailsbet held her back. "Was she truly poisoned by my father?"

Lady Maj stared at Ailsbet. "To the end, your mother loved him and tried to protect him."

"Lady Maj, did he kill her?" Ailsbet asked again.

Lady Maj stared into Ailsbet's eyes. "You know the truth already, Princess Ailsbet. You know what your father has become. How selfish, how mired in his own pleasures."

"She spoke of a prophecy," said Ailsbet. "Do you know what it says?"

Lady Maj's eyes fluttered. "I don't know of any prophecy." It was clearly a lie.

"Tell me of the prophecy," said Ailsbet harshly. "If you do not, I shall ask everyone in the court about it until I find out the truth."

That was enough, apparently, for Lady Maj. "It is forbidden to speak of it, on pain of death. It has not been spoken of for years, except in secret. It is a Weirese belief, though there are some in Rurik who share it."

"What is it?" Would the woman not spit it out? Ailsbet felt hot again.

"Only that the two weyrs will be magically combined again, and that the thrones will be one," said Lady Maj. "Some say a royal child will inherit both magics, taweyr from his father and neweyr from his mother, and with that power, he will be able to do miraculous things.

"Your mother believed in it all her days. It was one of the reasons she married your father. She thought because your uncle was ekhono that it meant the weyr in his line was more fluid."

"What?" said Ailsbet in astonishment. She had heard many rumors about her uncle, who had died young, but never this one.

"Your father's elder brother, Achter, was ekhono. I thought you knew."

Ailsbet shook her head.

"It was the reason he is never spoken of," said Lady Maj. "It was thought best for the kingdom and the new king."

"Is that why the king is so vicious in his treatment of the ekhono?" Ailsbet asked.

"He cannot allow there to be any doubt about Prince Edik's taweyr," said Lady Maj.

"But Edik has shown his taweyr," said Ailsbet.

"I've seen it. And he is young. He should easily expect to grow into more."

"Has he shown it? Are you sure?" said Lady Maj. "His tutors have reason to make sure their charge shows well before the king."

It had never occurred to Ailsbet to doubt that her brother would come into his full taweyr. But now she had to know the truth. Was any of the taweyr she had seen Edik's own?

Chapter Fourteen
Ailsbet

THE QUEEN'S FUNERAL was a quiet affair, and the king was in mourning but a day. Then he was dancing every night again with Lady Pippa, enjoying the luxuries of his court. Duke Kellin hinted at nothing about his mysterious errand for the king, though he seemed distracted, and stared at the king often from across the room, as if trying to understand him. Ailsbet dared not ask him directly what he had done, for she had her own concerns.

The betrothal with Lord Umber continued to be indefinitely postponed, whenever she asked her father for a specific date. Not that she was eager for it. Lord Umber treated Ailsbet with courtesy these days, but no more than that. She watched Umber carefully and wondered if he had heard rumors of a betrothal between Princess Marlissa and Edik, but if so, he showed no sign of nerves. He did not even seem angry with her, only distant.

The prince kept to his rooms unless the king commanded his attendance at court, so Ailsbet had no chance for a private conference with Edik until a spring fever struck the city and the palace itself. The king and almost the entire court fled the city for the western countryside, including Lord Umber. But Prince Edik, who was already ill, was left behind, and Ailsbet elected to remain with him.

The evening after the king and court had gone, Ailsbet knocked on the door to the prince's chambers and found Edik's groomsmen as far from the bed as they could be. They were eager to give her and her brother privacy, and they quickly left the prince's rooms entirely, promising to return when she sent for them.

Ailsbet found Edik's rooms as cluttered as usual, his clothes in heaps on the floor. Only his metal soldiers seemed well cared for, arranged along with the cannon and ramparts in wooden boxes. There was very little dust on any of the pieces. Ailsbet surmised that Edik still played with them regularly. And why shouldn't he? He was only thirteen.

Ailsbet knew her brother had not spoken for nearly a week after the queen's death and had refused to kiss Lady Pippa on the cheek at the funeral, as commanded by King Haikor. Ailsbet both admired him and feared for him for that. He had always been so spoiled, and so he had been allowed to indulge his emotions as she never had. And yet, it was not good for him. He could not take his father's place on the throne if he did not learn to disguise his feelings, as she had learned years ago. She wanted to know if he had been told of the impending betrothal with Princess Marlissa, and if so, what he thought of it.

"Edik?" she called. He did not answer her.

Stepping within, she saw his slight form move underneath the rumpled blankets. She pulled back the covers from his head and shoulders and was astonished at the sight. Her brother's eyes were ringed with black smudges, and his whole face was flushed with fever. His stupid groomsmen had allowed him to become dangerously dehydrated. Were they not afraid of the consequences if the king discovered their neglect? Could they have been told to let him die? No, surely the king would not do that—at least, not yet. He and Lady Pippa were not even married.

Ailsbet looked around the room. There was a basin on a table by the corner, but the water had several drowned insects floating in it.

Edik groaned.

She should have been here earlier, Ailsbet told herself, before her father and the rest of the court had gone. She moved closer. "Edik," she whispered. "It's Ailsbet. I'm here."

He waved a hand weakly.

"What is it?" The sound of his wheezing was horrible, and his hand and forehead were burning. "I'll get it for you, Edik. But calm yourself."

He fell back out of sheer exhaustion and Ailsbet turned to the basin of water. There was no vessel to hold the water, so she cupped her hands, straining out the insects, and dribbled it into his mouth.

He swallowed, then promptly fell asleep. She stayed at his side until he woke some hours later, the fever gone, wracked with shivers. She was exhausted, and her neck was cramped from having been upright for so long. She desperately wanted to sleep, but she forced herself to stay awake.

Edik whispered, "Father?"

Of course, he wanted his father. King Haikor had

always doted on Edik. At least, he had before he had become involved with Lady Pippa.

"Father is not here," said Ailsbet gently. "You know how afraid he is of the fever. He will welcome the news that you are well again."

Edik nodded and slept again. Ailsbet remained with him, dozing on a chair beside his bed.

In the morning, he woke again and asked her to talk to him.

"What about?" asked Ailsbet warily. It had been too long since they had spent time together. She had many things to tell him, but she did not know if he was in any state to listen to her.

"Talk about anything. Only—not the taweyr. I don't want to hear about the taweyr. That is all Father speaks of."

So Ailsbet spoke of Master Lukacs and his first weeks in Rurik, ten years earlier, when he had not understood any of the rules of the kingdom or the two weyrs. He had made Ailsbet promise that she would bring music to her people when she ruled them as queen, another of his misunderstandings about how the rules of inheritance worked in the islands. She had had to explain to him that the oldest child inherited only if he was male, and Master Lukacs had been utterly perplexed.

"Would not the kingdom be best served by the eldest and most experienced heir?" he had asked.

"He thought of us all as barbarians," said Ailsbet, smiling fondly at the memory. "With no music. And with our weyrs."

"Barbarians," murmured Edik.

"I wish I could write to him," Ailsbet said, musing. "And tell him that I think of him still. But I don't know where in Aristonne he is. Or if our father would allow letters to be sent from me in any case."

At this, Edik's eyes grew bright. "You can write," he said.

"Of course, I can," she said. "You have had tutors as good as mine, I should think."

But Edik looked away from her. "I can't write," he said.

"Well, not now. You are too weak now, but as soon as the fever is gone, it will come back to you."

"You don't understand. I can't write," repeated Edik. "I never have."

"Of course you have. Your tutors have shown Father many things you have written." Ailsbet said.

"They wrote for me," Edik said in a small voice. "I couldn't do it. There is something that stops me when I hold a quill in my hand. I cannot see anything on the paper but a jumble of letters staring back at me. They make no sense."

Her father could not discover this, Ailsbet thought. It would only give him more reason to doubt Edik's other abilities—his taweyr—and then there would be no hope for him.

"I must write a letter," Edik said. "Father commanded it. He will expect it when I am well. He will punish me if I have not finished it."

"I am sure he will want you to rest yourself and recover." But Ailsbet knew very well that Edik was right. Her father had no tolerance for weakness, no matter what the cause. And in his son and heir, even less.

"The letter," insisted Edik. His hands shook.

"Do you want me to help you write it?"

"Yes, please," said Edik.

Ailsbet fetched some paper and a quill from her own rooms, then set an inkwell by the bed. She handed the quill to Edik, but he could not hold it in his hands.

"I'll form the letters for you. Tell me what you would have me write for you. It will be your letter in everything else."

"It is to Princess Marlissa of Weirland," said Edik.

So he did know of the rumored betrothal.

"The king says that if I write a good letter, she will fall in love with me. And if she wants to, she can make me very happy, and I could not want for anything else," said Edik. "But what if I do it badly, and she throws away my letter and will not hear my name spoken to her ever again? What will the king do to me then?"

"She will not throw it away," said Ailsbet, though she supposed that did not mean that there was no chance the betrothal could be ended before it had officially begun. And that would make King Haikor angry, which would not be good for Edik. She tried to think of everything she had heard of Princess Marlissa. It was not much.

She told her brother, "I shall write, 'To Princess Marlissa of Weirland, may her neweyr live long and her kingdom longer.'" Ailsbet spoke the words aloud as she wrote them. They were not Edik's words exactly, but she had to help him along.

"Good, that sounds very fine. What else?" asked Edik.

"Tell her you admire her father. I have heard that she is very attached to him." Lord Umber had made some remarks on this topic, comparing King Jaap's refusal to marry again to King Haikor's eagerness after the queen's death. Ailsbet wondered what it would be like to have such a father.

But then again, Princess Marlissa had the neweyr in abundance, as Ailsbet did not.

"Her father? Who does not know how to use his taweyr?" said Edik with a sneer that sounded very like King Haikor's when he spoke of the other king.

Had he not just said he didn't want to speak of the taweyr? "He rules his kingdom differently, that is certain," Ailsbet said.

Edik picked at an old sore on the back of his hand. "Father says she has seen a portrait of me. What if she thinks I am too small and ugly to marry?" Though he had grown taller in recent months, he had spent much of his childhood conscious that he was smaller than his age mates in the palace, and she was sympathetic about that.

"I am sure there are other qualities in you that she will value, and you will grow into more," said Ailsbet. She knew Duke Kellin would have made sure that the initial offer of betrothal had been acceptable to the princess—and her father. Had she seen a portrait of Edik? She must know his age, as well.

Edik snorted.

"What is it?" asked Ailsbet.

"It is different for you. You know that any man

will marry you if Father commands it," said Edik.

He seemed utterly unconscious of the insult. Ailsbet bit back her anger and controlled her taweyr. "A man who is to be king must be valued for his wisdom and his foresight more than anything else."

But Edik put his hands to his face. "Has the fever ruined my looks?" he asked. "Am I hideous?" He would not stop until Ailsbet handed him a mirror. "Pale," he said with a sigh. "But I think I shall be well enough."

Ailsbet brought his attention back to the letter. "You could tell Princess Marlissa of the king's hounds," she said. Edik loved his father's hounds completely and protected them against his father's rough handling. Perhaps Princess Marlissa would wish to know this. In truth, Ailsbet didn't know what the other princess would care about.

"What would she care about my father's hounds? You must think about more womanly things, Ailsbet," he said. "I must flatter her and make her see me as strong."

"And what are womanly things, then?" she asked in return, smiling faintly.

"Jewels," said Edik with an impatient wave of the hand. "And gowns. Sweet words and a gentle touch." He said this with the disdain with which King

Haikor spoke of the neweyr and all things womanly, though the king offered such things freely enough to Lady Pippa.

"Those things will show you that Rurik itself is strong, but nothing about you," said Ailsbet.

"Maybe I should tell her a joke and make her laugh," said Edik after a moment's thought.

But Ailsbet shook her head, thinking dubiously of the jokes Edik might have heard in her father's court.

"Then what?" asked Edik. "How can I possibly fill a letter?"

Ailsbet thought of the Weirese prophecy her mother had spoken of. Surely, Princess Marlissa knew of it, as well. "Let her know that you think of both kingdoms, that you wish them both to prosper together. And the two weyrs, as well. She should believe you understand a little about the neweyr."

"The neweyr? Why should I think of that? It is the taweyr that matters. And Weirland should be glad to be part of Rurik. It will be much better served that way," said Edik.

Ailsbet was sure it was what their father thought, though she doubted Princess Marlissa felt the same way.

"Do you think she will have read many books?" asked Edik suddenly.

"I should think so," said Ailsbet, remembering what Lord Umber had told her of King Jaap's extensive library.

Edik's face fell.

"But perhaps she is bored by books," Ailsbet went on. "She already has people she can talk to of books around her. She will want to hear something different from you." She hoped that this was true, for Edik's sake.

"What, then?" asked Edik.

And so it went, suggestion by suggestion.

In the end, despite her earlier intentions, Ailsbet wrote the letter almost entirely on her own. When she read it aloud to him, she found that Edik had no more interest in it, as long as it was finished and he could pretend to his father it was his. Instead, feeling slightly better, he asked Ailsbet to play metal soldiers with him. She did so while her mind turned over the words of the letter again and again:

To Princess Marlissa of Weirland,
I write in hopes that I can show myself to
be a man worthy of your attention. I could tell
you many things to flatter you, but you must be
beyond such devices. It is your character that

matters, and the more I learn of your father, the more I hope that you are like him. He is not a king as my father is, but he rules with kindness and good judgment and I hope that you have many of the same qualities.

I am no scholar, to quote wise men of old. Nor am I a poet who can sway your heart with beautiful words or sentiment. You have seen my face, and I shall leave it to your own judgment if you think me fine looking or not. But it is not my face that will matter when I am king. As for you, it is your heart that I most admire, for it is your heart that makes you a true princess and will remain unchanged through the years.

My father's hounds are his prized animals. I know how to feed them, how to clean and groom them, how to make them feel happy and well loved. These are the tasks of a boy and not a king. But I am learning from them how to treat men, as well. And if you look at my portrait, I hope you will see the man I may be, if I have a woman at my side to inspire me.

Our two kingdoms have long been enemies, but it was not always so. Let us return to peace and prosperity together. Rurik will be greater with Weirland added to it, and Weirland will *be greater, as well. Your neweyr is renowned as strong, and my taweyr will be as strong as my father's. With them together, we shall look to the future. It will be the same with our two thrones, and with us.*

Prince Edik of Rurik.

After she copied the final draft, Ailsbet left the letter in Edik's chamber, curious to hear what happened to it. But when Edik had recovered, and the king and the court returned from the countryside, the letter was sent as she had written it. It seemed the king did not see the hints at the prophecy, or perhaps did not know the prophecy well enough to see them.

On the contrary, King Haikor laughed over the letter's length and teased Edik over his way with women. He seemed to think the letter was too short and very plainly written. But he announced officially that Duke Kellin had negotiated a betrothal between Edik and the Weirese princess and that the official binding ceremony would take place on the first day of autumn.

This, at last, seemed to reach Lord Umber, and he reacted by becoming more obsequious around the king, more eager to please, and the sense of humor that Ailsbet had once enjoyed became a tool to make the king and court laugh often. Ailsbet once shared a glance with Duke Kellin in the midst of one such incident, and she thought she saw a warning in his eyes.

CHAPTER FIFTEEN
Ailsbet

"LET US HAVE A SPRING HUNT," the king suggested one warm afternoon.

"It is my pleasure to serve Your Majesty," said Lord Umber humbly.

"Of course," said Duke Kellin.

Ailsbet sometimes wondered if she had been mistaken when she saw Kellin in the south last summer. The man who dared to flout King Haikor's orders and save an ekhono could not be the same nobleman who stood at the king's side so quietly day in and out. He never seemed to look for any benefit to himself for his services, and though he was never fawning as Lord Umber had become, he was always carefully dutiful. "We will go into the forest tomorrow and see who brings back the greater prize," said King Haikor to the court.

"And what will the winner of this competition receive?" asked Lord Umber.

"A hundred gold pieces," said King Haikor. "And a favor granted by the king."

"If I should win, I would not ask for any gold, only my king's ever-gracious goodwill," said Lord Umber.

"I am sure that you will do honor to your new king and kingdom, Lord Umber," said Duke Kellin.

"I shall do more than honor the king. I shall prove to him I am of such value that he may wish to have a new man as his favorite," said Lord Umber.

"That would indeed be a worthy prize for a man who proves the fiercest hunter," said the king. But a look passed between Kellin and the king that made Ailsbet sure the two of them knew more than Lord Umber.

Nonetheless, Lord Umber strutted about the rest of the day, unaware of any danger.

Ailsbet did not sleep well that night. She tossed and turned with images of Lord Umber being chased by her father on horseback, being caught and killed with the king's taweyr stopping his heart. She woke early and lay in bed, wondering what her father intended for Lord Umber. Had he ever intended Ailsbet to marry him?

In the end, Ailsbet went outside to see the men off. The other ladies of the court were already there. She had never made any close friends among them, and she held herself at a distance now. If they thought she was arrogant, she did not care. She did not intend to be distracted from what was happening between her father and Lord Umber.

She watched as Lord Umber boasted about what he would do to the boar that day, how quickly they would all be returning. The king nodded and clapped him heartily on the back. Duke Kellin stood at the king's side. His riding clothes were black, in contrast to the colorful raiment worn by all the others. It might have been his choice simply to remain in the background, or it might have been more than that.

Once the men were gone, the other noblewomen went back into the palace to continue their gossip. But Ailsbet stayed outdoors, pacing in the courtyard, imagining the scents and smells of the royal forest and the feeling of her own taweyr allowed to go free, until the party returned. She half-expected that it would be not a dead boar that returned to the palace, but Lord Umber's body.

But late that afternoon, when the party returned, Lord Umber had indeed won the hunt. He had a boar over his horse's flank, its eyes glassy with death, its tusks red with blood.

When Ailsbet looked at her father, there was a sly smile on his face. "A hundred gold pieces," he called out to a page. "Bring them to Lord Umber at once."

"But Your Majesty, I have no wish for such a reward," said Lord Umber.

The king would not hear him. "I shall not be known as a man who does not pay his debts," he said.

Ailsbet looked closely at Lord Umber, seeing his face was streaked with dirt and sweat, and his hunting jacket had been torn in several places. He limped a little and acquiesced to the king's suggestion that the boar be cleaned and trussed for the evening's dinner. She caught up to him as he headed to his own chambers. "What happened to you in the woods?" she asked. "Did my father attack you?"

"Of course not. I am a better hunter than he could hope to be. Can you not see my strength in every motion?" he said.

"You are injured," said Ailsbet.

He waved a hand at her. "A scratch. I am in no pain. There will be no lasting damage. The boar took me high." He put a hand just below his ribs on his right side. Ailsbet could see no blood seeping through his tunic, and she assumed that he must have been bandaged after the boar was dead, for her father always took the palace physician along on the hunt.

"But why is my father so pleased with himself?" asked Ailsbet.

"Because I am soon to be his favorite, and you and I shall be married," said Lord Umber easily, and he drew her close to him. "I hope that you have changed your mind at last, eh?" He stole a kiss before she could pull away, then laughed and stumbled down the hallway.

Ailsbet hurried away from him, back to the courtyard. She tasted bitter and sweet at once in her mouth, and she felt a prick of pain in her throat. She swallowed again and again, but her throat grew hotter and more painful. She could feel sweat break out on her face and had to focus on her footsteps to keep herself from wandering. She did not know where she was, still inside the palace or out.

She felt a hand on her neck, lifting her head. It felt cold and hard, and the pain in her throat worsened.

She recognized her father's face close to her own and would have pulled away, but she realized she did not have the strength.

"What did you do? Did you touch his wound?" the king demanded.

Ailsbet shook her head firmly, shuddering at the thought.

But King Haikor seemed not to believe her. He pulled up her hands and examined them. "I see no blood." Then he sniffed them. "No scent of it, either. Good."

She was in his royal chambers, Ailsbet realized. She could not remember if she had been here before. She gazed around at the sumptuous curtains in damask and silk, the braided hangings on the walls, and the great bed, the size of ten bears all lying together.

Ailsbet concentrated on what she could remember, before she had become confused. Earlier in the day had been the spring hunt. Lord Umber had won. Her father had seemed cheerful.

"What did you do?" asked Ailsbet, her words slurred. "To Lord Umber?"

King Haikor answered, "He thought he would take my place as king. My place. And then he came willingly into my forest, where the animals have long been taught to fear me and to answer when I call."

"Did you use your taweyr on him?" Ailsbet asked.

"I helped call the boar to him with my taweyr," her father answered. "A generous act, do you not agree? At the last moment, the boar went wild and gored him. But lightly, only lightly. I made sure of that."

It had all been staged. And Lord Umber did not understand any of it. "But why?" Ailsbet asked. "If you meant to kill him, why not do it openly? Why the hunt?" The man had already betrayed his own kingdom, and her father had killed other noblemen in court. Clearly Lord Umber's fortunate arrival in Rurik had offered a second way to take Weirland and was unnecessary now that Marlissa was to marry Edik.

Her father made a theater of answering her, walking slowly around her as he spoke, as if telling a story on a stage. "He thrust the spear straight into the boar's eye. The creature died instantly and fell forward, pulling him with it. Only then did he notice that he was wounded, for he saw the blood on the tusk. What was I to do but send the palace physician to aid him?"

Poison again, thought Ailsbet. It sent a message to others in his court who might consider crossing him in the future. If they ever believed that the king was showing weakness, it was likely just a ruse. He might be toying with them. They could never trust that he would not come for them when they least expected it.

Her father pinched Ailsbet's cheeks as if teasing her. "You kissed him, did you? Kissed him because you thought he had come back victorious, that you would sit in your mother's place and he would sit across from you on my throne?"

She did not know what to say. The king had arranged the betrothal. It had not been her choice. And now he blamed her for trying to make the best of it?

"Well, it is no matter." King Haikor said casually. "He did not want you, only my kingdom. And now he has what he deserves."

The sting of her father's assessment was sharper than the pain of the poison. "He is dying," she said, trying to decide if she should mourn or rejoice.

"And what of yourself? Do you not care if you are dying?" asked King Haikor.

She stared at him.

"How well did he kiss you? For how long did you taste his tongue?"

Ailsbet spat at her father's vulgarity, but he had already turned away.

He clapped his hands for his servants to remove her to her own chambers. As she left, he said, "It is not a fast-acting poison. He will die slowly. And you will not know if you are to die with him for weeks to come."

She did not die, but there were many hours when she wished she would. Her room stank of illness and sweat, and her maid came in often to wipe her brow and change her bedding. She did not know how much time had passed until she was nearly over the worst of it, and Prince Edik came to see her. He told her it had been three days.

"You should not be here. He will be angry," Ailsbet whispered to him.

"You came when I was ill," said Edik.

"That was different," Ailsbet said. She was not ill. She had been poisoned, by her father and by her own stupidity.

"Umber?" asked Ailsbet.

Edik shook his head

So the man was dead. By now, she felt only relief.

"She is coming," said Edik suddenly.

"Who?"

"Princess Marlissa of Weirland is coming at mid-summer to finalize the betrothal," said Edik.

And so Ailsbet would do what her mother had asked, and make sure that Edik and Marlissa were married and the two kingdoms were bound once more. What would happen to the weyrs she did not know. Perhaps it would not matter, if she went to Aristonne after the wedding. What place would she have here in Rurik then? Princess Marlissa would not want her there to threaten any heirs she and Edik had, and the other princess would have no use for a woman who had no neweyr.

CHAPTER SIXTEEN

Issa

I
N LATE WINTER, news came to Weirland that Queen Aske had died under mysterious circumstances, and Issa wondered if this would affect her betrothal to Prince Edik. But some weeks later, Issa received a letter from Prince Edik himself.

"Read it and think on it. Then come back and tell me what you think he has revealed of himself," said King Jaap. Their relationship, once so warm, had become rather distant. Issa did not know how to heal the breach or even if she wanted to.

"Thank you for the privacy," said Issa. She took the letter and went away from the castle to the Queen's

Garden. She sat on her favorite, moss-covered stone bench and read with only the scent of the lilacs to distract her.

It was a good letter, far better than Issa had expected. He did not sound like a child, as he had seemed in his portrait. He did not sound like his father, either, at least as Issa had heard King Haikor described. There was no arrogance in the letter, and there was a hint of warmth, of need. Perhaps he was as lonely in his world as Issa now felt in hers.

She looked up and realized it was nearly sunset. She was normally so connected to the neweyr that she did not lose track of time. She hurried back to her father in the Throne Room.

"And what do you think?" he asked.

"The handwriting is polished, the letters well formed," said Issa.

Her father made a face. "What else? We do not know if it was written in his own hand. He could have dictated it."

"Then it may be nothing is his," said Issa.

"That is possible. But I do not think that is a letter that King Haikor would have written himself, so I suspect the words, at least, are the young prince's. Or something like."

"You have already decided yourself what it

means," said Issa. "Why don't you tell me?"

"Because I want to have your opinion. And be sure that you are able to make your own judgments before I send you off to another kingdom alone."

Before he sent her off, because he would send her off. "He spoke well of you," said Issa.

"Another proof that it was not King Haikor who wrote it. He would choke on his own tongue before he would say anything in my favor."

"Is he mocking you, do you think? It could be King Haikor's sense of humor," suggested Issa.

"His sense of humor is not so subtle," said King Jaap. "Now, what else?"

"It seems humble," said Issa. "He says he is not a scholar, and that he has no intention of flattering me."

"You are not offended that he does not praise your beauty?" asked King Jaap.

"Are you?" asked Issa. But before he could answer, she shook her head. "No, I am not offended.

"He speaks of matters of substance. Of our kingdoms, of the different styles of ruling, and of the hope for the future," said Issa carefully.

"Yes. What of that?"

Issa thought for a moment. "The prophecy," she said. "He hints at it."

"Are you sure?" asked King Jaap. "It is never clear."

"It could not be, if King Haikor was to allow it to come to us. He hates the prophecy, or so you have always told me."

"Yes. He threatens death to any who speak it on the street in the capital city, let alone the palace itself."

"But Edik knows of it and believes it," said Issa. "It is part of why he looks to the betrothal with a happy heart."

King Jaap nodded. "Perhaps. I hope it is so. I hope that you and I shall find a meeting place in that, as well as in other things. But it is a good beginning."

"And the part about the hounds of the king—" Issa began. "Do you think that Duke Kellin told him of the gift I planned to offer him on my arrival?" She did not know if that would spoil the surprise.

"I do not think so. I think it is a genuine confluence of interest," said her father.

"Well, then," said Issa. She was not sure how to take that. It seemed a very good sign.

"Can you love him?" her father asked.

"I think I can," said Issa. But as soon as she said it, she thought again of the portrait. *Love* was a word that had many meanings. She did not know if the boy she had seen would ever stir her heart to thump wildly in her chest or make her wish for the touch of his lips. But she could be his friend, his confidante. She could find a kind of happiness with him, even if it was not the kind of happiness she had seen her mother and father share.

"Then can you forgive me?" her father asked.

Issa did not like to admit how angry she had been. She bowed her head. "I understand why you did it."

Her father lifted her head and stared into her eyes.

"Yes," she said.

"It will be difficult for you there. I understand that. You will have to learn to understand what is meant, and not what is said. Nothing is on the surface in Rurik. You will have to read faces and gestures and think ahead to survive. You will have to twist yourself into a new shape, one you have never conceived of before." It seemed to Issa that this, too, was part of her father's apology. Though it sounded a good deal like Duke Kellin's advice to her on that last fateful day in the library, and for that she disliked it.

"Streams twist, and when they do, they offer water to more places. Trees twist in the wind, and it strengthens their trunks," said Issa.

"If they do not break," said her father. He kissed the top of her head, then sent her on her way.

Back in her own chambers, Issa put the letter in her chest and locked it.

When it was full spring, with the roads to the land bridge still too muddy to travel on, King Jaap called all the noblemen of Weirland to the castle for a jousting tournament to disperse any buildup of taweyr that had occurred over the winter when the weather had kept the men apart.

The blue-and-green flag of Weirland that flew overhead was an old one and had been slashed and repaired multiple times. Her father was proud of it, since it had been made in the first year of his own reign. Issa felt a nostalgic twinge at the sight of it.

Issa and the other ladies of the court sat in the shade of a willow tree, in a good position to watch the tournament. At her side were Lady Willa, Lady Sassa, Lady Neca, and Lady Hadda, all close to Issa in age and all adept in the neweyr.

As they waited for the men's competition to begin, Lady Hadda put a hand on the ground and drew up a stunning tulip in a purple so dark it was nearly black, with edges of deep red.

Issa clapped at this use of the newyer, and the others joined in.

The ladies looked at one another. Who would best this?

It was Lady Willa, who drew up an enormous iris, with each petal a different color, from pink to pale blue to lilac and butter yellow.

Issa realized it was five different iris plants melded together at the stem and that before the petals opened, Lady Willa had chosen the color of each one.

Now Lady Sassa put both hands on the ground and leaned over it, as if her breath itself would cause a flower to grow. Then she stepped back to show a rosebush that she had grown waist high in just a few moments. The roses were the pale blue of the sky in spring, and the color of the Weirese flag.

Issa hesitated and she knew that all the ladies were waiting for her reaction. The rose was lovely, but it was also the flower of Weirland. Lady Sassa seemed to be making a statement about Issa's loyalty to Weirland, since she was leaving for Rurik in mere weeks.

Issa plucked one of the blooms and said, "I shall have to take this with me to Rurik to plant just outside the palace and remind me of home. Thank you, Lady Sassa."

With that, the tension dissipated, and the ladies turned their attention to the jousting field. Lady Neca's brother, Riob, was in the tournament, as was Sir Tomah, who was betrothed to Lady Willa. As for Lady Sassa and Lady Hadda, they seemed to be in love with every male figure that they could see and cheered for all. Issa knew how like them she had once been and how shallow she must have appeared. But she had been happy, as well, and she missed that.

For the jousting, her father cleverly paired rash noblemen who were rich in taweyr with others who had great physical strength. The contest would leave both with so little taweyr that they were no threat to the kingdom. The jousts were King Jaap's way of containing the taweyr that might otherwise be set against him. Issa thought her father generally had better relationships with his nobles than those in Rurik.

Lord Riob rode by with his worn and blackened helmet under his arm and waved to his sister. He wore his family's sigil of the boar on his breastplate, but no ribbon from a lady.

"So dashing, so muscular," said Hadda.

"I would not mind having those strong arms around me," said Sassa.

"You should be so lucky," said Neca. "My brother will not throw himself away on a pretty face."

"Oh? He wants land to go with it?" suggested Sassa.

"He wants a mind. And a heart," said Neca tartly.

"Ha!" said Willa. "No man wants that. They may say they do, but it is never more than bluster. Men want a pretty wife with a little neweyr to help them along, but no more than that."

Would anyone think she was pretty in Rurik?

"Make him come closer," Sassa begged.

Neca beckoned to her brother. For a moment, he seemed not to see her, but then he turned his horse toward them.

Lord Riob had a freckled face from spending a great deal of time outdoors. His hair was sandy with streaks of gold on top. He held himself well in his seat, and his back was straight and tall. Though his breastplate and helmet were little different from any other, there was something in the way he held himself that made him appear very regal.

"Princess Marlissa," he said, nodding to her first.

"You look very strong, Sir Riob," said Issa.

"Looking strong is hardly the point," said Lord

Riob soberly. "I must prove my strength on the field of battle."

"Are you afraid of the joust?" asked Lady Sassa. "I know I would be. Though, of course, I have no taweyr."

Lord Riob said, "I have learned to control whatever fear I may feel, milady."

Before Lord Riob could ride away, Hadda said, "Lord Riob, I see no ribbon under your armor. I could offer you one of mine."

But Lord Riob refused. "It is the king's name I fight for, and his house," was all that he would say.

"For the king's house?" said Willa. "Oh, then you should offer him your ribbon, Issa."

Issa looked to Riob. "Would you like one of my ribbons?" she asked, noticing how blue his eyes were against his freckled face.

"I would be honored, Princess Marlissa," he said.

Issa allowed herself to consider for a moment the possibility of telling her father that she did not want to marry Prince Edik of Rurik, that she would remain at home, loyal to her kingdom as Kellin was to his. She could marry someone like Lord Riob. Why not? Why should she be the one to make an alliance with Rurik? There was no guarantee that this would be the answer to the prophecy. It might be for nothing, after all.

Could she have no small happiness for herself? A handsome young man who could love her and laugh with her? An honest and uncomplicated man who had nothing to do with King Haikor and his heir?

Lord Riob came close enough that Issa could smell his clean scent. She flushed and held out the ribbon. He took it, slipping his fingers across her wrist. His skin was smooth and warm, and she looked away immediately.

"Thank you, Princess. I shall surely win now," said Lord Riob. "For I would not dare dishonor your father."

"I look forward to seeing you next to my father at the end of the day, on the dais with the other winners," said Issa.

"You can go away now," Neca told her brother. "You've conquered all the hearts there are to conquer here."

Lord Riob glanced once more at Issa, then trotted away on his horse.

Willa snickered. "He will win, because no one will dare to unhorse him, wearing the king's colors."

"He may not," said Issa. "My father has always asked for fair battles."

"Your father has asked that all pretend the battles are fair," said Willa archly. "There is a difference. Sir Tomah has told me the truth that is understood and never spoken."

"But my father has never taken first place," Issa protested. "Not once in all the years I have seen him."

"No. He is always in second or third place, never below that. Have you not noticed? My father told me the king is always very high in the rankings, and whoever is ahead of him one year will never be ahead the next year. It would be too dangerous for the king, if there were one man who bested him consistently."

"Are you saying that my father is a fraud?" asked Issa. She had her own complaints against him, but she would not hear others speak ill of him.

Willa shrugged. "He is the king. He cannot afford to have an accidental outcome here today. It is far too important."

Perhaps her father was not so different from King Haikor, after all, thought Issa. It was not a pleasant thought, and she felt ill at ease the rest of the tournament.

All the ladies watched as Lord Riob passed once, twice, and then three times, without being unhorsed. Issa's ribbon of green and blue fluttered in the wind.

"He won't even look at me," complained Hadda.

"And he never will," said Neca. "Not at a twittering idiot like you."

But Lord Riob did glance once in Issa's direction. He won another joust, and then King Jaap was set against him. This time, Lord Riob fell and the king was roundly applauded.

Issa looked at Neca.

"He was fairly beaten," she said. "I have no doubt of it."

"And you ask her for the truth?" said Hadda. "He is her own brother."

"Would you lie for him?" Issa asked.

Neca hesitated a long moment. "I would lie for my brother," she said. "But I am not lying now. Riob was exhausted. Your father is more used to conserving his strength. That is why he won."

Issa looked around at everything that was familiar to her here. When she was in Rurik, she would miss this simplicity. She would have to give up her simple gowns and her braided hair and her privacy. There would be servants everywhere and always the need for show. Yet she would never be at ease there, never sure of her place, even as queen. And it must be done. There was no choice now. She had agreed to it when Duke Kellin was here, and she could not go back on her word now.

At the end of the day, Lord Riob was awarded third place in the competition, receiving for his pains a large haunch of pork. King Jaap took second and donated his prize of a newly born lamb to the villagers. Lord Karod, who was the new lord of the traitorous Lord Umber's lands, took first place and received a fully mature bull, which he struggled to control as he stood for applause. Issa tried not to think of it as an omen of for the future.

Chapter Seventeen
Issa

As soon as the roads through to the land bridge were dry that summer, Issa was to leave for Rurik. Everything to do with the betrothal had been negotiated and agreed to on both sides, down to the colors she and Edik would wear and the words they would say. Sometimes Issa wondered if her father and King Haikor had decided for her how many breaths she would take at the ceremony. And yet the ceremony was not until the first of autumn, several months away.

On the morning of her departure, Issa woke up very early, unable to fall back to sleep. She walked through the castle in Weirland one last time, noticing the tiny details that she had always taken for granted, the dull wooden floors, worn down over so many years, the windows made of fine greased cloth rather than glass, the smoking fires with their ancient chimneys. She knew that when she came back to Weirland, it would be temporarily, as a visitor, and this was the last time it would be home to her. After this, she would be returning as the betrothed of Prince Edik.

There were sheep in the courtyard, and Issa knew their names. She had found them out from the shepherds only last summer. It seemed a lifetime ago. She would miss the sheep and the shepherds both. She would miss the feeling of neweyr all through the castle. It would take more than a month to reach the palace in the south of Rurik, and once there, she would have to think before she used her neweyr. What would it be like to have it so stifled?

Nervous, she went back to her room, where her trunks stood, already packed. The gowns she would have to wear in the Rurese court bothered her. She was sure that no garment made in her own land could be good enough.

Finally, after a last breakfast together, King Jaap held her hand as they walked out to the castle gate in the bright sun. It was a perfect day for traveling.

"They will take care of you," he said, nodding to the two dozen servants who were loading the pack-horses and donkeys and who would accompany Issa on the journey. Some of them were castle servants, two of her father's guards, one a maid who had served Issa on occasion.

Issa stopped a moment to be sure that the hound she was bringing for Prince Edik was properly secured in the basket tied atop one of the donkeys. It whimpered at her, and she put a hand out for it to smell and spoke a word of comfort.

Three of the servants who had come with them Issa recognized as ekhono she had seen in the underground courtyard years before, two men and a woman.

"What a terrible risk they take. Why would you command them to return to Rurik with me?" asked Issa.

"What makes you think that I commanded them?" her father asked.

"But—if you had given them a choice, I am sure—"

"They were all given a choice. These want to return to Rurik, to see King Haikor for themselves, under the protection of the king of Weirland. After all, he is the man who encourages the hunting of the ekhono."

"What if someone recognizes them?"

"They are well disguised, dressed as natives of Weirland. Perhaps they felt it was the price they must pay, to look back and see the world they were saved from."

This was bravery of the highest order, and Issa felt she must meet it with courage of her own. She lifted her head and took one last look at the verdant green fields, in full glory. She focused on the song of the plants, but something felt different.

Just before she mounted her horse, she bent down and touched the tiny purple flowers that were called heart's lace. She was astonished to feel a pinch of thorn. She looked more closely and saw that the thorny red scrub called red stone had hidden underneath the flowers. She sucked at her bleeding finger and told herself it was nothing, but the pain made tears spring into her eyes.

Her father helped her mount her horse, normally the job of a servant, but it allowed them a few last moments of privacy. "Did you know," said King Jaap, "King Haikor and I met once, when we were boys. I was the heir already to the throne, but he was a younger son."

"What was he like then?" asked Issa.

King Jaap smiled. "I thought him charming. He knew what to say to make others like him, even at an early age. He was smart, though selfish as children often are. And even then, he wished to control everything around him. If Haikor found someone who disliked him, he would focus all his energies on changing that person's mind. His elder brother had no sense of how to make others like him. Sometimes I think it is just as well that Achter did not take the throne."

Achter was the elder brother who, it was rumored, had been ekhono. He had died young, and Issa had heard that it was Haikor who had poisoned him.

"I caught Haikor practicing different voices near the river once," King Jaap continued. "He must have thought he was far enough from the palace that no one would hear him. He tried out a booming, deep voice, and a mysterious, changing one. He even tried to sing a melody, which was lovely. I thought that he had a unique gift, and that he should use it. But I have heard that after he became king, he never sang again."

"His daughter sings, I hear," said Issa.

"She plays a flute," said King Jaap. "But she did not learn music from her father. She learned from a foreigner, a music master from the continent."

"Is she like him in other ways, then?" asked Issa.

"So I have heard. Far more like him than his son. I suspect you will need to know her well in time. Married or not, she will be a force in the court to balance yours."

"Mine?" said Issa.

"Of course. You will have power if you are betrothed to Edik. Even more when you are married."

"But I shall still be a princess," she said, uncomfortable with the thought of holding power in the Rurese court.

"Yes, and Ailsbet is a princess, as well. She may resent you for that. She has been the only princess in Rurik for some time."

And since Ailsbet was unweyr, Issa would not be able to talk to her about neweyr, would not be able to compete to see who could coax the most beautiful bloom out of the earth, as she did with Lady Willa.

She kissed her father on the cheek and then forced herself not to look back as the horses clopped forward. She could feel tears drying on her face, but she did not wipe them away. She must learn not to give her emotions away too easily when she was in Rurik. This was the beginning.

The party rode slowly that first day and stopped for the night some miles from the castle in a wood. Issa could almost imagine that she was simply staying overnight in a visit to the countryside. She slept well and led the whole party on her horse, enjoying the feeling of the neweyr all around her. She played with the puppy, which had adjusted well to the travel.

But the next evening, the terrain turned rocky and arid as the retinue approached the land bridge, and Issa felt the anger of the ocean. The neweyr here seemed no more than an echo. Even the living plants gave off only a faint sense of it.

Issa's ears rang, and she wanted desperately to return home.

At a small stream, the party stopped their horses and dismounted. Issa ate a hearty stew for dinner and for dessert, a biscuit and some fresh berries. She could taste each rainfall in the berries, each bright spring day that had passed in their fruition.

"Your Highness," said the ekhono woman.

"What is it?" asked Issa.

"I was only wondering if you will save the neweyr in Rurik? It's dying, from what I hear. King Haikor's taweyr oppresses everything, and even the crops are being affected. The fields do not produce as they should, and there are people starving in the country-side."

"You have no neweyr yourself. How do you know about the Rurese neweyr?"

The woman said, "My mother and sisters talked about it often before I came to Weirland. I cannot feel it myself, but the effect on the people of Rurik must matter to all those who are about the kingdom, whether or not they have neweyr."

"Is that why you wanted to come back with us? To see how Rurik does now?"

"Oh, no, Your Highness," the woman replied with a slight tremor of fear in her voice. "I wanted to come back to show myself I could. That I wasn't afraid."

Issa admired her courage. What a difference from what Issa had to face: power and responsibility, and a betrothal to a young prince. Was that so very terrible?

"Tell me about the taweyr," she said. "How did you know that you had it instead of the neweyr?"

At first, the woman looked as if she didn't want to answer. Then she said, "I thought I was unweyr for a time. I didn't show anything. Then the taweyr came out one day when I was arguing with my father, and I struck him down. I was afraid he was dead and started weeping over him. 'Like a girl,' he said, and we both laughed and cried. After that, we went to tell my mother and sisters, and he told them he'd have to bring me here to keep me safe."

"Do they ever come to visit you?" asked Issa.

"Oh, no. They can't. Sometimes my father sends me messages, or gifts, things he thinks I would miss, like the round stones from the river, or a feather from the hawk we trained together."

"You won't see your family then, when you are here?"

"They have a farm to work and the other children to care for. And that's hard enough in Rurik now, with the neweyr as it is."

"Do you ever wish you had the neweyr instead of the taweyr?" asked Issa.

"Of course. A thousand times. It would make everything easier, wouldn't it? But I am who I am."

"But if the weyrs come together, what then?" asked Issa.

"You mean the prophecy? I've always thought that meant the end of the world. When the two islands come together again, when the two weyrs are one—it's the same as saying when the sun falls out of the sky or the ocean doesn't gnaw at the weyr anymore."

"I see," Issa said, and tucked herself into her bedroll after seeing to the prince's puppy. But she did not sleep for some time. She could not stop thinking that the woman might be right, that the end of the world was more likely to come before Rurik and Weirland could ever be truly joined.

While it was still cool the next morning, the party proceeded onward to the land bridge. Issa had thought she was prepared for it, but as the bridge came in sight, the ocean filled her ears. Her legs felt dead to her, and her whole body had to be forced to work. Her eyes did not blink without conscious effort. Her lungs did not take in air unless she made them. She could even feel her heart skipping now and again, and it left her in agony.

For the first time in her life, Issa wished that she had no weyr, if it would make this moment easier. To be unweyr in a place like this would be a gift.

With a deep breath to steady herself, Issa stepped onto the land bridge. It was only a little wider than the span of a large horse, and none of the party was willing to go closer to the edge, so everyone walked in single file. Issa focused on each footstep, fearful that she might slip and fall. The servants led the horses, which were afraid of the sound of the ocean and the height of the bridge above the cliffs and could not be calmed with neweyr.

The sound of the puppy's sudden whining filled Issa's ears as she stumbled along.

"It is—the same—every time," gasped one of the male servants who walked behind her. The man looked gray and ill. Issa suspected that she must look even worse.

If she had ever doubted, here was proof that the ekhono were nothing like the unweyr. The one unweyr her father had sent with her had come exactly for this purpose, to make sure everyone crossed the land bridge safely. He was ahead now, coaxing animals and servants along one by one.

"How many—times—have you crossed before?" Issa asked the unweyr servant, trying to focus on something other than the ocean's rage.

"Eighteen," said the man.

Issa stared at him in astonishment.

The ocean here rose up against the white cliffs on both sides of the bridge and sprayed in magnificent plumes of white foam and waves of watery needles. To look down and see the shore far below made her ill.

The salty, angry smell of the ocean was overpowering, and there were no birds overhead, nor any other animals that Issa could see or hear. The roar of the waves themselves was the only, constant noise.

This was the point at which, a thousand years ago, King Arhort had split apart the two kingdoms and the two weyrs at the early death of his beloved wife. He had not been able to save her with his neweyr, and he felt that if he was in pain, the whole world should be in pain with him. If he could not save the life he wanted with neweyr, he would never use it again, only the taweyr, which matched his dark anger. And after the kingdoms were sundered, every man could only use the taweyr, and every woman the neweyr. Except for the ekhono.

Suddenly, Issa felt the hand of the unweyr man on her and he pulled her over the last part of the land bridge. "Safe, Princess?" he asked as she stepped off the bridge onto the steady land.

She nodded and let herself take in the first breath of Rurik. She felt enormous relief at being away from the ocean, almost as if she was weightless. This was not her home, but there was neweyr here, if not as strong as what she was used to.

They continued for a few more hours, each step away from the bridge making Issa feel better. Then exhaustion seemed to hit the whole party, and they stopped in the dim light of early evening.

Issa asked the ekhono servant she had talked to on the land bridge, "Is it worse for those who have more weyr?"

"Yes." He looked at her a moment. "There are

many tales of those who have died near here, or who have thrown themselves into the water. There are rituals described in great detail for avoiding such an awful fate. Some of the servants were chanting them as we crossed. Did you not hear them?"

"I heard nothing, nothing at all," said Issa. She shuddered and pulled her cloak more tightly around her, but she could still hear the ocean roaring at her again, tearing at her neweyr and laughing at the prophecy she hoped to fulfill.

Chapter Eighteen

Issa

AFTER THE MONTHLONG JOURNEY through the craggy north and wet and muddy center of Rurik, Issa and her company arrived at the city of Skorosa in midsummer. The long travel had given Issa some understanding of the effort it had cost Duke Kellin to visit his brother. The royal party had become lost for a time, and Issa had feared that they would never reach the palace. But in the end, they were only two days late coming into the city.

They entered the city at midday, under a hot, cloudless sky that made Issa feel as if she were utterly exposed. The city of Skorosa itself was unlike any place Issa could have imagined. So many buildings, so many people crowded all together. She was sure that all of Weirland did not hold so many. All this time, she had thought the neweyr was in danger because of King Haikor, but she wondered now if the land itself might be insufficient to the needs of the people who lived there.

The buildings on the outskirts of the city were ramshackle, with thistle or daub and wattle roofs, as in Weirland. There were children running everywhere, clothed and not, dirty-faced, singing and pointing at her. She was a little frightened by them, and she kept a tight hold on the puppy for Prince Edik.

Then Issa and her retinue reached a more bustling part of town, its narrow streets crammed with horses and wagons. She could see signs for taverns, bakeries, seamstresses, and any number of businesses. There were also plenty of merchants hawking their wares in the middle of the street. Some seemed angry, shaking their fists at the party for passing without stopping to make a purchase.

As the party drew closer to the palace, they passed elaborate homes of white and gray stone, with stained-glass windows and white columns on either side of their entrances. There were no buildings like these in Weirland. Even the servants on the street seemed better dressed than Issa was. She glanced down at herself and wondered if her gown would stand out in King Haikor's court. She had worked so hard to find the best that was in Weirland, but now she was anxious once more. She handed the puppy back to one of the servants and heard it whimper as the basket lid was closed over it.

Then Issa reached up to be sure her hair was still neatly pulled into one sleek braid down her back. Eventually, she would have to wear her hair in the elaborate styles worn by the women in the court of King Haikor. But for her reception at court and her first meeting with Prince Edik, she would be seen as a Weirese princess first.

At last, Issa and her retinue rode up to the gates of the palace itself. The Tower that King Haikor had erected to hold prisoners was so tall that Issa could see it swaying slightly in the breeze above her. The stone was gray at the top, but toward the bottom it became gradually darker. It looked like a huge burning candle, and she felt as if she might easily be caught in that fire and consumed. The Tower dwarfed the rest of the palace, which was smaller and lighter in color, and rambling in shape.

In a moment, the gates were opened, and Issa and her company dismounted and walked inside behind the keep master and his men. The air beneath the gate was cool, and Issa reminded herself she must look the princess here, so she held her head high as she moved through the courtyard. But by the time she reached the keep itself, her legs felt sodden and dragging, as if she had walked a mile through the river Weyr.

The keep master bowed and relinquished the lead to the palace guard. He led them forward, up stairs and through corridors, until at last the party entered the famed Throne Room of King Haikor. The walls were covered in dark, carved, wooden panels, and the windows were made of colored glass in the red and black of Rurik. There were weapons mounted on all the walls, spears, swords, and scimitars, scythes, and battle-axes, including one that looked like it was still covered in dried black blood. Issa knew that the weapons could be swung off the wall by anyone with taweyr.

Sitting on the enormous throne was King Haikor, and at his right side, a boy with arms, legs, and a neck that all seemed too long for his body. He looked as if he had grown a great deal recently, and he seemed gawky and unsure of himself. He wore a gold crown on his glossy black hair, and she guessed this must be

Prince Edik, though he bore little resemblance to the boy in the portrait.

To the king's left was a woman hardly older than Issa herself, buxom and small-featured, her hair teased into an elaborate coif complete with birds and flowers. Issa might have thought she was the other princess, but to the right of the young prince stood a tall young woman with bright red hair, a pale face, and a long nose. She wore a haughty expression, and while her eyes met Issa's easily, there was no warmth in them. She was so like her father in appearance that Issa knew immediately this was Ailsbet, princess of Rurik.

Issa could well believe that a woman like this could be unweyr, for there was nothing feminine or kind or inviting about her. She turned back to look at Prince Edik, who seemed as nervous as Issa herself. He, at least, would not frighten or intimidate her.

She stepped forward and curtsied to King Haikor. As princess of Weirland, she did not wait for him to raise her up, but she let him take her hand. He kissed it formally, and then offered it to his son.

Prince Edik's eyes were a fine and shining blue. "Princess Marlissa of Weirland," he said, his voice cracking on the last word.

"Prince Edik of Rurik, I greet thee," said Issa. She

turned to the servant behind her, who handed her the basket with the sleek black puppy. She offered it to Prince Edik and saw his face change completely. He bent his head down and let the puppy lick it, whispering words of encouragement to the small animal. He was obviously thrilled, and Issa knew she had chosen well, though Kellin ought rightly to get some of the credit for that.

"You are welcome to my kingdom and to my palace," said Edik formally, his eyes dancing.

Now Issa offered King Haikor the gift from her father, which was a dagger with a white stone hilt carved with the great stag of Rurik.

King Haikor took it and twisted it, a gleam in his eye.

King Jaap had chosen well, but the other king's response did not make Issa comfortable.

"This is Lady Pippa," said King Haikor, with a wave of his hand to the gaudily dressed noblewoman who was young enough to be her older sister. "My companion."

"It is an honor to meet you, Lady Pippa," Issa murmured politely. She had not thought to bring a gift for her and felt a moment's pause.

But Lady Pippa smiled and greeted Issa eagerly. "Princess Marlissa, you are welcome to Rurik. We are so delighted to have you here and think—"

"And this is my daughter, Princess Ailsbet," said King Haikor, cutting off Lady Pippa.

The tall princess curtsied briefly to Issa.

"I have waited long to see the princess of Rurik," said Issa.

Princess Ailsbet said nothing in return.

Issa turned back to her servants and found the ekhono woman was handing her the gift she had brought for Ailsbet from her father's library.

"It is a collection of some of my favorite poems," said Issa. "I have marked some of them for you." She opened one of the pages and held out the book.

The other princess raised an eyebrow and then stared down at the book with disdain. "It is not a poem that would be suited for music, is it?" she said.

Issa felt a fool. She knew that Princess Ailsbet was musical. Why hadn't she brought her something more appropriate to that? But the moment was over, and her impression on the other princess was made. She could only try to do better later.

"Princess Marlissa, we hope to see you at dinner this evening," said King Haikor. "I am sure that you would prefer to rest now. The journey must have been exhausting."

Issa had just the presence of mind to whisper

"Thank you," to the king. She felt herself trembling as if she were on the land bridge again, with the water howling beneath her, the ocean tearing at her power.

Then suddenly, Issa heard a different, familiar voice. "Princess Marlissa."

She looked up into the eyes of Duke Kellin.

"The king asked me to help you feel more at home here, since you and I are acquainted already."

But Duke Kellin would make her feel more self-conscious than ever. Issa was suddenly aware of her disarray after her long weeks of travel.

She reached for the faint pull of the neweyr and embraced it, gradually feeling stronger. "I only need time to rest," she said.

"Of course," said Kellin. He nodded to a servant and asked him to show her to her rooms. Then he bowed and was gone.

Issa desperately wanted to call him back, but she knew she could not. He was King Haikor's man here, and she dared not reveal what else she knew of him.

When she and her retinue were headed to her rooms, Issa heard the ekhono woman from Weirland complaining angrily about King Haikor's treatment of Issa. "He makes it very clear how weak he finds her and Weirland itself. She should return home immediately." The woman looked red in the face, and her fists were clenched, as if she were ready to fight.

It took a moment for Issa to think of why the woman, so controlled before, had changed. It was the taweyr here in Rurik, and in the palace itself. Without neweyr to balance it, the taweyr made the woman overly aggressive.

"I am well. You are well. He has not harmed us," she said calmly. "Beware the taweyr here."

The ekhono woman took a breath and seemed to steady herself. But after a moment, she said, "King Haikor has more than one kind of poison."

Was it any wonder that his court is as it is, Issa thought. How did his noblemen survive it? How did Kellin keep himself so calm?

Issa slept fitfully that night, dreaming of a joust between King Haikor and her father. She called out again and again to stop the spear from entering her father's chest, but started awake before she saw the end of the dream.

Chapter Nineteen
Ailsbet

Ailsbet envied the other princess's poise. She had meant to say some words of welcome of her own, and thank her for the gift of the fine book. But Princess Marlissa was so perfect, every movement so graceful, every part of her dainty and feminine. Next to her, Ailsbet felt huge and ungainly, and when she opened her mouth, the only thing that came out was her own anger and mistrust.

When the Weirese visitors were gone, King Haikor laughed. "What a gift she brought you," he said to Edik. "That little black puppy is good for nothing but to be dinner for my true hounds."

Edik shook his head and held the young hound close to his chest while the king turned to Ailsbet.

"And you, a book for a princess? As though you had nothing better to do with your time than read," said King Haikor. "But in Weirland, I suppose there is nothing else to do. And a woman there does not think of beauty."

Ailsbet rather preferred a woman who thought of more than beauty.

"The dagger she gave to me was fine enough, but did you see how she had her hair braided like that, in one single plait down her back? Like a peasant woman, except that in Rurik even peasant women have better taste. What did you think of her, Edik?"

Edik shrugged. "She was old," he said.

That made King Haikor laugh again. "Old indeed. Old in the way her lips press together, in the way her eyes squint, in the way that she looked in judgment on us all. I daresay that if she caught you having a bit of fun, she would never forgive you. She will only get older and more disagreeable, I am afraid. But you must do your duty to your kingdom. It is what princes are made for. And kings." He nudged his son.

At this, Ailsbet had enough, and she returned to her own rooms and her flute. She played indifferently, however, unable to find her usual focus.

A knock on her door startled her, and she found Duke Kellin outside. She was sure from his expression that he had some distasteful message from her father.

"What is it?" she asked. She reminded herself that she had seen him with the ekhono girl on the coast last summer. She knew his secret, and he did not know hers. She had power over him, and no reason to be afraid.

"It has been some time since I had a chance to speak to you, Princess Ailsbet," said Duke Kellin. "I only wanted to tell you that I am sorry for your loss."

Ailsbet blinked at him, for a moment too surprised to speak.

"Your mother and your betrothed," said Kellin. "Lord Umber."

No one had spoken of Queen Aske since the funeral in the winter. It was as if King Haikor had never been married before, as if Lady Pippa were the only noblewoman on whom he had ever bestowed his favor. As for Lord Umber, he was only mentioned when King Haikor wished to embarrass Ailsbet.

"You did not know my mother well, and you did not like Lord Umber," said Ailsbet. "How can I believe you are genuine?"

"I did not like Lord Umber, it is true. But that is no fault of yours, and his loss must have been painful."

His sympathy, whether real or not, made her uncomfortable. "You don't know me at all," said Ailsbet coldly.

"I should like to know you, if you would let me," said Kellin.

"And why should I do that?" asked Ailsbet. Was this the beginning of his courting her, so he could assume the power that had belonged to Lord Umber as the betrothed of the king's only daughter?

"Because you need a friend?" said Kellin. Seeing a hint of a smirk on his face, Ailsbet thought he must be amusing himself with her.

She thought of all the ladies of the court who had pretended to befriend her, through her childhood. She had seen through them, even when she was very young.

"I have lived my whole life without a single friend," said Ailsbet. "Why should I need one now?"

The smile faded from Kellin's face. "Let me tell you what I know of you," he said. "You are indeed strong enough to live alone your whole life."

He knew how to flatter better than anyone she had ever met. Ailsbet was annoyed with herself for almost liking this man.

"You do not wish to be known as your father's daughter. You wish to be known as yourself. You are defiant in order to prove yourself."

It was true enough. "And you are happy to be the invisible hand behind my father?" asked Ailsbet.

"Nothing would make me happier than to be invisible."

"I don't believe it," said Ailsbet flatly. "No man wishes to be invisible."

"Then I am no man," said Duke Kellin. "My grandest hope is that the history books forget me and that my name is never mentioned again once I am dead. I hope that even those who know me will have difficulty remembering my name."

Ailsbet shook her head. "I know that is not true," she said.

"Oh? And how is that?" asked Duke Kellin.

"I saw you," she burst out. "On the southern coast, when you were supposed to be on your way to Weirland to arrange for the betrothal."

"I don't know what you mean," said Kellin stiffly.

"The girl. The boat. The ekhono hunters," said Ailsbet.

"You must be mistaking me for someone else. Perhaps the ekhono hunters frightened you, and you became confused," said Kellin blandly.

"It was you," she said. "I was not confused. And I aided you. I sent the ekhono hunters away."

"Why should ekhono hunters come for me?" asked Duke Kellin, still trying to pretend his innocence.

"Because the girl you were helping into the boat to Weirland was ekhono. And I suspect that if I were to begin to ask questions, I might find that more than one ekhono hunter has had an encounter with you over the last few years, though they may not have known your true identity. If I had them all together, what stories would they tell of you, I wonder?"

Kellin stared at her, his lips pressed together. Finally, he bowed his head. "What is it you wish, then, Princess Ailsbet?" he asked.

She was annoyed with him. "I don't wish for anything. If you imagine that I am trying to win some favor from you, you are mistaken. I do not need your favors."

"Then why speak to me of this?" he asked.

"I only wanted you to stop lying to me. My father loves to be lied to, and all the rest of the court has become used to it. But I am not one of them."

"I serve my kingdom," said Kellin.

Ailsbet had heard him say the same thing before. "Not the kingdom my father imagines you serve. That kingdom hates the ekhono."

"I serve the kingdom of Rurik as it should be," said Kellin, his tone softer.

"Ah," said Ailsbet. "And that is a kingdom with ekhono accepted as any other?"

"Yes."

"This is the reason you wish to remain anonymous, then? Because it is the only way to help the ekhono?"

Kellin nodded.

"Good," said Ailsbet. "I am glad of that. And in Weirland? Did you speak to the ekhono there? Did they greet you fondly?"

"My brother is ekhono," said Kellin after some hesitation.

"Your brother?" Ailsbet did not know why she was surprised, but she was. The idea of Kellin having a brother felt strange. He seemed a man without any ties.

"Kedor is his name," he added.

Now she had everything she needed to ruin

him. One word to her father and Kellin would be dead.

It made Ailsbet feel strangely close to him.

"You could do much for the kingdom in the future," said Kellin.

"Me? I am only a princess, destined to be married off to someone even more invisible to history than you," said Ailsbet.

"Perhaps," said Kellin. "And perhaps not. Your brother is young and malleable. You could be the voice that counters what your father tells him. You could stand behind him when he comes to power, whisper the truth in his ear about the ekhono."

"That is why you are here. Not for my father. But for my brother," said Ailsbet.

"Not only your brother," said Kellin. "For you, as well. You have the potential to wield a great deal of power, if you choose."

"Invisible power," said Ailsbet.

"Power nonetheless," said Kellin.

And with that, Kellin left her chambers, leaving Ailsbet to consider what it might mean for her to have power. She had never wanted it, and she wanted it even less now. But Kellin was right, that was the only way that the ekhono could be safe in the long-term. And it was not only the ekhono who were unsafe. The whole kingdom had become suspicious, grasping, and terrified since her father had taken the throne.

Ailsbet was ekhono herself. She should care for her own kind, should she not? But still, she wanted her music. And she hated power.

Chapter Twenty

Issa

ISSA SLEPT BADLY her first night in Rurik. The sounds were completely different. She did not hear the baaing of the sheep outside the castle nor the chatter of the birds overhead. Instead, she heard the creak of the stones in the Tower as the wind whirled around them and the sound of the boats coming up the river to the port. The noises were not unpleasant, but still she woke up feeling tired and listless.

King Haikor had sent her four new servants to attend her. She had not asked for more servants, but it seemed the king thought no noblewoman, let alone a princess, could manage with only two maid-servants. The other servants who had come with her from her own country were not suited to attending the princess and had returned to Weirland. To send the new maids away would risk King Haikor's displeasure, so they remained. They made Issa feel even more a stranger here. Their accents were sharper than she was used to, and they seemed always to be hurrying her along.

That morning, she spent hours having her hair done in the Rurese style, brushed and oiled, then wound into four tiny crowns in a row at the top of her head, while the rest of it was curled and left to hang on her neck—where it itched horribly. Then her trunk was opened and her gowns drawn out. They were shaken and cleaned and shaped. The servants looked at them dubiously. Then one asked if she might offer the princess a gown of her own as a gift. When she brought it, Issa realized that it had to be her best gown, but it was more elegant than anything she owned herself.

"Thank you," said Issa. Refusing the gift might offend the servant, she realized, and she could not appear in court in clothing coarser than the servants' garments. King Japp had given Issa some gold for the journey and expenses. She would have to spend it on a new wardrobe.

At last, she was dressed, and she followed her servants to the Throne Room. The palace was so large that Issa wondered if she would ever learn all its twists and turns. She could live all her life here, she thought glumly, and still fear that she would lose herself.

Prince Edik was waiting for her and after a moment of hesitation, Issa moved to his side.

"Are you well?" he asked quietly, patting the hound.

She nodded. "Very well, I thank you."

"You ate well? You slept well?" he asked.

"Yes," she assured him. There seemed little else to say to him. Issa stood, trying not to fidget, as King Haikor called Duke Kellin forward.

"Do you bring me a name?" demanded Haikor loudly, as the duke knelt before him.

Issa could see more than one nobleman near her trembling. One shook so badly he fell down.

"I do, Your Majesty," said Duke Kellin.

"What is it, then? Who has betrayed me?" asked King Haikor.

Duke Kellin glanced up and caught Issa's eye. His gaze was cold and he gave no hint they had ever met before. "It is Lord Werecks."

Instantly, the man cried out, "No. I swear, Your Majesty. I swear it is not I."

Issa turned and saw him. He was a thin man of middle age, balding on top, but with a wealth of hair on his chin and upper lip. He wore a fashionable, bright blue-and-magenta doublet that made his pale cheeks stand out.

The king's guards had already reached his side.

Issa glanced at Edik and saw that he seemed undisturbed by this, as if it happened every day. Perhaps it did.

Issa wished her father were there. King Haikor's court was a dangerous place. Who would be next? It seemed a matter of the king's whims. And Kellin was helping him.

But she imagined her father would tell her that she must let King Haikor deal with his court in his own way. A king sometimes had to do distasteful things to prove his power. And when men broke the laws, they must be punished.

While the court looked on in silence, Lord Werecks fought the guards, kicking and spitting. "It is not I! He lies! I shall tell you the truth, if you let me. I shall tell you everything," he said, gasping.

The guards slammed him down before the king, his head hitting the floor. Blood sprayed from his nose, spreading out on the polished marble floor in a pool.

Issa looked up and met Princess Ailsbet's eyes, but she could not tell what the other princess thought of this. Did she approve?

"You have the proof?" asked King Haikor.

"I do, Your Majesty." Duke Kellin opened a leather satchel. "There are papers there, letters written by Lord Werecks in which he discusses his plans. Maps he has made of the dying neweyr, places he believed he could take easily from you or other landowners. Also papers he has signed for debts incurred over the last year, more than two thousand gold coins."

Kellin spoke with cool precision, as if this were no more than a business transaction. He must have a good reason for what he was doing, Issa told herself. Lord Werecks must be a traitor, not only to King Haikor, but to the land itself, to the weyrs.

"The gold was for a new home for my young wife!" Lord Werecks said, his voice muffled. "And an inheritance for my newborn son. That is why I wished to buy land. That reason and no other."

But King Haikor paid no attention to the man. "I thank you, Duke Kellin, for your faithful service to the kingdom."

Duke Kellin gave the papers to one of the king's men, then stepped past Lord Werecks and offered to take the man to the Tower himself, if the king wished it.

King Haikor nodded, clearly pleased. "I shall give you two guards, then, to carry the burden, but you shall guide them to the Tower and hand him over there."

Kellin accepted this, and he led the guards and Lord Werecks out of the court.

Issa did not know why Kellin had done what he had, but she trembled in response. She saw Prince Edik, who was now at the far end of the court, near the door, and moved toward him. He was holding tightly to the black hound and she heard him whisper the name *Midnight* into its ear.

A good name, she thought, though she was still distracted by what had happened to Lord Werecks. Many of the noblemen and ladies in the court had moved to the windows to watch him being led across the courtyard to the Tower.

Issa was jostled away from Prince Edik and found herself standing by Princess Ailsbet, who said, "And here we are together."

"Indeed," said Issa, not sure if she should stare out the window or try to avoid seeing Lord Werecks.

"He frightens me like this," said Ailsbet.

"Your father?" said Issa.

"Not my father," Ailsbet whispered. "Duke Kellin."

Issa froze. She dared show no emotion when it came to Kellin, and especially not to Edik's sister. But before she could respond, she heard a sound like a tree trunk being split in two by a vicious storm.

Issa looked out into the center courtyard and saw Lord Werecks sprawled on the ground, his head at an unnatural angle. He looked as though he had flown into the sky and then dropped from some height.

He was clearly dead.

"He must have fought against Duke Kellin," said a lady.

"He did not look as if he had strength enough to threaten a gnat," said another.

Issa tried to tell herself that this was mercy, of a kind. What else could Kellin have done for the man? But a part of her wondered if she did not know Kellin at all.

The next week at court was a blur of meeting the nobles of Rurik, some of whom were already at court, but others who had come to pay a visit to court from the outlying counties. Issa spent hours on her feet, feeling as if she had become a statue, nodding and curtsying and looking pretty, but saying very little. King Haikor seemed to enjoy watching her struggle with the long days of meeting. There was always food and drink, but little time to consume it. While Prince Edik was often at her side, Issa had no chance to speak to him privately. As for Kellin, he was sometimes gone with no explanation, and that always made Issa feel out of place. Even if she could not speak to him, knowing he was there steadied her.

Throughout all of this, Princess Ailsbet would not even look at Issa. Did the other princess dislike her so much? It was a surprise, therefore, when Ailsbet came privately to Princess Marlissa's bedchamber the day after an especially long court meeting, several days after Issa had met with a palace seamstress and had ordered three gowns, to be finished as soon as possible.

"You look like a tree in the spring," said Ailsbet at the sight of Issa's new pale-green gown.

"You are kind," said Issa, suddenly self-conscious. Why had Princess Ailsbet come to her now? To mock her?

"But it is true. You are like a storm or the seasons, a force of nature. You are the neweyr itself, I think. My brother, Edik, is in awe of you."

But Ailsbet was not, Issa thought. "And you who have no neweyr think to compliment me on my wealth of it?" she asked. Ailsbet did not react to this, but nonetheless, Issa felt immediately guilty for what she had said.

"I am a musician," said Ailsbet. "Did you know that?"

"I did. But I have not heard you perform on your flute. It is a flute, is it not?" Surely, this was not the real reason Ailsbet had come. "Why are you here?" Issa asked.

"I came to warn you," said Ailsbet. "About Kellin."

Issa gaped at her. "What of Kellin? Is he in danger?" Was King Haikor angry with him for killing Lord Werecks? Had someone found out that Kellin's brother was ekhono?

Ailsbet smiled faintly. "Indeed," she said. "You and he are both in danger, I fear."

Issa was silent. She had hardly looked at him and had certainly not teased him as she might have in Weirland the year before.

"Your feelings for him are too obvious," said Ailsbet.

"I do not know what you mean," said Issa immediately. "I have no feelings for him. I do not speak to him. I do not look at him."

"That is precisely the problem," said Ailsbet. "You treat him differently than anyone else. You cut him as if he has wounded you. It will not be long before others notice and begin to spread rumors about what it means. They will begin by saying he has some ancient grudge against you, that he has offended you in some way. But they will not stop there. They may come to the truth by accident, they are stupid enough for that. But they are also persistent, and they will gossip until they see you react, as you are doing now."

"Oh," said Issa softly, and sank to her bed. She had been trying so hard to do her duty, to act properly, to be the princess of Weirland that everyone in King Haikor's court expected.

"You are supposed to be betrothed officially to my brother in less than three months' time. I know he is only thirteen years old, but he is not a fool."

"I did not think he was," said Issa. "But—"

"Is Kellin so irresistible? I find him rather cold," said Ailsbet.

It was an interesting comment from a woman whom Issa had thought cold herself. "He is not—I do not—there is nothing between us," Issa got out.

That was the truth. Whatever she felt for him, it was surely a passing thing. A childish fancy, no more. And Kellin felt nothing in return for her. His duty to the kingdom would not allow it.

"Are you so naïve as to truly believe that? Perhaps you are," said Ailsbet. "It makes me wonder what the court must be like in Weirland."

"I intend to be a good wife and queen for your brother, Edik," Issa said earnestly. "I shall show him all the love that is due him."

"Due him?" echoed Ailsbet.

"As my betrothed," said Issa. "Will you tell me about Edik? What you see of him as a sister?"

"He sees things," said Ailsbet carefully. "He may seem oblivious to what goes on around him, but he is not. He is smart, but he does not judge quickly. He takes the measure of those around him. He does not have much choice, but he knows whom he can trust and whom he cannot."

Issa was surprised that she was getting more helpful information about Edik's character from this chance encounter with his sister than she had found in the last week and more in Rurik. "And whom can he trust?" she asked, daring to hope for more.

"Not many," Ailsbet admitted.

"And you? Whom do you trust?"

"I trust myself," said Ailsbet.

Of course she did. Issa bowed her head. "I shall do my best to control myself. I thank you again for coming to me and offering to help. Please—do not tell your brother." Or your father, she thought.

"I did not do it for your thanks," said Ailsbet, and she left without another word.

CHAPTER TWENTY-ONE

Issa

THE NEXT EVENING AT DINNER, Princess Ailsbet made it clear to the whole court that she had an interest in Kellin. She smiled across the room at Kellin, then moved closer to say a few words in his ear before flitting away again, still smiling. For all Ailsbet had said the day before about warning Issa not to reveal her feelings too clearly, it seemed that Ailsbet had decided to take Duke Kellin for herself.

Issa turned to find Lady Pippa and two other noblewomen deep in conversation about Duke Kellin and Ailsbet. She stepped closer to them. She had been wondering how to make a place for herself among the ladies of the court. They had all nodded to her when she was introduced, but then they turned back to their conversations, and she had not spoken to any of them since. In Weirland, Issa had never had to learn to draw attention to herself. She was naturally the center of attention there, and she had always felt at ease. It was a rude awakening to come here and be no one, even with the betrothal to Prince Edik in the offing.

"You see how Duke Kellin rarely breaks a smile?" said the other lady, whose name was Viona. "He does not know how much that will attract Princess Ailsbet. She is tired of humor after Lord Umber."

"Umber betrayed her father, in the end. But Kellin stands stalwart at his side, loyal and true. Any woman would fall in love with such a man," said the other lady.

Then Lady Pippa said, "Ailsbet would fall in love with any man who looked at her twice. And with a man who refused to look at her—she would fall in love with him doubly."

The two noblewomen laughed and Issa tried to join in, though she feared her laughter sounded brittle and false. Lady Pippa turned to her. "Princess

Marlissa," she said. "We did not realize you were here."

"Princess Ailsbet seems very different from the other women of the court," Issa said. "Do you think it is because of her lack of neweyr?"

"She is different because she thinks she is above us all," said Lady Viona.

"And because she cannot be without that flute in her hand. I wonder sometimes if she needs a flute more than a man," said Lady Pippa.

Issa flushed. "Is there no one in Rurik who appreciates music as she does?" she asked. She knew nothing about music but had assumed it was not the same here. She remembered her father saying that the king sang so well.

"Don't tell us you are a musician, as well?" asked Lady Viona.

"No," said Issa.

"Good," said Lady Pippa. "One musician is one too many, as far as I am concerned. A lady at court has certain obligations, don't you agree? She must think of others. Not live in her own world." Lady Pippa touched a finger to her temple.

"But does Princess Ailsbet have no friends? No confidantes?"

Lady Viona stared pointedly at Issa. "Who

could be a friend to such a woman?" she asked.

"Because she has no neweyr?" asked Issa.

"Because she makes no effort. She thinks she can stand apart from us. Well, let her. Duke Kellin will not be under her spell long, I think. She is the king's daughter, to be sure, but he knows that he needs a woman who will help him at court."

Issa walked away, wishing fervently then that she had brought Lady Neca with her, or even Lady Hadda or Lady Sassa. Anyone of her court who was familiar to her. She could talk to them, passing a pleasant evening without worrying what it looked like to stand apart from all the others. What if King Haikor's court came to think she thought herself too good for them?

Shortly thereafter, Prince Edik stumbled off to bed, barely awake. Midnight, the hound, was in his arms, sleeping soundly.

Issa was left on her own to watch Kellin dancing with Ailsbet, his hands on her waist, his head next to hers, whispering things that Issa could only imagine.

Later, he came to stand by her. "Princess Marlissa," he said formally, as if to make clear that she could never be anything more to him than that.

After a moment, Issa found her anger dissolving into self-pity. She had known it would be difficult to marry Prince Edik. Seeing Kellin again had changed nothing but what she felt in her heart. She must still do what was best for her kingdom. Kellin came to ask her to dance with him later that evening, but she refused him, claiming exhaustion, and went to the far side of the Great Hall. She did not know what to do around him anymore. She could not act coldly, but she could not act as she felt, either. She did not trust herself to find a middle ground.

"Come walk with me in the halls," said Ailsbet. Issa had not seen her come up behind her. "It is as much privacy as we are likely to get tonight."

Issa did not know if she wanted to have another private conversation with Ailsbet, but she supposed she did not have much choice. They went out of the Great Hall.

"Well?" said Ailsbet.

"You are the one who asked me to come speak with you," said Issa.

"Because you are revealing too much. You look like a mourning dove in there, every glance a song of despair."

"You think me weak," said Issa.

"Hardly weak," said Ailsbet.

"I am not like you," said Issa. She was new to hiding her emotions.

"You did not see me when I thought myself in love," Ailsbet said, shaking her head. "I was a fool then, too."

Issa supposed that was a compliment, of sorts, from Ailsbet. "A clever way you had of asking what I felt for Kellin, so you could have him for yourself."

Ailsbet did not answer for a long moment. "That is not why I came to you last night," she said.

"Then why?" Issa demanded.

"To see what you were like. To see what you were worth."

"And what did you decide?"

"That you were the sort of person whom it is nearly impossible to help," said Ailsbet. "And it is as true this moment as it was that one."

Issa raised a hand, and the sound of the slap rang out like music.

"I only meant that you will take nothing," said Ailsbet. "You must always be in charge. But you are distraught now. You should sleep."

"Don't tell me what I should do," said Issa, and she raised her hand a second time.

It did not fall on Ailsbet's face, for the other princess caught Issa's wrist and held it tightly.

Issa tried to pull away, but she found she could

not. She tugged at her hand, but it was not merely a matter of Ailsbet's strength. There was something hot and immovable that held her, something Issa could not fight against.

It was the taweyr, Issa realized. Ailsbet was not unweyr. She was ekhono.

"I hate this place, all of it," said Issa. "The taste of the taweyr is everywhere, and I can never feel the neweyr. No sense of quiet or peace, no connection to the earth, no sense of continuity."

"I have no neweyr to mourn its absence here," said Ailsbet, something they both knew very well now, though it seemed to be a secret to the rest of the court, and to King Haikor. Then she let go of Issa at last. "Excuse me," she said. Abruptly, she turned away from Issa and was gone.

Issa was left to wonder what she should make of this secret she now held in her hands. But if she had power, Ailsbet held equal power against her. She could ruin the betrothal with Edik by simply hinting that Issa had done something improper with Kellin, and Issa would be sent home in disgrace. As for Kellin, there could be a much worse fate waiting for him. And still they had done nothing.

Issa wandered the halls of the palace alone for some time before she found her way back to the

Great Hall. But once there, she had no heart to remain, and found a servant to help her back to her own chambers. Princess Ailsbet was long gone, and Duke Kellin did not even look at her.

Chapter Twenty-two
Ailsbet

THE NIGHT AFTER her unpleasant encounter with the princess from Weirland, Ailsbet placed herself at Duke Kellin's side at dinner. He was handsome, to be sure, and he was intelligent. But she knew very little of him, except that his brother was ekhono.

"And how are your crops this year?" Ailsbet asked. Despite Princess Marlissa's accusations, she and Duke Kellin had hardly exchanged anything but pleasantries, and she did not know what to say to him.

"Very well, I thank you," Kellin responded blandly.

"You do not lack in neweyr on your estate?"

Ailsbet asked. Did he have any other family at all?

"We lack in nothing, Princess. Your father's rule has made us very prosperous," said Kellin.

"And how do you enjoy the palace? You have been here two years now, I believe. But I suspect I could still show you some of its secrets. I know some of the best walks in the palace, places not everyone knows."

"Very tempting," said Duke Kellin. "I shall consider your offer when I have time away from my duties with your father to indulge in such ease."

This stung Ailsbet. Did he think her whole life was ease? "Perhaps I could advise you about other concerns. I know my father's nobles as well as I know his palace. I have seen them year after year."

"Indeed, I should appreciate your advice greatly," said Kellin.

But thereafter, he seemed to ignore her when Ailsbet tried to speak, turning to speak to the nobleman next to him, who had a great deal to say about how to use taweyr on a male horse to make it ride faster. Ailsbet went to bed frustrated and annoyed that she cared about Kellin's opinion at all. She had not cared about anyone's opinion of her for years— since Master Lukacs left, in fact.

The following day was dark and rainy, though still

warm with summer. On a whim, Ailsbet brought her flute to court, though she knew it might bring her father's displeasure upon her. Before dinner, Kellin came to her side and asked, "Will you play for me? Or must I offer you a trade for such a demand?"

"No need for trading," said Ailsbet. "I would be glad to play for you."

Kellin clapped his hands immediately and shouted for silence. "Princess Ailsbet will delight us with her music," he said to the court. He nodded to her.

Once she had begun, Ailsbet felt exposed, but she could not stop. The music had an energy, almost a mind of its own, that she could not control, and she found herself playing a tragic love song.

King Haikor clapped when she was finished. "A little dreary, my dear. But perhaps the weather is upsetting you."

Ailsbet turned away from her father.

"Princess Ailsbet," Kellin said afterward, when only she could hear him. "It was beautiful. I thank you. I wish I could hear it again and again."

"You do not," said Ailsbet. "It would distract you from your duties."

"Yes," said Kellin. "But there is something about that music—it makes me feel differently. Calmer and more connected."

Ailsbet looked around the room and saw that Kellin was not the only one affected. The court seemed less fractious, at least for the moment. Her father's expression was calm, and so were those of all the other noblemen. Was it possible that her music had had an effect on the taweyr? Ailsbet knew that her music stilled her own taweyr, but she had not realized it worked as well on others.

After dinner, Duke Kellin asked her to dance with him. She felt the whole court was staring at her.

"Are you attempting to prove your courage?" Kellin asked.

"Is that what you like about Issa? That she is courageous?" asked Ailsbet.

"She is courageous," said Kellin calmly, "in the most important matters."

"And this is not important?" asked Ailsbet.

"This is a show. Like your father's many shows," said Kellin. "You are like him, do you know that?"

"I am not," said Ailsbet hotly.

Kellin raised his eyebrows. "Oh, but you are. You hate him because he disdains you. And so you disdain him in return."

"I do not know what you mean."

"You disdain his lack of music. Even when you dance, you are mocking him. You do not think this is true music." He waved a hand at the handful of brightly dressed musicians who played gold and silver instruments without much sound.

"They are not," said Ailsbet. How could there be any debate about that?

"You see?" said Kellin.

As Kellin moved away, King Haikor called Ailsbet over. She froze, knowing that tone of her father's voice. "You do not choose your own husband, Princess," he said.

"Of course not," said Ailsbet, trying to remember how other ladies made her father believe that what they wanted was also what he wanted. "I know that you choose for me. But surely I can hint, as Lady Pippa hints about the jewels she wishes for?"

She lifted her eyes to catch King Haikor winking at her. "You like him, do you?" he asked.

"I like him very much, Father," said Ailsbet, lying. In fact, she feared she had become dead to true feelings after what had happened to Lord Umber. She found Kellin—interesting.

"Hmm. Then we shall see. Perhaps he deserves a reward for his service to the crown," said the king.

He was in a good mood, thought Ailsbet, watching as the king waved at Lady Pippa. "The smell of wedding is in the air, eh?" he said, and slapped Ailsbet heartily on the back.

Ailsbet turned and saw Issa's haunted expression and felt guilty. It was hardly her fault that the other princess had agreed to marry Prince Edik in five years' time, but Ailsbet still wondered why her relationships with other women never ended well. Or, why they always ended. She could not be with other women of the court, and perhaps now she knew why. It was because of the taweyr.

CHAPTER TWENTY-THREE

Issa

OTHER THAN IN THE PRESENCE of the court that summer, Edik and Issa spent no time together. He did not invite her to walk outdoors with him in good weather. He did not even dance with her after dinner, unless his father suggested it. Then he seemed so focused on his steps that it would be cruelty to distract him. He was not a graceful dancer, though he was young and perhaps might grow into it.

Issa would ask him about his tutors, but he would tell her only about his training with the taweyr in the courtyard. She would ask him about his metal soldiers, but he said that they were for children and he did not play with them anymore. He did love Midnight, but he would not speak about that, either. She had as little idea who he was as when she had first seen his portrait.

Prince Edik could be quiet and watchful. He would speak in his father's tones, with the proper words of a courtier. But then his attention would waver and he would fidget in his seat and speak as coarsely as any of the guards. When his father ignored him, he seemed to have no idea why.

Sometimes, Prince Edik took a bit of his own meat from dinner and fed it to Midnight under the table. He tried to keep his hound away from the others, but the king subtly encouraged his own animals to tease and pick at the newer, smaller one.

King Haikor laughed at their antics and told Edik he should do the same, even when Midnight whined at him and bled where the other hounds had scratched him.

Issa was horrified and tried to help by adding a little neweyr to the creature's food the next day. It seemed to help, and for days, Midnight stood his ground against the other, larger hounds.

But a few days after that, the hound was found dead in the middle of the Throne Room after dinner.

Prince Edik wept bitterly, and when his father told him to be quiet, he grew sullen. Late that evening, after the king had departed, Issa saw him sneak back into the room and take Midnight's body with him.

Silently, Issa followed him outside the palace to the courtyard, where Edik set the animal down gently, then turned his anger to the ground itself, tearing at it with his hands until he had dug a hole large enough for the animal. It was not a proper grave by any means, but he mounded up the dirt on top and then patted it gently, weeping silently all the while.

Issa returned to her own rooms and wept for the grieving boy. She wondered if she should have left the puppy in Weirland. It would still be alive, and perhaps Prince Edik would have grieved less to have never loved it. But what a cruel world Edik lived in, that everything he loved was taken from him.

It was not always so easy to feel for the prince, however. Edik could be as cruel as his father, especially when King Haikor was watching him, and Issa saw these moments far more often as the summer passed.

One day, Prince Edik lost a jeweled pin that he often wore on his tunic. He searched for it when King Haikor was not in the Throne Room, and he boxed the ears of one page boy who interrupted him.

Issa did not understand why he valued it so highly.

"It was our mother's," said Ailsbet, who had seen Issa watching the prince. Then she added, "It may be all that he has left of her."

This was the boy she was to marry, when he became a man. But what kind of man would he be?

That evening, Issa's gaze was caught by the sight of Ailsbet and Kellin standing close together, their shoulders brushing against each other, and she felt a hot rush of pain. It should be her hand almost touching Kellin's. It should be she who leaned in and spoke to him intimately. But he had never shown her a moment of answering feeling in Weirland or here. And even if he had—it would not matter.

She looked away and met the eyes of Prince Edik, feeling a sudden panic at the thought that the prince could guess her feelings.

As the prince came closer, she blurted out, "Your hands are very white and fine," an attempt at a compliment. But as soon as she said it, she knew it was the wrong thing. It was not at all a compliment for a boy trying to be seen as a man.

Prince Edik put his hands behind his back. "Your braids are coming undone," he told her, in equal frankness.

Self-conscious, Issa put a hand to her head and felt

several braids falling down from the pins that held them.

"My mother never braided her hair," added Prince Edik. He had grown since the portrait, but he was still no taller than she was.

"It is a different tradition," Issa said. "I understand that."

"It is my tradition, and it will be yours when we are married. Then you will let your hair go loose, or pin it up properly," said Prince Edik. "For I shall be your husband, and the neweyr must always follow the taweyr as the wife follows her husband."

Issa felt her cheeks grow hot. As she lifted her hands to cool them, Prince Edik reached for them, examining her palms closely until Issa pulled them away. "And when we are married," he continued, "you will oil your hands every day and perfume them until they please me. For a princess has no place touching with her own hands the land that provides for her."

"But the neweyr——" said Issa.

Prince Edik cut her off. "White hands are the sign of royalty. But perhaps in Weirland, you are not used to true royalty."

It so incensed Issa that she had to turn away. But that was a mistake, for she caught a glimpse of Kellin touching Princess Ailsbet's loose red hair, the two of them laughing intimately together.

Sitting behind her, Edik spoke close to her ear: "You see, you are far too modest in your habits. In Rurik, women in love smile and laugh and flutter their eyes," he said.

"I am sorry. I do not know you well yet. And I have many responsibilities," said Issa. How else could she excuse herself?

"And I have none?" demanded Prince Edik.

"No, I did not mean that. I only meant—" She stopped.

"I have as many duties as you do. I must use my taweyr many times a day. My father has great need of me. Just because you do not see it does not mean you should not respect it."

"Of course, I respect your taweyr," said Issa. He was so much younger than she was, and she felt she had to treat him gently.

"I do not believe it," Edik said, belligerent. "Have you ever noticed when I used it?"

"I'm sure you have not noticed when I used my neweyr, either," Issa said.

There was a moment of frozen surprise. "You have used it here? In the palace?" said Prince Edik. "Without my father's permission?"

Issa hesitated. "I meant no offense to you or your father. I beg your pardon for what is so natural." She could hardly avoid using it every day. It was her habit to use it when she woke to find out the weather, to smell her favorite flowers, even though there were none in her chambers.

"If it is so natural, then you can show it to me. Here. Now." There was a hint of mockery in his tone.

"I think that is not necessary," said Issa.

"And I think it is. If you think the neweyr is so much a part of you that you cannot bear not to use it, then prove it to me. Prove it is so much more powerful than my mother's." His arms were crossed over his chest petulantly.

"I did not say it was more powerful than your mother's," said Issa. "I never meant to cast aspersion on her or her neweyr." But clearly, he thought she had.

"Make my father's hounds dance," Edik commanded her.

It was then that Issa saw that Edik wanted this less as a reminder of his mother than as a rebellion against his father, who had moved on so easily after her death.

"Or plant a tree at the foot of my father's throne. Do it boldly and unmistakably," said Edik.

"If I planted a tree at your father's throne, it would grow for many years until it swallowed the throne that will be yours one day," said Issa.

Prince Edik shrugged. "Then something else. Could you grow a flower in your hands and give it to me?"

Issa could do that. But she felt she had gone too far in coddling him tonight. "When we are married," she said, "you will command me in many things. I shall wear the gowns you choose and say the words you write for me. But the neweyr is not a prince's nor even a king's. That will remain mine always."

At this, Prince Edik's face went as fiery red as his sister's hair. "I shall show you my taweyr now, for all to see."

He looked around the room and saw his sister with Duke Kellin.

"You, Kellin," said the prince, stepping forward.

Duke Kellin looked up, unafraid. Issa could see no way to send him warning. Her heart pounded in fear for him.

"Spar with me. Show your taweyr, if you think you are worthy of my sister, the princess of Rurik."

"As my prince commands me," Kellin said immediately.

Prince Edik began to shift his weight from one foot to the other.

Duke Kellin stood before him calmly.

Prince Edik slammed his fist forward, into Kellin's stomach. The duke groaned but held his place.

Issa could see no taweyr in what he had done. That was only a physical action. But what did Issa know of how to use the taweyr? Or how to stop it?

"I could send you flying across the room if I wished it. I could kill you with a thought," threatened Edik. He was a foot shorter than the duke and must weigh less than half. Even his voice was still a child's.

Issa thought Edik must be depending on Kellin to allow him to win, because he was the prince.

"Come, give the prince a battle," King Haikor called out. "There's no honor in it for him if you bow down and make obeisance, Kellin."

"He is your son and heir," said Kellin.

"He is prince of Weirland," said King Haikor, "and as such, he needs a little honest battle of taweyr now and again. Teach him to believe he can lose, Kellin. For only then will he truly have the courage to win." The king waved out the wide, lead-paned windows to the fields where the most famous battle of the war against Aristonne had been fought and won only twenty years earlier.

"You give me permission to unleash the full strength of my taweyr against him?" asked Kellin.

"As if you would not otherwise—" Edik began.

"I do," said King Haikor.

"It will make no difference," shouted Edik.

"My prince," said Kellin.

Prince Edik ran at him again.

Where was Ailsbet? Why did she not try to stop her brother? Issa saw her standing nearby. She looked angry, her face flushed, her fists clenched.

Duke Kellin slid to the side, easily evading the prince's attack. Edik had to throw up his hands and stop himself.

The prince whirled. "Show your taweyr!" he shouted.

"There is more than one use of taweyr, my prince," said Duke Kellin smoothly. "A subtle trick turns away an obvious one. Not all battles are on an open field."

This response only made Prince Edik angrier. He barreled forward again, this time knocking against Kellin's chest. The prince stumbled but did not fall, and when he stood again, there was a trickle of blood falling from a shallow cut on one cheek.

Edik put a hand to his cheek, his eyes wild. "You will regret that!" he shouted.

Issa looked over at Ailsbet again. She had a dark expression on her face and seemed to be holding her breath.

Prince Edik ran again toward Kellin, and Issa saw in the corner of her eye a flickering of Ailsbet's hand. At that moment, the duke flew across the room and landed heavily on his side, unconscious.

Prince Edik cheered for himself, and then others joined in.

But Ailsbet looked ill. She moved toward Kellin as if she had lost all her strength.

"Kellin?" said Ailsbet.

The prince waved a hand. "I could kill him if I wished it," he said casually, striding away.

"Yes, we all know," said the king, sounding bored. "But I find Duke Kellin a useful tool. If he dies because of this night's contest, you will have deprived me of his service, and I shall expect compensation."

Issa began to tremble, and Prince Edik put his arm around her possessively.

Issa was glad that no one else was watching her. They were looking at Ailsbet, who was weeping and shaking uncontrollably. Only Issa knew why she was weeping. It was because she had been forced to use her taweyr against Kellin to protect her brother. She must have worked very hard to avoid killing them both.

King Haikor motioned to the servants to help Kellin. He was carried off between the two of them. Ailsbet followed behind, in control of herself once more.

"I showed him not to treat me as a boy," Edik said to Issa.

"Indeed you did," said Issa, afraid to contradict him now.

"He will be well in the morning. Father will send a physician to him. You will see, Princess Marlissa. There is no need for you to cry." He patted at her shoulder, but Issa told herself that this time, at least, there was a reason for her to weep.

Chapter Twenty-four
Ailsbet

As she sat in Kellin's bedchamber, Ailsbet was conscious of the fact that it was her own taweyr that had hurt Kellin. She had not meant to do it. She had only meant to help Edik, and then she had lost control. Afterward, the taweyr had fallen away from her in a rush, and she was left panting and exhausted. No wonder her father had become more irritable and irrational in his later years, living with this pressure of the taweyr day after day. How did any man stand it?

Stupid, stupid Edik, showing off for Issa. Even now, Ailsbet could not understand why Kellin had done so little in his own defense. She could hardly wait for Kellin to wake up so she could scold him on this point.

Near dawn, Kellin had still not opened his eyes, nor spoken. He had fallen hard, and there was a terrible bruise on the left side of his head. The physician also suspected that one of his ribs had been broken, because of the hot swelling on his left side there, though Ailsbet did not have the chance to view that damage under his shirt.

The physician insisted that the window in Kellin's chamber be curtained, and Ailsbet felt oppressed by the emptiness of the room. There was nothing here to tell her about Kellin. Even in his own room, he was hidden under a cloak of mystery.

Some time later, the physician began to pack up his things.

"You cannot give up," said Ailsbet. "You must do something for him. I shall offer you anything you want. Just help him."

The physician raised his bushy eyebrows. "I am leaving because he is better, not worse. If he has made it this far, he may be too stubborn to kill. Summon me if he wakes so I can ask him what his secret is," he added drily.

"You are not lying to me to make me feel better?" Ailsbet asked.

"Princess," said the physician impatiently. "I know that your tender feelings for him mean that you can hardly think. But I swear to you that he is doing well. He will wake soon enough and tell you himself how he does." He nodded and then left.

When the physician was gone, Ailsbet allowed herself to move closer to Kellin. She held his hand to assure herself he was still alive.

Some hours later, she felt Kellin stir and saw that his eyes were open. She started and pulled away her hand.

Kellin groaned, "Head hurts."

"You are a fool," she said. It was only the beginning of the lecture she had stored up.

"Doubly a fool," said Kellin. "The prince?"

"He is not hurt."

"The princess?" said Kellin.

"Princess Marlissa is also uninjured," said Ailsbet. Issa had never been in any danger.

"I meant, did she show what she felt for me?" said Kellin. It was the first time that he had admitted that he knew what Issa felt, and that he knew Ailsbet also knew.

Ailsbet shook her head. "Nothing that my brother

or father saw. Or anyone else, I think. You and Edik fighting with taweyr was as entertaining as anything my father has ever paid for."

"Edik and I?" said Kellin.

Ailsbet tensed, ready to deal with an accusation that she was ekhono, but Kellin asked, "She has not come here?"

"I think she must have decided that she does not love you so very much, after all," Ailsbet said. "A man who gives up his life so easily cannot be worth the trouble."

"It would be better for her," said Kellin.

Ailsbet did not argue with him on that point. She stood and stretched. She could feel the taweyr inside herself once more, not uncontrollable, but there, like a banked fire.

"I should call the physician," she said. "To tell him you are awake."

"No," said Kellin. "Not yet. First, tell me what you remember from last night."

Ailsbet looked at him suspiciously. "You engineered that. As a test for me," she accused.

"You think I control your brother? If I had meant for you to show your taweyr to me, it would have been privately, not in front of your father and the whole court."

So he had known about her taweyr before then? It seemed that every time she thought she had the better of him, he found out something just as dangerous to hold over her.

"Do you think Edik has no taweyr, then?" asked Ailsbet.

Kellin sighed. "He is too young to be sure. It may yet come to him in full force."

"And do you think my father suspects anything with regard to me?" asked Ailsbet. It was surprisingly easy to talk about her taweyr with him.

Kellin shook his head. "Certainly not. His reactions last night were all of a father enjoying his son's display of power. But we must make sure it does not happen again. You must deal with your taweyr properly and mask it when necessary."

"And how do I do that?" asked Ailsbet.

He shook his head. "It is not something I can tell you about. We will have to be in a place where you can use it. I have some experience with the ekhono. But you need training, to learn control."

"And how will we do that without my father knowing?" asked Ailsbet.

"We will have to be away from the palace on some excuse."

Ailsbet reddened. She had immediately thought

of an excuse. If they married, then her father would send them to tour the kingdom. It would be the perfect time to practice whatever Kellin had to teach her. But she did not want to say it out loud. Neither, it seemed, did Kellin.

"For now, tell me when you feel desperate," said Kellin. "I can take some from you. That is easy enough."

Like her father taxing taweyr from his nobles. It did not look pleasant, but it would do what she needed, she supposed.

But Ailsbet was not desperate with anything now, except frustration with Kellin. She shook her head, and he let it go.

Kellin fell asleep soon after, and Ailsbet was about to steal out of the room when he started awake suddenly and called after her, "Don't let her come! It is too dangerous."

Ailsbet turned back. "She will know the danger already," she said. "She is not a fool."

"Women like a doomed love," said Kellin with a hint of a smile.

"Well, she cannot be in love with you anymore. You are too much trouble," Ailsbet said.

"What a song you could make of this," said Kellin.

"Are you giving me advice about my music?"

asked Ailsbet, smiling. "I don't write music with words. It is—cheap."

Ailsbet brought the physician to him again, and when he was gone, Princess Marlissa came into the room without a knock.

"Issa, what are you doing here?" said Ailsbet.

At the sound of her voice, Kellin stirred awake. "Issa?" he said, and smiled. "You should not have come. "

Issa held her head high, but her eyes were shadowed. "I have come on behalf of Prince Edik. He wishes to know if the duke yet lives."

"He will live long enough to annoy us all many times again, according to the physician," said Ailsbet. She opened the bed hangings, and Issa ran to him immediately. She touched his hand, but Kellin pulled away.

Ailsbet turned and stared out the window, thinking of an intricate song that required almost all of her attention.

"You must go," said Kellin after a long while.

"In one moment." Princess Marlissa said. "Prince Edik asked me to come. He was worried that he might have killed you. He is very proud of himself."

"Good. Tell him how weak I still am. He will like that."

"I shall tell him I slapped your face for your arrogance."

"Oh, yes, he will like that, too. But now you will have to do it," said Kellin. He pointed to his cheek. "Someone is sure to come in and see me, and if there is no mark, then the truth will come out."

"No." Princess Marlissa sounded stricken. "Don't ask me to do that."

Ailsbet thought it was time for her to intervene. She tugged on Marlissa's arm. "Come back tomorrow," she said. "I shall slap him for you today, and gladly."

"No, do not come back," said Kellin. "Not ever. Wait until I return to court."

"Tomorrow," said Ailsbet. "You can castigate him again and make the walls ring with the sound."

When Princess Marlissa had closed the door to the outer chambers, Ailsbet returned to Kellin.

"You are going to make sure you leave a mark, aren't you?" he asked, his dark eyes wide.

"With pleasure," said Ailsbet. This was one use of her taweyr that she did not need to conceal.

Chapter Twenty-five
Issa

THE NEXT DAY, Prince Edik insisted on going to see Duke Kellin for himself, and Issa had to go with him. Ailsbet stood aside as Edik strode into the duke's chamber and yanked open the hangings around the duke's bed. "Kellin, I have come to offer you my forgiveness," he said loudly.

"I thank you, Prince Edik," said Kellin, lying back on his pillow. "For your kindness in coming to visit me."

"And now if you hear of any saying that I have not yet proven strong in taweyr, you will have to speak against them."

"Of course," said Kellin, as Issa tried to pull Edik away.

"You don't sound convinced," said Edik. "Let me show you my taweyr again. There can be no doubt here, among women, that it is mine and mine alone."

"Surely there is no need for that," said Issa.

"My prince," said Kellin. "I have long shown myself to be your friend and supporter. I know that your taweyr is as strong as any boy's your age."

"As any boy? You mean as any man of any age," said Edik.

Kellin would never have made that mistake if he were not ill, thought Issa.

"But—" began Kellin.

It was too late.

Edik lifted a hand to Kellin and then thrust it out, as if expecting the force of the taweyr to carry it forward.

But his hand sagged.

"What is wrong?" Edik demanded. "I have done this before. Dozens of times."

"You are a little weak, that is all. Depleted," said Kellin, shrugging. "It happens to those who have expended a great deal of taweyr."

"It does not happen to my father," said Edik. "And

it has never happened to me before." He shook his head and thrust his hand out again.

Again, there was no taweyr. "You are still young," said Kellin. "The taweyr is not always sure at that age."

"The ekhono." Edik looked about wildly, ignoring Kellin. "They must be here, even now. They have stolen from me."

"Edik, no," said Ailsbet.

"I must go at once and tell the king," Edik said. "He must know the danger to us all—" He didn't finish, but rushed away.

"Go!" Ailsbet urged Issa. "Who knows what he will do?"

Issa chased after Edik into the Great Hall.

What Edik had said as he burst in, Issa did not know. But the king looked up in annoyance at his son. "Yes, what is it?" he said.

"There are ekhono in the palace," said Edik, in great heaving breaths. "They have taken my taweyr. And they may take yours, and every other man's here. We must find them and stop them!"

"There are no ekhono in this palace," said King Haikor. "I have made very sure of that, Prince Edik. Do you think I would not be able to sense them around me?"

"But how could you be sure?" said Edik. "The ekhono may have stolen even that ability from you."

This was dangerous for Edik and dangerous for her, as well, thought Issa. If Edik angered the king, another could be set in his place as heir. And then what of their betrothal? What of the prophecy?

But King Haikor was focused only on Edik's challenge. He lifted a hand, and a sword flew to him from the wall. It was long and studded with rubies at the hilt, a sword he had once used in battle.

"No!" shouted Issa.

But King Haikor did not even turn in her direction. Just when Issa was sure that he would run his son through at the neck, he stopped, the blade gently slicing a tiny point of the prince's skin. A trickle of blood ran down to his shoulder and into his tunic.

"If your taweyr has been taken, you will not be able to stop me," said King Haikor.

Prince Edik swallowed hard, and the blade dug a quarter inch farther into his neck. "Please, Father," he said.

King Haikor's arm twitched. "I must be sure," he said, and the sword pressed into the skin once more.

Issa ran forward, heedless of her own safety, and thrust Edik out of the way of the sword, as blood poured down his neck. Issa pressed her fingers to him, focusing on her neweyr.

His wound had not been caused by taweyr, but only by the naked steel blade. Issa poured neweyr into Edik, sealing the wound in his throat. If he lived, that was good for her and for Weirland, surely. The betrothal would continue.

"Neweyr in my own court?" said King Haikor. "You must know I have strictly forbidden it."

With a deep curtsy, Issa begged the king's pardon with all the proper language she could summon. "For the sake of your son, whom I knew you would have wanted saved. I promise it will never happen again, Your Majesty." She kept her head low, her voice humble.

King Haikor touched her chin with a finger and looked her in the eyes. There was something in his eyes that made her think of the ocean at the land bridge, rapaciously hungry and grasping, never satisfied.

Edik groaned, and Issa bent down to him.

"Get up," said King Haikor to his son with little sympathy. "You have not an ounce of taweyr in you now, Edik."

Did that mean the king would say he was no longer heir?

But King Haikor's anger was not directed at Edik. "Someone has taken it from you, for you had it in quantity when you battled with Kellin. So who have you seen since then? Give me the names!"

"Only—only my groomsmen," said Edik. "And Duke Kellin."

But the king shook his head. "Duke Kellin is no ekhono. He has shown his taweyr time and again. It cannot be him. Therefore, it must be your groomsmen." He clapped his hands and two servants ran to kneel before him. "Bring me Prince Edik's groomsmen immediately."

Issa felt herself going faint as she realized what this meant. The king thought the groomsmen were ekhono and would punish them accordingly. She had been so relieved that Edik and Kellin had survived their battle, and that her betrothal would go forward. She had not thought of the consequence to others.

"As for you, go to your rooms and rest," King Haikor said to his son. "Once the ekhono are dealt with, then your taweyr will return to you. Come to me when you wish me to test you again, to prove yourself."

Edik bowed his head and motioned for Issa to go with him. She had no choice. She could not save Edik's groomsmen. She had to be content that she had saved Edik. And she had kept Ailsbet's secret, as well as her own.

Chapter Twenty-six
Ailsbet

THE FOLLOWING DAY, Ailsbet returned to her own rooms to bathe and dress. She fell asleep without intending to, and thus it was late that night when she went to check on Kellin again.

The duke's servants allowed her in, but when Ailsbet called for him, he did not answer and when she opened the curtains around his bed, she discovered it was empty. Her first instinct was to chastise his servants for not knowing where their master was in this early stage of his recovery. He should not have been out of bed, surely, and the physician must have told them this.

Then she stopped herself. It was entirely possible that Kellin had not told his servants where he was going. Whatever he was doing might need to be kept secret, but that did not mean that she would be satisfied he was well without seeing him for herself.

She wondered if whomever Kellin married would spend most of her nights awake, waiting for him, and unsure if he was well or not. Did she want to be that woman? Pondering this, she fell asleep on the chair by his bed. Some time later, she started awake at the sound of Kellin's footsteps. He looked exhausted. "So. Will you demand to know where I have been?" he asked.

"Will you tell me?" asked Ailsbet.

"I shall tell you something that sounds true, if you wish it. It will make a good story to share with others, if you wish for a laugh," said Kellin.

Ailsbet shook her head, relieved that she had found him well enough to walk despite his recent injuries, and returned to her own rooms. Perhaps the physician had exaggerated his need for rest. She could not believe that Kellin had an assignation with another woman. He was too careful for that. No, it was something else that he was involved in, likely far more dangerous.

In the morning, she heard that all four of Prince

Edik's groomsmen had disappeared in the night. No one had seen them flee or had any idea where they had gone. They had slipped beyond the gray stone walls of the palace, likely to the east where the walls were crumbling, and King Haikor was in a fury that his guards had been so negligent as to let them go. He had even held two of the gate guards for questioning.

Now Ailsbet knew where Kellin had been, and why.

She returned to his rooms soon after breakfast and found him just dressed, his hair still wet. "You helped the groomsmen escape," she accused him. "But how did you know they were in danger?" She had heard rumors that her father had blamed them for the theft of Prince Edik's taweyr.

"They were easy targets," said Kellin.

"But it is ridiculous," said Ailsbet. "Edik has always been too young to show his taweyr. I don't understand why so many have bothered to pretend otherwise, when it would come to him naturally in time."

Kellin shook his head. "It was simply too tempting for those in your father's court to help it along. With your father's brother being ekhono, and your own lack of neweyr, it was more urgent for Edik to appear normal, and more than that—strong in the taweyr, adept, and even early with it. It keeps your father's nobles from beginning to make plans for the day when your father is weak or dead, and a young Edik is all that stands between them and the throne."

"Does this mean my father suspects the truth about me being ekhono?" said Ailsbet, daring to say aloud words she had only hinted at before.

"Even if he doesn't, he may decide that you and Edik are useless to him now that Edik's taweyr is revealed as a sham."

"But Edik should still have years—" Ailsbet protested. It was a matter of physical development. Girls came into their neweyr as they grew into a woman's body, and they did it earlier than boys. Why should Edik not have as much time as anyone else?

"He should, but he will not now. Your father must have known he was taking this risk all along. Now the nobles will always suspect he is being helped along, that his taweyr is exaggerated. I cannot see how he ever will be safe as heir again." Kellin sounded angry.

"You were counting on him to be heir," she said.

"He was my hope for a better future," said Kellin. "If Edik were king of Rurik, he would remember his love for you, and it would change his view of the ekhono."

That was Kellin's plan, the reason he risked so

much and worked so hard at her father's side?

"And now?" Ailsbet asked. "What will my father do?"

"Oh, your father is never caught off guard. He has another heir waiting in the wings," said Kellin. "Or near enough," he added.

It took Ailsbet a moment to understand this. "You mean if Lady Pippa bears him a son," she said. "But surely such a son would be too young to threaten Edik and me. It would be years yet before he showed his taweyr."

"But a babe who has not been shown a fraud or without weyr is better than either of you," said Kellin.

It felt like a blow to the heart. Ailsbet had not cared much for power herself, but if Edik were to lose all, what would happen to them? "It is his own fault," she said. "He did this to Edik." Or if not, her father had encouraged it.

"Yes, he did. And it does not matter. Your father sees you as pieces in a game," said Kellin. "Do you not know that already? If he has to lose one piece, he does not mind so long as there is another that he can make stronger."

Ailsbet's mind whirled and she felt hot with taweyr. She wanted desperately to fight Kellin physically, though she knew that none of this was of his doing. "But even if there is a baby, it is not born yet. He does not know if it will be a boy or a girl."

"He will have others," said Kellin. "With Lady Pippa or another noblewoman who can give him what he needs. I do not even know if he cares anymore if the child is legitimately born to a woman named queen."

"But he will have to wait twelve or fourteen years or even more for another son to show his taweyr clearly," said Ailsbet. "What if he does not live that long?"

"That is exactly the right question," said Kellin, nodding at her with approval. "Ailsbet, you see this more clearly than anyone in your father's court. And you see it with eyes that are not colored by your own desire for power."

"Power?" said Ailsbet. "I want none of it."

"But that does not mean that it is not yours already," said Kellin softly. "You have many advantages over your brother. You have taweyr in plenty. If you admitted it, no one would think that you were pretending. You could take the throne here in Rurik, where taweyr is so valued above neweyr."

Ailsbet could not believe that Kellin was suggesting this. She shook her head. "I am ekhono. There is no way that I could ever be anything in my father's kingdom. As soon as the truth comes out, I shall be shunned at best, killed more likely."

"If your father is still alive," Kellin answered. "But what if he is not? What reason could there be after his death for his prejudices against the ekhono to continue?"

"They are not only his prejudices," said Ailsbet. "And they existed long before he came to the throne."

"No, but if you showed yourself to be the best ruler, and you had powerful nobles to support you—" Kellin said.

It seemed he was offering himself, but how many others would there be? She had believed that she and Kellin were friends, but this was not what she had thought that friendship meant. "It does not matter," she said. "I have no interest in the throne. Even if I could reveal myself, it would not matter. I do not want to play with politics."

"It is not a question of what you want, Princess Ailsbet," said Kellin, using her title. "It is a question of what Rurik needs."

If she had not known what he felt for Issa, she would have wondered if he, like Lord Umber, meant to woo her for his own power. Would any man ever see her for herself, and not for the title she bore? "You are speaking treason," said Ailsbet.

"Am I?"

"The only time I would be able to announce that I had taweyr would be if my father—" said Ailsbet.

"If he were dead or so weak that he needed you."

"But Edik—"

"Even if Edik comes into the taweyr, he may not have enough of it to rule with the iron fist that your father's nobles have become used to. You do. It is always strong in the ekhono. Otherwise it would be easier to hide, and they would be less threatening to the rest of us."

He spoke truth, but Ailsbet wanted none of it.

Kellin continued speaking. "And taweyr or not, Edik does not have the personality to lead the kingdom. You know that."

"He is still growing," said Ailsbet. "He may yet prove as strong as my father."

"Yes. I have told myself the same thing over and over again. Surely, no man in the kingdom wishes as much as I do that Edik would grow into a proper king. But if he does not, there must be another choice."

"He is to marry Princess Marlissa. They are to unite the kingdoms." And possibly the weyrs, as well, Ailsbet thought. It would be a perfect end, and it would have nothing to do with her.

"Perhaps," said Kellin. "I have promoted that alliance from the first. But if Issa and Edik marry, do you think they can hold two kingdoms? I fear your father never meant for them to do so. He wanted an excuse to have Edik on the throne in Weirland, perhaps, but not both of them here."

Ailsbet gaped at him. "You love Issa." Or was that another part of his ruse? "How can you give away Issa's power so easily? She and Edik are the ones meant to rule both kingdoms, not me." That was what the prophecy said, was it not? Ailsbet had no neweyr. Even if she married Kellin, she could not expect a child of theirs to have both weyrs, could she?

"This is not about Issa and Edik or my feelings for her. This is about what is best for both kingdoms. It always has been."

Ailsbet supposed she should not be surprised. She had already seen how ruthless and single-minded Kellin could be when it came to doing her father's bidding. Now Issa would be sacrificed to his vision of the future as much as he himself would. And if she allowed it, Ailsbet would be, as well.

"Issa will still betroth herself to Edik, at least for now," said Kellin. "But a king like Haikor never has only one plan to maintain his power. That is why he will marry Lady Pippa, when she has proven she is carrying his child."

"Then there is nothing left for me to worry over," said Ailsbet. "Issa and Edik will have all the power they can hold on to."

"Except that your father stretches himself too far, and he does not see you clearly enough. He does not understand what an asset you might be to him. Even I did not realize that until I began to spend time with you."

It had been a mistake, Ailsbet thought, to let anyone close to her, Kellin most of all. She should have remained hidden in every way if she wished to be free of all this.

Kellin continued, "You have all your father's best qualities, Ailsbet. You are clear-minded, and you see others' faults. You understand how the court works and who moves whom. You need to learn more, of course, but you have the foundation."

"Of what?" Ailsbet shook her head. "All I want is my music. I do not even want to be a princess."

"This is not about being a princess," said Kellin. He did not use the word *queen*, but it rang in the air nonetheless, unspoken.

Ailsbet had never thought the man ambitious before now. He had made his move openly to court her, if that was what he was doing. If she married him, and if he made her queen, then he would be king. Was that what this was all about, and not helping the ekhono? Was he merely another Lord Umber?

"I am ekhono," she reminded him.

"And for now, that bothers the Rurese people. Because your father has made it so."

"Is this why you saved my brother's groomsmen? So that there would not be a spectacle involving the ekhono before you make your move?"

"It is not I who will make the move," said Kellin. "It is yours to make. I have said it before, and it remains true. I serve the kingdom, not myself."

Ailsbet did not know whether she believed him or not. "I have never believed myself capable of ruling, and now that I know I am ekhono, I believe it less than ever."

"You should trust yourself more. And your people. You should see how flexible they are. They value strength in a ruler, and they value the weyrs as they should."

"No," said Ailsbet. "How many times must I say it?"

"Until I believe it, I think," said Kellin. "And until you do."

She waited a long moment and shook her head again.

Kellin shrugged. "As you say. It will be Edik, then. We must make sure that your father gives him time to show his taweyr, and to grow in other ways. Princess Marlissa may help."

Yes, that was how it should be, how it must be. The throne had always belonged to Edik. And Marlissa would make a far better queen than Ailsbet ever would.

There was a knock at the door, and a messenger came to inform Kellin that two of Prince Edik's groomsmen had been discovered by the king's spies. Both had been brought to the Tower and formally accused of being ekhono, and of stealing Edik's taweyr. In the next week, they would be executed in public as ekhono, the fate that Ailsbet herself had begun to fear.

"I am sorry your work was all for nothing," said Ailsbet, though, in truth, she was relieved that Kellin's plan had proven him flawed. It meant, surely, that he must be wrong about her, too, and about Edik.

"There were four groomsmen," Kellin reminded her.

So he had saved two. Perhaps she could do something for the other two herself.

Ailsbet left Kellin and went to see her brother. She noticed there were new groomsmen within his chambers, and new guards without, one of whom was missing two front teeth and looked hardly older than her brother.

"Have you heard what will happen to the captured groomsmen?" Ailsbet asked. Could he put himself in the place of his guardsmen and imagine what that would be like? Could he conceive of what it would be like to watch it—to hear it?

Edik closed the door to his chambers and pushed a trunk against it. He looked thin and pale. "They stole from me! My groomsmen took my taweyr!" he cried. "They deserve punishment!"

"Edik, what proof do you have that they took your taweyr?" asked Ailsbet.

"Who else could it be? I have no taweyr, so they must be ekhono."

"Think, Edik," said Ailsbet. "Have they shown at any other time that they are ekhono?"

"They are too clever for that," said Edik. "They came to destroy my taweyr. It is a great ekhono conspiracy."

He had several swords hanging on his walls now. Ailsbet had not noticed them before. New gifts from their father, the king? Edik touched them lovingly.

"Perhaps there could be another explanation," said Ailsbet. "One that has nothing to do with your groomsmen."

"Of course, there is no other explanation," said Edik.

"But what if you have not truly come into your taweyr yet? What if it was true that others were using their taweyr for you?"

"That is impossible," said Edik flatly. "Of course it was my taweyr. I felt it. I knew it was mine."

"Then think about this: you could beg our father for their lives. You could ask him to set them free."

"For what reason?" asked Edik.

"For the sake of mercy?" said Ailsbet.

"And when has our father done anything for mercy?"

"Then do something else for them."

"What?" asked Edik. "They are guilty. I cannot save them from their fates now."

"Were they never your friends? Did they never do anything kind to you, laugh with you or tease you? Did you never meet their families or hear them speak of sweethearts?" asked Ailsbet.

"They are servants. I owe them nothing," said Edik, turning away from her.

"Edik, beware," said Ailsbet. She had told Kellin that Edik could be a proper king, that he only needed to grow older. But now she did not know if that was the case. "There is danger waiting for you that you do not wish to see," she added.

"I see the danger of the ekhono," said Edik stubbornly.

"That is not what I mean. Our father is a king first, not a father." She did not spell it out for Edik, but surely he must understand her.

"The ekhono hate me," said Edik, ignoring Ailsbet's hints completely. "They want to destroy me. I must destroy them first."

There was altogether too much destruction in Rurik, as far as Ailsbet was concerned. But it seemed no one listened to her.

Chapter Twenty-seven

Issa

IN THE THRONE ROOM the next day, King Haikor invited Issa to attend the execution of the prince's groomsmen on the Tower Green. Please no, Issa whispered silently.

"I think Prince Edik would be glad of your place at his side," said King Haikor. "It will be an opportunity to show your loyalty to your future husband and your abhorrence of all those who act against him."

Issa knew that when she became queen in Rurik, she would have to attend executions. But she had hoped to leave that for some years yet.

"Or perhaps you are too weak for this. You do look pale and pinched," said King Haikor.

"I have slept poorly these last weeks," said Issa, "in this new and unfamiliar place, with so many new things to learn. But I am adjusting quickly." She was learning how to put on a mask, as Princess Ailsbet had.

"So you will be well enough to come to the execution, then?" said King Haikor.

It was the last thing Issa wanted to do. But when she glanced at Ailsbet, she saw that the other princess was not asking to be excused. Issa could hardly be seen as weaker than Ailsbet.

She still believed Edik's groomsmen were innocent. But there was nothing she could do to save them.

"I shall come," said Issa.

"Good. So there is some mettle in Weirland, after all," said King Haikor.

The following morning, Issa woke long before dawn. Still, she lay in bed until one of her own servants came to help her into her new gown, made from blue silk, the color of Weirland. They did not speak of where Issa was about to go. Nor did anyone speak of breakfast.

At last, Issa walked down the stairs and out through

the inner courtyard, which was beaten-down dirt, with no touch of neweyr left in it, no hint of green growth. She looked at the clean stones, untouched by moss and ivy, and felt a pang of homesickness that she suspected would never really leave her, even if she returned to Weirland.

Then she caught sight of the gangly figure of Prince Edik, waiting for her. He lifted a hand and waved, and she felt relief. She and Edik had something in common, after all. These were his groomsmen, and he must regret their death as she did, even if he thought it was necessary.

Issa could see Kellin and Ailsbet sitting close together, looking at ease if unusually solemn, as if it were merely another day in court. A makeshift throne had been brought out for King Haikor to sit on, not the elaborate one from the Throne Room, but one that was finely carved with stout legs and raised him high above anyone else. The throne sat upon fine Caracassan rugs, which had been spread on the grayish ground. The name *Tower Green* was now more of a reminder that there was no grass near the palace, nor much of any living plant.

The river Weyr could be seen clearly from this vantage point, reaching out to the ocean beyond, and there were already commoners gathered across the river to see the execution. Their attitude of celebration made Issa ill.

"You look a little better now," said King Haikor.

Issa nodded and took her place next to Prince Edik.

"Now you will see how we deal with traitors in Rurik," said Haikor.

Edik shuddered, the first sign Issa had seen that he regretted what had happened to the groomsmen, and for that she felt a sudden warmth for him and put a hand on his arm.

"A man faces death proudly and gladly," said King Haikor, his gaze on Edik as harsh as on the grooms-men as they were led out of the Tower.

"I think a man is no less a man for grieving at a loss, when it must be faced," Issa said, for Edik's sake.

"But what you think makes a man does not matter here, does it?" said Edik quietly. "Nor what I think."

After that, Issa had nothing else to say to him. The commoners on the other side of the river roared as the two young men struggled against the Tower guards and wept on the short path to the block where the executioner stood, tall and hooded.

The lower part of the Tower had been built gen-erations ago, but King Haikor had added to it early in his own reign, so that it rose higher than any other part of the palace. It swayed with the wind, a symbol of the taweyr, in a land where only the taweyr mattered.

The two groomsmen looked up and caught sight of Edik. They cried out for mercy.

Issa could feel him tense beside her, and he opened his mouth, but did not speak.

The executioner knelt both of the groomsmen down on the Green. Edik looked away, biting his lower lip until it bled. .

But the executioner made quick work with his axe, and soon the two men were dead. Their bodies would be burned later for all to see.

"It is finished," Issa whispered. Only then did Edik look upon the men he had betrayed, and Issa could not tell for whom the hatred in his eyes was meant.

Issa turned to Ailsbet and saw there were tears on her cheeks. It was the first time Issa had seen the other princess weep. The tears ran down her face and dripped onto her gown, and she did not seem to notice them.

King Haikor stood and waved at the commoners across the river, who cheered for him and for the executioner. Then he thumped Edik on the back. "This is what it means to be a prince," he said, and the warning was clear in his tone. "A prince rejoices in seeing traitors receive their due."

They all walked toward the palace then, but Haikor returned to his Throne Room, and Edik remained outside a moment longer with Issa. He said softly, his head bowed, "I have never had many friends, and now I have none."

"You have me," said Issa.

Edik turned away, his shoulders hunched, and walked back to his chambers, alone. And then Issa saw Kellin, who had his eyes on Ailsbet and his hand on her cheek, wiping away her tears. He was not hers, thought Issa. And he never would be, no matter how much she might wish it.

Chapter Twenty-Eight
Ailsbet

Later in the afternoon following the execution of Edik's two groomsmen, Ailsbet was astonished when the ambassador from Aristonne dropped a note in her hand. The face of Ambassador Belram was pockmarked from a long-ago illness, but he wore fine clothes with the continental cut. He spoke to King Haikor in a precisely accented tone, but he tended to fade into the background of the court for long stretches of time. He had certainly never spoken to Ailsbet before.

Ailsbet was not able to read the note until that evening, after she had retired to her own chambers.

The paper was thick and fine, of a perfectly uniform ivory color. The smell of the ink was unfamiliar, and its color was almost brown rather than black, so she thought the ink must be very fine. The words themselves were formed in a delicate hand, with ornamentation that made it difficult to read. It was an invitation to meet Belram two hours past midnight at the stone wall behind the kitchens.

She debated whether to go. After all, there was no reason for her to think the ambassador of Aristonne wished her well. The location was a dark, vacant one. If Belram meant to harm her, he could do so without any fear of being overheard, and it would be hours before she was found. Ailsbet had done nothing personally against Aristonne, but she feared that hurting her might be a way for the current prince of Aristonne to wreak vengeance against her father, even if it was twenty years after the battle at which the young King Haikor had defeated that prince's father.

But the ambassador was no assassin. He was at least a foot shorter than she was, and Ailsbet was fairly certain that she could protect herself against him without any assistance. If the prince of Aristonne wished her dead, he would have sent someone else.

Perhaps the ambassador meant to propose marriage to her before Duke Kellin did, to take her away from her father's court and offer her a place at his side when he returned to the continent. She would have her chance to escape. It was surprisingly tempting.

Whatever weyr she held would end as soon as she crossed the ocean to Aristonne. She would not be forever holding back the taweyr to prevent its discovery, nor wishing she had the neweyr. She would find Master Lukacs. She would be in a world where music mattered to everyone as it did to her, where her talent would be truly appreciated and allowed to grow.

Two hours after midnight, she went to the wall behind the kitchen and found the ambassador holding a scroll in his hands.

"It is a gift from Prince William of Aristonne," said Belram with a bow.

"And what does Prince William of Aristonne want in return for this?" asked Ailsbet suspiciously.

"He wants only your happiness," said Belram, his voice revealing nothing.

Ailsbet eyed the man. "Do you think I am a fool?"

"No, Princess."

"What has Prince William heard of me?" she demanded.

"He has heard that you are mistreated by your father and overlooked by all in your father's court," the ambassador responded. "Even Duke Kellin does not see your true worth."

Ailsbet was taken aback. Kellin was the one who had suggested she could become queen. What more could Prince William see in her? "Does Prince William expect me to send information to him?"

The ambassador fingered his beard. "Prince William has no need of a spy," he said.

Ailsbet shook her head. "Do not expect me to believe that Prince William has forgiven all that has gone in the past." Prince William had been only three years old when his father and his kingdom's whole fighting force had been destroyed in battle by her father's army.

"I did not say that Prince William has forgiven anyone. But you are not to blame for your father's war."

"I am princess of Rurik," said Ailsbet.

"You are that," said Belram. "Though I think it brings you more pain than happiness."

Ailsbet did not dispute this. "My father—"

"Prince William despises your father and would sooner see him dead than standing in the same room with him. That is not in question."

"But he sent you to sit with my father at his court and act as his emissary?"

Belram shrugged. "Your father is king of Rurik. I could hardly come and ask to speak with you without first speaking to him. And if ever I paid you attention openly, what would your father do?"

Ailsbet was not sure she knew the answer.

The ambassador continued, "He would make Prince William pay a ransom to send you a note, and then ask him for half his kingdom for your hand in marriage."

Ailsbet put a hand to her throat. "I shall not marry Prince William," she said. She was nearly betrothed to Duke Kellin, and while she did not love him, at least she knew him. She knew nothing about Prince William.

Ambassador Belram tilted his head to one side. "Prince William does not ask you to marry him, Princess Ailsbet. Please, open the scroll."

Ailsbet pulled off the ribbon and unrolled the scroll. It was written on rougher paper than the earlier note, with splotches of darker color, and the writing was not as fine, instead seeming rather hurried. And familiar. In the dim light from the torches on the wall behind her, she scanned the contents.

It was not a formal letter or a poem as she had expected.

It was a song, purely instrumental. A song for the flute, in fact.

The notations were written in the coded marks of Aristonne's system of music, which Ailsbet had learned from Master Lukacs.

This was the last song that she had learned from Master Lukacs, the one she had mastered just before he left more than four years ago. She had no need to read the music. It was all here, every change she had made to the original song when she had played it that last time with Master Lukacs, marked in his impatient hand.

"Prince William waits for you. For Ailsbet, the musician. Not Princess Ailsbet of Rurik. Do you understand?"

She nodded. Could she leave behind her place as princess, give up all power and political intrigue and be only a musician? Or was this just a way to get her to Aristonne, where she might be forced into a marriage with Prince William, despite his protestations to the contrary? It might be much worse than her situation here in Rurik. But it might also be much, much better. How could she assess the risk when such a prize was dangling before her?

"You have only to send a message," continued the ambassador. "I shall wait for you with a small vessel, on the dock at the wide end of the river. There will be a black-and-white flag flying the swan of Aristonne."

Ailsbet nodded. She had been there a few times, watching the boats from the continent unload their goods with the help of the unweyr, who were not affected by the ocean.

Ailsbet rolled up the scroll and held it against her chest.

"You must give no hint of what I have said to you," warned Belram. "You must not speak to me or look at me differently. Your father might suspect something, and if he were to find out the truth—"

Ailsbet knew as well as he did what the consequences might be. The ambassador could end up in the Tower himself, and her own life would be in danger.

"Tell me of Prince William. Are you his friend?" asked Ailsbet. Before now she had thought of Kellin as her only hope for a refuge within her father's court, her only way of surviving. But perhaps Prince William was not such a terrible alternative.

Belram stared at her. "I was his father's friend. But

Prince William would not call me the same. He has been heard to say that a prince cannot afford to have friends. The moment he has a friend, he will look at that man differently, will favor him over others without noticing it, or will punish him in order to be seen not to favor him. A prince who has a friend is inviting others to twist him one way or another. A friend is a hostage at best and at worst is an invitation to betrayal."

Prince William sounded like a man whom she might honor for his principles. A cold man, as cold and dispassionate as she was herself. Could she make a marriage with him if she had to?

"Is Master Lukacs not his friend, then?"

The ambassador smiled. "Ah, Master Lukacs is his fellow musical enthusiast. The prince allows himself this one weakness, you see. But I tell you the truth when I say that Prince William would throw all his musical instruments and scrolls into the fire if he had to, to save his kingdom."

"And Master Lukacs?" Ailsbet was imagining a fire of scrolls, and Master Lukacs jumping into it to save them.

"The prince would throw him into the fire, too. And me. And you," said the ambassador.

Ailsbet looked into his face, and she saw that he

was entirely serious. "He sounds a harsh man. You serve him anyway?"

"With all my heart," said the ambassador, without hesitation. Then he slipped away, and Ailsbet walked back to her own rooms, humming to herself.

Chapter Twenty-Nine

Issa

IN THE WEEKS FOLLOWING the groomsmen's executions, the king grew more enthusiastic than ever in the pursuit of the ekhono. There had been two more servants accused who fled, and she heard of more than a dozen burnings in the city of Skorosa. No one from the palace attended these, and Issa was both relieved and guilty about this. She wished she could talk to Edik. She had tried to bring up the subject of his groomsmen's execution, but he had simply walked away from her and refused to speak. He did not say much about any other subject, either, and had become so quiet at court that the king mocked him for it. But even this did not change him.

At last, it was less than a week until the first day of autumn, when Issa would make her final oath of betrothal to Prince Edik. Issa spent all day being fitted by a seamstress for her betrothal gown, feeling hot and irritated and trying not to take her frustration out on the hapless woman, who kept pinning her through the fabric of the gown. Though she thought she had accepted her choice, Issa still felt a pang that evening, as she watched Kellin and Ailsbet with their heads together, laughing intimately.

Was it just a game between them? They seemed so happy in love, yet she felt as if she were being stabbed with thorns with every word they spoke. Was this what she would have to endure every day? Could she fall enough in love with Edik to take away the pain of this?

Now King Haikor called Kellin to him. "Shall we have a double ceremony, then? A prince and a princess of my house officially betrothed on the same day?"

Issa steeled herself to show no emotion. She found a bit of mold growing along a crack in the floor, and pressed some neweyr into it. The mold blossomed in green and white until Issa withdrew her neweyr entirely, and it crumbled to dust.

There was a long moment's silence. Then Duke Kellin said, "If all can be made ready in so short a time?"

"If I command it so, it will be. After all, there will already be food prepared and the invitations sent," said King Haikor.

Duke Kellin glanced at Issa, and then his face went blank. "You honor me, Your Majesty."

"Princess Ailsbet?" said King Haikor. "Is this your wish, as well?"

Ailsbet bowed her head and came to kneel at Kellin's side before her father. She glanced up at Issa, who had to turn away.

"Are there any who object to this?" the king asked the court.

Of course, no one objected.

"The wedding date will be decided later, but not too far off. Anyone who looks at you two can see that you are eager. And there is no reason to wait, since you both are of age."

No reason at all, thought Issa.

"I assure you, there will be a handsome dowry laid upon her, Duke Kellin," King Haikor added. He clapped his hands and declared that it was time for dancing. Soon there were feet stamping in rhythm as Kellin and Ailsbet twirled around the room.

Issa felt ill. She could see Edik across the room, staring at her. She knew that she must congratulate Kellin and Ailsbet properly, as a princess should.

Before she could, Prince Edik came after her and asked to dance with her.

She should do it, she knew. But she could not bear it. "I request leave to go to my room and rest. These past few weeks have been very trying for me," she said, her voice unsteady.

"Are you ill?" asked Edik kindly.

"No, only tired," said Issa. "Very tired. Please excuse me." She did not wait for Edik's response, but fled down the corridors toward her rooms, where she flung herself onto her bed and wept.

A few moments later, the door opened behind her. She thought it would be one of her servants and was a little ashamed of how she must look, her hair in disarray, her face ravaged by tears.

She looked up and saw Kellin.

He closed the door behind him. "What do you think you are doing to me?" he demanded.

"What I am doing to you?" Issa echoed.

He crossed the room in two steps. "You retreat from the Throne Room nearly in tears after the mention of my betrothal to Ailsbet, daring me to come after you in private. Did you think once of the danger to me? To yourself? To Ailsbet? You tease me and taunt me with your eyes, and so I have to come, knowing that every minute you wait here for me is another minute that we shall never have again."

"I—" Issa tried to begin, but she could not finish. Not when he was looking at her like that, his eyes angry and condemning. He had never said anything to her of his feelings before now. She had begun to believe that she was the only one who felt anything.

"I hate him," said Kellin. "Do you know that? The boy whom I pity and hope will one day make every sacrifice worthwhile, I hate. Because he has the right to dance with you, to stand by you, to whisper to you. He will be married to you all too soon. If I had the hope of that for even one day, I should not care about any other day."

Issa had nothing to say. Kellin was the one who had come to Weirland as King Haikor's emissary. He was the one who had proposed the betrothal and had pressed on her the importance of her seeing Edik truly, as the man he might one day become. And now he threw that in her face?

"You will kill us," he said, and then he leaned closer to her, inch by inch, until at the last it was she who had to cross the distance between them.

The kiss was hot and hard. Issa found her hands

were in his hair, pulling at it, and his fingers were on her neck, pressing her back against the wall, until she was pinned against it and could not move except for her lips against his.

It should have been wonderful. It should have been perfect. Instead, it was the most exquisitely painful thing she had ever experienced. Because she knew it had to end.

Every moment she tasted his lips against hers, the strength behind his embrace, the honesty that cost him so much, she knew she would have to let him go.

Soon, soon.

And then it was done.

He breathed heavily. "We should not have done that," he said.

"No," she said.

Then he kissed her again, this time more tenderly. She could taste the cinnamon from dinner on his lips and his tongue.

"And now what?" he asked, breathless.

"I suppose we must go on as before," she said.

"Pretending," he said.

"Yes." She could not look him in the eyes. There was no hope for their love. She could not marry anyone but Edik. And Kellin had his own responsibilities, to his kingdom, to his own estate, to Edik, and to

Princess Ailsbet now. There was the prophecy to consider, and a thousand other things, all having nothing to do with them. It was so complicated.

"We do it for our kingdoms. And for the ekhono. And for the weyrs," said Kellin, making it sound more simple than it seemed to her.

He left her there alone, and she recited the prophecy again. One child with both weyrs? Two islands becoming one? She wished she had no doubts about it. For her sacrifice to be worth it, she needed the prophecy to come true.

Chapter Thirty
Ailsbet

*E*ARLY THE NEXT MORNING, Ailsbet went to Issa's rooms and knocked cautiously. Issa answered the door, looking as if she had not slept all night. Her face was blotched with red and her eyes had dark circles under them.

"What is it?" asked Issa.

"What happened last night?" Ailsbet said. "I saw Kellin hurrying toward your rooms. He must have spoken to you, and he will not see me this morning. He has barred even his servants from his room."

Issa flushed.

"What did you say to him?" Ailsbet asked. "Did

you hurt him? Condemn him? You knew that he could not refuse to marry me in front of my father."

Issa lifted her chin. "He admitted at last that he loved me."

Ailsbet shook her head. Issa had made things worse for all of them. "If I ever fall in love, I hope that I shall retain some sense."

"If you ever fall in love, you will be betrothed, or married, to Kellin," said Issa.

"Marriage never stopped my father from pursuing any woman he thought he loved," said Ailsbet.

"You are not like your father in that way, I don't think," said Issa. "You are not like him at all, in your personality, however much you look like him."

"I can be as ruthless as he is," said Ailsbet.

"Not for your own selfish reasons, however. That is not why you are marrying Kellin. But perhaps once the prophecy is fulfilled, everything will be different, for all of us," said Issa.

Did anyone truly believe that now? Ailsbet wondered. "That is your final choice, then?" she asked. "You choose not to have Kellin? To give him to me so that you can fulfill the prophecy with Edik? What if the prophecy still does not come true? How will you live with yourself then?"

Issa's head bowed, and she said no more. Ailsbet

left her rooms and went out to the courtyard to watch her father's guard battle with swords and taweyr. She could not join in, but watching the conflict, hearing their grunts and the clash of steel on steel fed her taweyr in a way she had not allowed before.

That night, Ailsbet went to see Edik. For all her doubts about his suitability as a king, she wanted to warn him about the possibility of his own lack of taweyr, about Lady Pippa and the danger of her becoming pregnant with the king's child.

"I'm in no mood for company," Edik said, greeting her at the door. After a moment, though, he stepped back, letting her in.

"You seem unsettled. Why?" Ailsbet asked.

"I am afraid of Princess Marlissa," he said simply.

Ailsbet was astonished at this. "What is there to fear in her? She never has a harsh word to say, and she treats you with perfect respect."

"That is what I fear. She makes no mistakes, and I make so many. I know she must think badly of me, yet she never says a word. How can I believe anything she says? She will marry me, and then she will hate me, and all the while she will be smiling." This was far more rational and endearing than anything Ailsbet had heard Edik say in weeks.

"I'm sure she will open up to you in time,"

Ailsbet said. "You have only just started to become acquainted. And you are always with dozens of others in the court, never alone. There are five years until you are married, and by then you will have grown into a man closer to Issa's equal than you are now. Then when you are wed, you will have time to spend alone with each other. You will see her as she truly is, and she will see you."

"That terrifies me even more. What if she sees me truly and she hates me? Better to show her a false face."

Ailsbet smiled.

"Are you laughing at me?"

"I only want what is best for you, Edik," said Ailsbet.

"And what is that?" asked Edik. "Do you know?"

"Edik, I did not come to war with you. I wanted to make peace. To give you some advice before—" Before she either left Rurik for Aristonne or was betrothed to Kellin.

"All these years, I mocked you for having no weyr. But now I think you are well quit of it," said Edik suddenly.

"What do you mean?" asked Ailsbet.

"You have never dreamed of going to the continent as I have? Not to Aristonne, of course. They would never let me in there. But I think I would like to travel to Caracassa or the Three Kingdoms. Or anyplace where the name of Rurik is only a legend and little more. Where the weyrs are only stories."

"Are you serious?"

Edik laughed. "I dream about it," he said. "Of leaving here and going someplace where I am not a prince, where I could live my life without thinking about taweyr and death and taxes."

Ailsbet felt a surge of love for her brother. He was not so different from her, after all.

"But, of course, it is impossible. Father would never let me go," said Edik. "Not while I am living and his only heir with taweyr."

No, thought Ailsbet, he would not. It seemed there were advantages in being a useless princess. Her father would not pursue her.

Chapter Thirty-one

Issa

On the day of the double betrothal, Issa woke feeling muzzy-headed and languorous. It was still dark outside her window, but she could hear movement in the outer chambers. She wished for silence to calm herself, then pushed aside the bedcovers and stood to face the day. In addition to her own servants, King Haikor had sent six maids to help her, and they chattered incessantly through the morning.

Even with the additional maids, it took three hours until she was fully dressed. The shimmering green gown she wore was made from yards of silk, adorned with seed pearls and precious gems. Her slippers were crusted with matching jewels and were tight around her toes. Her shoulders ached from the weight of the gown, and her neck and head were sore from the ministrations to her hair.

She had seen the end result in the mirror, the way her hair had been teased high above her head, with little ringlets all around her neck and flowers tucked into a wreath that looked almost alive. It could have been alive in truth, if she were allowed to use her neweyr, but on today of all days she did not dare to flout the king's orders. She would have felt steadier if there had been anything that felt familiar about the day's routine, but it seemed as if she had entered another realm, even more different than when she had first come to the palace in Rurik.

When she stepped out of her rooms, Issa found two guards waiting for her. They helped her climb the steps to the ramparts so that she could look out onto the city.

King Haikor had commanded that all the shops in the city be closed for the day. Issa could smell food being cooked in the palace kitchens, to be passed out to the thousands who lined the streets, which were covered with flowers. Issa felt a pang of guilt at the sight, knowing the neweyr that had died in them as they had been pulled from their stems.

The sun shone brightly, almost blinding her as she smiled and waved to the crowds. She could see Edik on the other side of the gate, and Ailsbet with him, as extravagantly dressed as she was, in a red gown that shone brighter than her hair. How the gown had been made so quickly she did not know, but King Haikor must have paid well for it. She did not look nearly as uncomfortable as Issa felt, however.

Kellin was with the guards down below. He was dressed in a uniform and cape, half-armor studded with rubies and gray feathers. He looked wonderful, and he was staring at her quite openly. King Haikor himself was already waiting for them within the Throne Room.

There were cannons shot off, one for each of Edik's thirteen years, and then a pause followed by seventeen cannons for Princess Ailsbet's age. Issa was conscious then that she was now eighteen, five years older than Edik. Would the difference in age always bother her? Kellin was two years older than she was, at twenty.

They waited for the haze of smoke from the cannons to die down. Then, at last, it was time for the ceremony itself. Issa walked down the ramparts and into the Throne Room, which was nearly silent after the noise outside. She and Edik were to be betrothed first, then Kellin and Ailsbet.

Issa knelt before King Haikor with Prince Edik's shoulders touching hers. His neck was thin against the stiff collar of his uniform, and the sapphire crown on his head looked heavy and uncomfortable.

Behind them, the Throne Room was filled with nobles and some merchants upon whom the king wished to show favor. By the time they were all in their proper positions, it was past noon.

The binding official stood in front of King Haikor, upright, a dark hood over his head so his face could not be seen.

He looked too much like an executioner, Issa thought, as she had seen one recently. The black hood was the same, though an executioner was taller and wider, strong enough to kill with an ax alone, if his taweyr failed to stop the heart. The hood was meant to show that all those who stood before marriage were the same, no matter their rank.

It was all Issa could do to breathe. One of the guards behind Issa nudged her, reminding her to bow before King Haikor, giving him a final obeisance as Princess Marlissa of Weirland before she was transformed into Princess Marlissa of Weirland and

Rurik. A betrothal was in many ways as binding as a wedding.

Then Edik took her hand in his gloved ones.

"The highest of the land have gathered today," said the binding official. "We are here to see a contract made between this man and this woman."

Issa felt Edik stiffen beside her. She wanted to smile at him, to reassure him that he had no reason to fear. But she could not make herself do it.

"This is a binding contract to be held until the death of the one or the other. King or queen, lord or lady, duke or duchess, man or woman, it is the same."

Issa tuned out the droning words and stared behind the official's head at the bloody history of Rurik depicted on the walls.

She heard a cough behind her and realized that the official had stopped speaking.

It was Edik's turn.

"I swear to abide by the contract of this betrothal and to be united in matrimony with you, Princess Marlissa of Weirland and Rurik, when I reach my majority. May we be joyful together in our impending nuptials and always mindful of our duties to our peoples and always conscious of the history of our kingdoms that has drawn us together." Edik was nervous and stammered more than once, but he was sincere.

Issa thought that he might not be the man she loved now, but she had hope that she might come to love him in time.

When he was finished, he placed on Issa's middle finger a large ring of sapphires and diamonds, fumbling slightly as he did so. It was his mother's ring, which King Haikor had given to her at their wedding.

Then it was Issa's turn: "I swear to abide by the contract of this betrothal and to be united in matrimony with you, Prince Edik of Rurik, on the day you reach your majority. May we and our kingdoms be joyful together as we sow peace between our peoples, and may the future bring to both our kingdoms the finest imaginings of all our hearts."

The binding official took up Issa's hand on one side and Edik's on the other. He pulled them to their feet and then pressed their hands together. "As the weyrs are opposite hands, so are you two. Affianced to affianced," he declared triumphantly.

There was a round of applause, and bells rang out somewhere in the distance. Issa felt numb as she turned to Edik for a kiss and felt his cold lips on hers. When he pulled away, King Haikor congratulated his son heartily and clapped him on the back.

Then it was time for Ailsbet and Kellin to be betrothed, and they went through the same ceremony, nearly word for word.

Afterward, Issa felt confused, as if it had all happened in a dream. None of it felt real to her, though she knew when King Haikor clapped Kellin on the back and kissed his cheeks, that Kellin was farther from being hers than he had ever been.

Bells rang out again, and Issa could hear distant shouting, as if her hearing had suddenly returned. The betrothals were finished, and Issa and Edik turned together to face all of those who were gathered inside the Throne Room.

Kellin and Ailsbet were nearby, waving and giving thanks. With Edik at her side, Issa nodded and smiled and kissed cheeks and gave embraces until it was all a blur.

At last, she was in the Great Hall for the grand dinner. There were fifteen courses (including a full roast peacock, its bright feathers returned to its carcass). The feast took four hours from beginning to end, though Issa could only take small bites of the most delicate dishes, roasted fish and poached eggs, or fruit compotes.

After the feast, King Haikor stood and clapped

his hands to get the attention of the court. Issa stared at Lady Pippa, who rose to stand beside him, noticing that she seemed slightly thicker around the waist than before. Issa glanced around the room, wondering how many others had seen this. Of course, King Haikor would want more heirs, but Issa had not thought it would happen so soon.

What did this mean for her and Edik's betrothal? Or Kellin and Ailsbet's?

"There is another joyous announcement to be made," said King Haikor. "After our two betrothals today, there is to be a royal wedding. And this time, not a prince and princess to be joined, but a king and queen." He bent down and kissed Lady Pippa, and the applause from the court was thunderous.

Issa looked down and saw that Edik's hands were clenching the sides of the table.

She whispered into his ear, "Do not show anything but happiness." Did he understand the danger he was in?

"This should be my day, mine and yours. Why could he not have waited?"

"He is the king," said Issa. And he had never been known for his patience, she thought.

"Lady Pippa is to take the queen's chambers now, and she will be called queen-in-waiting," said King

Haikor. "She will be queen when we are married in one month's time."

Issa clenched her jaw and held tightly to Edik's hand. She thought of the five long years until she and Edik were married and wondered when Kellin and Ailsbet's final binding would occur. The king had seemed so eager for them to marry, but he had not yet set a date. Now it seemed likely that would be postponed until after the king's own wedding.

The dinner went on with more toasting to the king and his bride-to-be, and Issa only pretended to sip from her cup. As the celebration was winding down, she realized Edik had fallen asleep in his chair.

At the same moment, Issa and Kellin stood to excuse themselves from the table. Edik woke but was too groggy to do more than wave to Issa. Ailsbet stood and moved to Kellin's side, eager to seize the opportunity to leave.

"Congratulations on your betrothal, Princess Marlissa," said Kellin formally as the three neared the door.

"Thank you," said Issa, "and my congratulations to you on your betrothal. You and Princess Ailsbet." She wished she sounded more genuine, but she was not at her best and did not know when she would be again. In time for Kellin and Ailsbet's marriage, perhaps.

Chapter Thirty-two
Ailsbet

THE FOLLOWING DAY AT DINNER, King Haikor filled the room with energy and his excitement about the coming birth of his new heir. There would be an autumn hunt two days hence in celebration, he announced. The last hunt Ailsbet remembered was the one at which Lord Umber had been killed, but no one spoke of that. This time, the ladies of the court would be invited, and King Haikor specifically announced that Prince Edik would come. To prove his place as King Haikor's heir, presumably, with his taweyr.

"You must be wary," said Kellin, when he walked

with Ailsbet to her chambers after dinner. "In a hunt, with animals about, it will be difficult to keep from showing your taweyr."

Ailsbet knew that he was right. This would be one of many occasions when she must avoid revealing herself as ekhono. Was that the life she wanted? No. She must leave. As long as Kellin watched after Edik, she could go with nothing on her conscience.

After the hunt, Ailsbet decided, she would get final word to Ambassador Belram and flee Rurik for Aristonne. But until that moment, she would let no one know of her intentions. Not a hint, even to Kellin.

"Do you wish me to take some taweyr from you, as your father does in tax?" asked Kellin.

Ailsbet shook her head, thinking of the men she had seen giving her father taweyr and how weak they were afterward. "I have kept my taweyr secret for years now. I think that I can manage this time, as well."

This one last time, she thought.

"I know that you have done it before. But on a hunt? Your father has not allowed you on hunts since you were a child."

"True," Ailsbet admitted.

"Since you came into the taweyr, perhaps," said Kellin. "But you know that the weyrs in Rurik are out of balance. The taweyr is too strong in the forest. It is like a deluge. Irresistible."

"What should I do, then?" asked Ailsbet.

"If you will not let me take some of the taweyr from you, then keep away from the men," said Kellin. "Stay with the women and the tamer horses."

"If you insist," said Ailsbet.

"Or stay at the palace," said Kellin. "It would be safer for you here. And if you stay, then perhaps Issa would be allowed to stay, as well."

"My father will certainly expect all four of us to be there, to prove his grip on the throne is strong," said Ailsbet.

Kellin sighed. "I should have given you instruction before now."

Ailsbet could feel her taweyr rising up, and she pushed it back down. She had no intention of letting Kellin see how close she was to losing control.

"Tell me something. A hint, if I get in trouble," said Ailsbet.

"If you get in trouble, there is no help for any of us. The taweyr will burst out of you," said Kellin soberly. "You must stop it before there is the least hint of trouble."

"Then tell me how to do that," Ailsbet spoke impatiently.

"It is not so easy as that. We must be away from the palace to practice. Just keep yourself from getting angry."

Ailsbet took a breath. "If ever—" she began, hoping to give a hint of a good-bye to Edik through Kellin.

But a pair of servants came by and interrupted, and once they were gone, Kellin had already begun to think about something else. "What was it you were saying?" he asked.

"Nothing," said Ailsbet, changing her mind. "Nothing at all. I shall see you at the hunt."

"Until then," said Kellin, leaving her at the door of her chambers.

Ailsbet went to Edik's room. He looked as though he had been crying.

"I hate hunting," said Edik.

"You have to be there," said Ailsbet.

Edik nodded.

"You must say nothing to Lady Pippa. And only answer Father with obedience."

"I hate him," said Edik.

"You hate him now, but you will grow older and stronger. And he may grow softer in his later years."

"Softer? Ailsbet, the taweyr makes him more unpredictable, angrier. Sometimes I wonder if I shall be glad never to get it back. I feel well quit of it now."

"Don't say that," Ailsbet said.

"Why not? It poisons him as much as he ever poisoned our mother. Who else will he kill? We are all in danger near him. If I could leave here, I would."

Ailsbet's heart pinched in her chest. She was taking the easy way out for herself, by leaving Edik behind, an Edik who was becoming wiser and more mature. Was she a coward? But she would leave the kingdom to him. It would be her proof that she trusted him.

"You have Issa," she said.

"I have Issa," said Edik. "If she marries me in five years. But I don't expect her to admire me after what she has seen of me so far."

"She wants to help you and Rurik," said Ailsbet. Did Edik know of the prophecy?

"She can help pick up the pieces that I make of it and myself," he said sourly.

"There will be no pieces, Edik. All will go well," said Ailsbet. "You will see. You have learned a great deal and now you know where the dangers are. You will think like a prince and say and do what is right."

"I shall try, Ailsbet," he said.

Staying with him would not help him, Ailsbet

decided, and it might well make it worse. Her taweyr had already confused things. Edik's grooms-men might still be alive if Ailsbet had not made the mistake of using her taweyr for her brother. How many other lives would she save by leaving and giving up her taweyr?

"Once Lady Pippa has a son," said Edik. "Then it will not matter what I do, will it?"

"It may not be a son," said Ailsbet.

"Then she and my father will try again, until they succeed," said Edik.

"And what if their offspring are all sickly and die?" said Ailsbet. "You cannot know. Lady Pippa is so young, and our father is so old. Such a match often results in children who do not survive."

"And we are left wishing for the death of an innocent child, are we?" said Edik bitterly.

But Ailsbet was not waiting for that. She was not waiting at all anymore. She had chosen her path, and now nothing could stop her from having her freedom.

Chapter Thirty-three

Ailsbet

WHEN AILSBET ARRIVED at the stables for the hunt, Princess Marlissa was already there, ready to mount her horse. There were more than a dozen other women already mounted, waiting patiently for the king. The men of the court were waiting to mount until the king arrived, and Ailsbet glanced out over them, counting more than thirty, mentally measuring their physical strength and their taweyr against her own. She did not know for certain, since she had never battled against them, but she had heard what they said about one another, and she had seen enough of their posturing to guess how much was true.

King Haikor came out next, wearing several gold chains around his neck, along with an elaborately embroidered red-on-black hunting coat. Ailsbet wore a far plainer black riding skirt. She thought her father would look better wearing something simple, but he did not ask her for fashion advice. Apparently, he had asked Lady Pippa, who was dressed in something similarly overwrought. She had come out to see everyone off, though she would not be riding in her condition.

Prince Edik was there, as well, sitting anxiously on his horse. His face was pale, and he looked small and out of place. Ailsbet waved to offer him some comfort, but he did not appear to see her.

When Kellin arrived, he greeted the king and prince warmly, then turned back to kiss Ailsbet gently as her betrothed. He whispered as he lingered near her, "Do you remember what I said about the taweyr?"

"I remember," said Ailsbet. Did he think she was an idiot?

"Be careful," he said.

"I shall. Am I usually so careless?" she asked sarcastically.

Kellin stared at her, and Ailsbet thought she saw a

glimpse of hurt in his eyes. But then he was gone, to join the men.

Soon all the hunters were mounted, and the noise of jingling harnesses and voices and horses was so much that Ailsbet could hardly hear herself think, let alone carry on a conversation.

"To the hunt!" said King Haikor at last. He set out quickly, so the others had to nudge their horses into a gallop to follow him. His mount was larger than any of the others, almost a draft horse, and it could not keep up this speed for long, but for a little while it made Haikor look, if not young, then at least like a much younger version of himself.

Ailsbet watched as Edik, with Kellin close at his side, chased after the king, with the other men not far behind. The women, while allowed on the hunt, knew they were not to get too close to the men, for fear of interfering with the taweyr. Ailsbet took care to stay with them, though at the very front of the women. Issa was close on her heels, though the other women remained far back, talking animatedly with one another as they would have at court.

Kellin looked back several times to see Ailsbet, and he nodded with approval. But she could feel the taweyr in the air. It had never been like this, not even when she was in the south country and had first realized she had the taweyr. Then, it had felt rich and thick, and easy to take hold of. Now it felt as if it were pressing on her, like heavy air being forced into her lungs. She had to concentrate on her breathing to keep from using it. It was not only King Haikor's taweyr, but the taweyr of all the men around him, and it was different out-of-doors than inside the court. The taweyr was freer here. It wanted to be free, and she had to stifle it.

Ailsbet normally thought of herself as a good rider, but she found herself struggling to relax on the horse, trying to force the animal to her own pace. It would not listen to her, and the more she fought with it, the farther back she fell from the other women.

The royal forest was just on the west side of the palace gates, away from the river, near the hills where the battle with Aristonne had been fought. The trees were old oaks that had been growing for many generations, tall and thickly leaved so that there was little light allowed beneath them. The forest floor was dark, nearly black, and the heat was oppressive, made more so by the moisture trapped in the air.

Ailsbet relaxed for a moment and found herself alongside Issa.

"It is so strange here," said Issa, her face troubled.

"So little neweyr in a place where I would have expected so much."

"My father thinks of the woods as his own," said Ailsbet. "Is it difficult for you?"

"I am used to so much taweyr by now," said Issa. "But I am disappointed that it is this way even here."

"Perhaps it will be good for Edik," Ailsbet suggested.

Issa sighed. "Have you spoken to Edik about his taweyr?"

"He says he feels it returning to him. That might mean he is coming into his own taweyr at last. But then again, he is sure that he has had it all along, and that it has been stolen from him. He thinks he has only to wrest it back."

"You see no similarities between him and yourself?" asked Issa.

"In the taweyr?" Ailsbet shook her head. "I know so little. He should speak to Kellin about it." Since she would be gone. "Perhaps you could ask Kellin to bring it up with him."

"Kellin and I do not speak anymore. It does not seem wise," said Issa.

"I do not think that is the right course for you. On the contrary, you should speak to Kellin as often as you can, and in full view of others," said Ailsbet. She did not know if she and Issa were friends, but she felt she owed her some last, parting gift of advice.

"But when we speak—" Issa reddened. "We always do more than speak."

"You must practice not falling into temptation," said Ailsbet. Just as she must do, herself, with her taweyr.

"It is easy for you to say," said Issa.

Easy for Ailsbet to say? No, it wasn't. Just because she was not in love, that did not mean that she did not have feelings.

After this conversation, Ailsbet rode out ahead, spurring her horse past Issa and the other women, until she was nearly closing in on the men. The smell of the forest was intoxicating, and the sight of the animals darting out all around her only made her want to follow them. She let go.

She realized that this was where she felt truly herself. She loved the feeling, hot and heady and open. It made her feel as broad as the whole forest, and not crammed into a tiny space in a castle.

There was music all around her, natural music. She could hear it in the wind that whipped around her face, rushing through her hair. She could hear it in the cawing of birds overhead, in the thumping of her own heart, in the cadence of the horse's hooves, in the dance of her father's hounds just ahead of her.

She could hear everything as she never had before. She heard the horn calling out ahead of her, signaling to the hounds that a stag had been sighted.

But Ailsbet already knew he was there. She could see the weight of him, the color of his golden hide, the tines on his antlers so heavy that it did not seem he could stand upright. She smelled the blood in his veins, and felt the thirst in his dry throat as he passed by the river crossing, not daring to stop. He was afraid, but he was also full of excitement. His senses were keener than ever before, and he loved the feel of his hooves against the dirt of the forest floor, challenging him every second to go faster.

Ailsbet felt his urgency, his heat, and his speed. She pushed her face into her horse's neck and dug in her heels. She smelled the forest and the taweyr and the freedom and the wholeness that was here.

There was a voice calling behind her, but Ailsbet ignored it. She could not ignore the rush of blood in the men ahead of her, like the stag himself. That was where she belonged, with them.

She could hear her father shouting at Prince Edik to hurry, to go ahead, to ride close behind the hounds. She could see and hear and smell and feel and taste so many things at once. Death was all around her, though its presence made life seem more real.

Every male creature in the forest stood out for her like a beacon in the darkness. Ailsbet could see them turn and stare at her as she passed. They were blood and death, war and violence, mastery and victory, bloodthirst and terror.

Then came the moment when Ailsbet had broken free of the trees and the women were so far behind her she did not think of them. She looked up and there was the great golden stag in all his glory before her, with a true crown on his head. No need for jewels here, the twisting tines of the rack were a beautiful, unconscious pattern that nothing man-made could match. Ailsbet wanted that crown for herself.

The men had turned one way, but the stag had doubled back. She was only yards away from him, closer than anyone else.

She did not see Edik or King Haikor anywhere.

But Kellin was there, staring at her with a look of utter shock on his face. He covered it, and then tried to chase after her, but this only spurred her on faster. She would not allow him to beat her to the stag. She had to kill him and claim her victory.

The stag stared at her as if he understood her thoughts, and then he fled.

Ailsbet followed close behind, keeping her head low so the wind passed over her easily.

She could feel the stag losing strength. He was hot and lathered, and his heart was beating wildly. In a moment, he would fall, or he would have to slow, and she would be there to offer him death with taweyr.

Ailsbet could feel the hounds closing, nipping at her horse's hooves.

Then she turned a corner, and the hounds went the wrong way. She let out a cry of happiness that was cut short when the stag stumbled and fell, and her horse leaped over him. The stag regained his feet as she quickly pulled back on her reins, and then she was looking into the eyes of the wild great creature.

She slid off her horse. Now the stag was conquered, and he was begging her for death. That was the way of the natural world. She had no weapon to kill him with, but she did not need one. She pressed her hand to his chest and she twisted his heart inside.

His eyes rolled up in his head and he fell forward toward her, his great body knocking her over, trapping her legs.

The king's hounds came up around her, barking.

Suddenly, Ailsbet felt ill, as if someone had

slammed a bar of iron into her stomach and chest. Her breath caught in her throat, and she did not know if she would breathe again.

"Princess Ailsbet!" called out a familiar voice. Issa.

She wanted something urgently, but Ailsbet could not think what.

She could not move.

The men on horses drew up behind her, but like the hounds, they did not come too close.

"No!" bellowed King Haikor. "It's not possible. Not my daughter!"

And then Ailsbet realized what she had done. Kellin had warned her. He had offered to take her taweyr, but she had wanted to keep it. And so the taweyr had taken control of her. Now she had shown herself here, in front of everyone. Could there be any doubt how she had killed the wild stag?

"Ekhono," was the shout all around her.

Issa stared at her, as Kellin came up behind her, too late to help. Ailsbet could see the sorrow on his face, mingled with guilt. And she did not care. Though she was exhausted now, drained of taweyr, she was still glad that she had done what she had. She had never known that the taweyr could feel so good.

Ailsbet could feel her father's cold, controlled

taweyr like a ring around her, closing tighter and tighter around her neck, dragging her out from underneath the stag.

"She didn't mean to," said Edik, confused. "Let her be. It must be the ekhono. They gave her my taweyr."

But King Haikor pushed his son aside and thrust Ailsbet to her knees. "Ekhono," he spat at her. "In my own palace, there you were. You have always been there, stealing taweyr from me and from your brother. And I never guessed it. All the problems in the last years, I thought were from rebellious lords lurking at the edges of my power. I kept searching for them and executing those who demonstrated the least hint of defiance. But I never looked at you."

Of course not. She was his daughter, and therefore insignificant. He had never imagined that she might matter.

He slid off his horse and stood above her. Spent and exhausted, Ailsbet used all her remaining strength to lift her head and stare back at him.

"You are not my child," said King Haikor. "You never were."

This hurt more than Ailsbet had expected. "My mother—" she began.

"Your mother cuckolded me. I do not know who your father was."

"That is ridiculous. Everyone knows I am your daughter," said Ailsbet.

"You are not my daughter. No daughter of mine could be ekhono. So there must have been some mistake. And now you will pay for your crimes. To the Tower with her," he cried to his guards.

The ropes that had been brought to string up the great stag and display him were instead turned on Ailsbet. King Haikor used his own taweyr to bind her hands. And Ailsbet could not fight back. Not now that her taweyr was spent. She did not know how long it would take to come back. A day? Or more? She did not know how much she had used. There was far too much she did not know.

Chapter Thirty-four

Issa

*I*SSA WATCHED AS PRINCESS AILSBET was taken away, hands tied behind her back, pulled along by the invisible force of King Haikor's taweyr. She was limp and silent, an animal carried back from the hunt to be slaughtered and drained. King Haikor had followed on his horse, looking murderous. Would Ailsbet survive the trip to the Tower?

Issa would not trust King Haikor for anything.

Prince Edik glanced back at Issa, and then at his father. Could he see Issa's guilt on her face? She had known the truth about Ailsbet and had not told him or even hinted at it, and so he had been surprised like this about his own sister. Issa could not bear to face him now, and he moved forward without her. The whole court went with him.

"Let me see you safely back to the palace," said Kellin a moment later.

And so she and Kellin had a private moment, and it was the least romantic thing she could imagine.

"I asked to take some of her taweyr before the hunt, but she wouldn't let me," Kellin said. "She could not control it in the forest. Think what she might do with that power, if she were allowed. She could be a queen of the like that we have never seen before."

Issa felt a pang of jealousy. Did he think Ailsbet would be a better queen than she?

"And yet she is made into a criminal, like any other ekhono."

"I shall help her," said Issa.

"What?"

"Somehow, I shall make sure she is free and safe. I shall make Haikor give her up." And then she could offer her refuge in Weirland, like the other ekhono.

"That is unlikely, Issa," said Kellin. "King Haikor cannot afford to let it seem that you can sway him on this point."

"What is the good of being a princess?" demanded Issa. "All my life, I believed that it was so that I could use myself for the sake of others." Kellin reached for her hands, but she drew away from him. "If I can save her, I should risk what I must."

"Issa, Haikor has hated the ekhono all his life," said Kellin. "And to see his own daughter show herself so publicly like that—he must destroy her."

"Then he will destroy me as well," said Issa fiercely. Nothing that she had believed in seemed to matter anymore, the prophecy, the betrothal with Edik, the treaty with Rurik. At this moment, even her feelings for Kellin seemed false, since they had to be hidden and kept secret. The only thing that was real and honest in the time she had spent in the palace was what Ailsbet had shown of herself. Issa felt that she owed the other princess for that.

"No!" said Kellin. "You must stay away from her. You must give every impression of disgust when she is mentioned in your presence. For my sake, if not for your own. And for Edik's sake."

She could not simply throw herself away, Issa realized with reflection. She still had a duty to her kingdom and her people. "Help me help her, then," said Issa.

Kellin put a hand to her chin and lifted it. "You are right. We will not give up the fight."

At that, Issa felt a new strength that had nothing to do with the neweyr.

"In the Throne Room," said Kellin. "I shall speak first."

Issa nodded. He was not trying to stop her. He simply thought he had the better chance.

They made their way back to the palace, then parted at the stables.

Issa went to her rooms and changed out of her riding clothes into one of her new court dresses, a dusky rose-colored velvet. Then she went to the Throne Room.

It was not as full as usual, but King Haikor was there, with Lady Pippa at his side, both still in riding clothes. What surprised Issa was that Prince Edik was standing before his father, head held high, his body rigid with grief and anger.

"I shall not listen to your defense of her," said King Haikor. "And the fact that you say anything for her sake tells me only that my betrothed, Lady Pippa, has been right about you all along."

Issa felt a sick twist in her stomach. She had never imagined that Edik would do anything but return to his own chambers after the hunt. But here he was, fighting for his sister with no help.

"You are no more my son than she is my daughter. I should have seen it from the first. You do not look like me. You are not like me in any way."

"If I am not like you, then I am glad of it," said Edik.

No! Issa wanted to shout. She turned and saw Kellin, with her own despair reflected on his face. In thinking only of Ailsbet, they had both failed. They had believed that Edik was weak, and here he was, proving them wrong. He was thirteen years old, and he had not come into his full taweyr, but he was proving himself as brave as any man.

He knew the consequences. He knew that he could well die this day, this moment, at his father's hand.

Haikor put up a hand and looked sharply at Lady Pippa.

Whatever she had tried to convince the king to do, Issa would never know. She could only guess.

Haikor closed his eyes and seemed to make a decision. "Edik of Rurik, stand and listen to my decree," he said. "You are not my son. You are henceforth banished from the kingdom of Rurik for the rest of your born days. If ever you are seen here again, you will be brought to the Tower for execution."

Issa groaned. Edik, banished? What would he do? Where would he go? Could she bring him to Weirland with her?

King Haikor continued, "You are to give up the title *prince of Rurik*. You may keep your own name, if you choose to. You must never refer to King Haikor as your father." No mention of Princess Ailsbet as his sister.

"If you agree to these terms, you will be granted the sum of a thousand gold coins to ease your passage."

A thousand gold coins? Edik could go anywhere he chose with that, even to Aristonne.

"You must give up your betrothal to Princess Marlissa of Weirland. She is no longer bound to you but free to marry another," said King Haikor.

Issa was surprised for a moment, but then realized it was not that King Haikor was trying to spare her feelings. He just wanted to strip Edik of another part of his identity. And to make sure that Edik would not flee to Weirland and plot against him there.

"You will leave now and prepare yourself to flee the palace," Haikor continued. "You may take your own clothing, but no jewels and no crown. Nothing belonging to your mother, nothing given to you by your father, no remembrance of your place as prince."

Edik's clothing was filthy, his hair matted, and his face was smeared with tears and dirt, but he held his head high.

"You may not speak to anyone except to answer 'yes' or 'no' while you yet remain on the soil of Rurik. You may not ask servants for aid. You may not elicit conversation or sympathy from your peers," King Haikor added.

"I agree," said Edik, as if he were impatient to have this over with.

"Then go now. You have until dawn."

Edik brushed past Issa as if he did not recognize her. It seemed as though the part of not speaking to anyone would be no hardship to him.

In one day, the king had lost both his heirs. The only one he had remaining was the one in Lady Pippa's belly.

She had no reason to be here now, Issa thought. Her betrothal was over. She was free again. She could marry Kellin. The prophecy could no longer be fulfilled. Why could they not have happiness, then? As long as they did not feel guilt over leaving Ailsbet behind.

"King Haikor, I must ask you regarding your daughter," said Kellin when the Throne Room was quiet again.

Everyone stared at him.

King Haikor raised a hand. "I have neither son nor daughter," he said sharply.

Kellin's eyes met Issa's for a moment. Then he turned back to Haikor.

"To execute a princess would set a bad precedent," said Kellin in an even, reasonable tone. "My only concern is for Your Majesty, of course. But the crown you wear must be seen as inviolate, your blood superior to others. Even if she is no longer a princess, think of what ideas it might give."

King Haikor thought a moment. "Are you suggesting that there might be a rebellion against me, Duke Kellin?" he asked, a note of danger in his voice.

"No, nothing of the kind. I would never—"

"Then there is no threat to me. I should think that executing a princess, as you call her, would be a good warning that no one is above my law."

Kellin set his jaw. "I shall speak plainly, Your Majesty. If you banish Edik and execute Ailsbet, think of the succession of the crown. As of this moment, you have no legitimate heir." He nodded to Lady Pippa.

"And even if the infant is born soon, it will not be fit to rule in your place for many years. If anything were to happen to you before then, the kingdom of

Rurik would descend into chaos. It would be very easy for Weirland or one of the kingdoms of the continent, even Aristonne, to sweep us into their power," he continued.

The possibility of Weirland taking control of Rurik, or Aristonne, Haikor's lifelong enemies, would surely be enough to make the king reconsider his decisions, thought Issa.

"I intend to live a long time yet. And there are other heirs, though not as closely related, perhaps," said King Haikor. "You have had your head turned by the ekhono woman somehow, though I cannot think it is because of beauty, for she has none. But now that she has revealed herself, you must see it all truly. Whatever you felt for her was false. Who knows what she took from you or forced you to feel?"

"Then remember that she is a woman," said Kellin at last. "A little mercy for her, Your Majesty?"

King Haikor said, "She will die. She is an affront to my name and my place. I shall not hear her name spoken in my presence again."

There seemed nothing else Kellin could do. He took a breath and bowed deeply. "As you wish, Your Majesty." He looked up and added quietly, "May I ask when she will die?"

"When I find an axe sharp enough and a man able

to wield it at my bidding. Though it would be faster, neither I nor any other man would dare use taweyr directly on her. Think what it might do to us," said King Haikor. "But when she is dead and burned, her ekhono power will finally be destroyed."

At this, Issa fled to her rooms. She did not think that Haikor even noticed her. Kellin had done what he could. Now it was her turn.

She waited until the small hours of the morning and then slipped out of her room. Her hands shook as she walked across the courtyard, toward the Tower.

Chapter Thirty-Five
Ailsbet

The Tower was cold and uncomfortable. Ailsbet knew it was ridiculous, but that was all she could think of, that and the ache of hunger in her stomach. She was going to be executed. She should be worried about that, and about her brother, Edik, and what he would face in her father's court without her. And Issa and Kellin. She should worry about the two islands and the two weyrs, and the prophecy itself. She should worry about the music that she would never write or play for the court of the Prince of Aristonne because she would be dead.

Instead, she tossed and turned through the dark

night, wishing that she had a cushion to lie on instead of the bare stone bench. Shivering, she held her arms around her shoulders and tucked her knees into her chest. She tried to find the heat of the taweyr inside of her, but she had used too much of it and it was gone.

As the sun brought color to the sky, she looked out her window onto the Tower Green below and saw that everything seemed miniaturized, as if they were all part of a set of metal figures, like Edik's toy soldiers. It made her dizzy and she had to hold herself upright. She felt as if she could not breathe. The air was too thin; there were clouds wisping by; even the birds and the treetops were below her.

She closed her eyes, and felt the Tower sway with the breeze, hearing the stones straining against the mortar that held them together. Suddenly, she turned away from the window and fell to her knees, retching, though there was little left in her stomach but water. When she was finished, she turned her back to the window and did not look outside again.

She had seen the Tower every day from the palace. She had always thought how impressive it was. It was quite a different experience when one was inside of it.

Yesterday, she had climbed the steps herself, with the king's guards behind her. She had counted the steps, four hundred and thirty-five, and had asked if she was at the top of the Tower.

"The very top," said one of the guards. And then he had locked the door behind her, and she was left to face the stink of some previous inhabitants and to slowly add to it herself. The smell of fear was rank and moldy and sour.

Ailsbet had thought silence would be bad enough, but the sounds of the Tower were far worse than no music at all. It was the kind of music a tortured man would make, sighings and groanings and then, at unpredictable intervals, a scream that might or might not have been human.

How did her father make sure the prisoners did not use their taweyr to escape? No doubt he drained them before sending them here, and then killed them before they had time to recover it. Or he starved them until they were too weak to use it.

Suddenly, Ailsbet was startled at the sound of footsteps, followed by a thumping on the door.

"Stand back!" called a guard's rough voice.

Ailsbet took a deep breath, then looked up as the door opened. To her surprise, there stood Issa.

"No," gasped Ailsbet. Issa was the last person who should be here. "Take her away!" she told the guard.

He smirked at her. "You're no princess anymore, to tell me who comes and goes now. She paid me to let her in, and so I let her in. No one will ever know, once you're dead." He closed the door behind them, and Ailsbet was chilled at the sound of the lock clanging back into place.

"You shouldn't have come," she said.

"You sound like Kellin," said Issa.

"You should listen to him," said Ailsbet. "Kellin knows King Haikor well." If Issa could maintain her betrothal with Edik, perhaps that was the best that anyone could hope for.

"Kellin is not well loved of the king today," said Issa. "He spoke on your behalf. He thought you should be banished as your brother will be, instead of executed."

"My brother will be banished?" said Ailsbet. She had hoped that Edik would not be touched by this scandal. But she should have known that her father would make sure everyone suffered because of his displeasure.

"At least, he will live," said Issa.

Ailsbet shrugged. She knew already that she would not. "And what of you?" she asked.

"I don't know. Now that the betrothal is at an end, there is no reason for me to remain here."

"Yes, go home. You will be safe there."

"For a little while, perhaps," said Issa.

King Haikor wanted Weirland, thought Ailsbet. What Issa had hoped to prevent would come regardless: the two islands at war, the two weyrs more apart than ever before.

"And I shall be without Kellin," said Issa. "When I need him most."

"Why without him? He should go with you. You should both go, as soon as you can." Kellin could not want to stay here now, no matter how loyal to Rurik he claimed to be. With Edik banished and Ailsbet gone, with the feckless Lady Pippa at King Haikor's side, there would be no safety for anyone.

"I shall not go until you are free," said Issa.

Ailsbet shook her head. "It is useless to do that. Take care of yourselves while you can. I am a lost cause."

"Kellin and I shall not go until we are certain there is nothing left to do for you."

"I thank you for coming, and for trying to help me. But now you must leave," said Ailsbet. "Go to the door and call the guard back. He has not gone far. Go home to Weirland and take Kellin with you. Be happy there. Truly, that is the best thing to do for me. I shall think of you until the very end, and I shall share a little of your happiness."

"There must be some way to save you," said Issa stubbornly. "Kellin is still your betrothed. Perhaps he can once again petition the king to save you." She knew Kellin had not been successful yesterday, but she still thought that as the king's favorite, he might have another chance to sway King Haikor.

Ailsbet shook her head. "Please. I do not want to die knowing that I stole anything from Kellin. Rather ask him to spit on the memory of me, to refuse to say my name, to declare that he hates me now for my betrayal of all he thought of me, and that he will be at my execution to laugh in my face."

"Kellin does not hate you," said Issa.

"Then he can act the part. He is very good at acting," said Ailsbet. "And he knows how to protect himself well. He has been doing it for a very long time."

"He has never been protecting himself," said Issa. "It is always someone else. His brother, Kedor, or me or you or the kingdom of Rurik itself."

Ailsbet did not argue.

Issa put a hand on Ailsbet's. "It is so cold here. So cold and hard."

"Yes," said Ailsbet.

"How do you bear it?"

"When there is no other choice, it can be done," said Ailsbet.

"How I envied you!" said Issa. "Your strength. Your independence."

"You envied me?" said Ailsbet bitterly. She could not see how that was possible.

"You do not see yourself clearly if you do not see why," said Issa.

"But you are the one who has the enviable life," said Ailsbet. "You have a father you are not ashamed of. People who love you. You have the proper weyr, and you know how to use it. You have Kellin."

"And you have your music. And your certainty. You have the courage to show your true self, to challenge your father."

"That was not courage," said Ailsbet. "I did not know what I was doing. The taweyr drove me. I assure you, if I had been in control of myself, I would not have done it. I would have been safe instead of courageous."

Issa let out a laugh. "I do not know if I believe you. You have never been safe, Ailsbet. And I always have been."

Perhaps she had been, but it was not true anymore,

Ailsbet thought. "You will live to change the world," she declared.

"Or to see it end," said Issa.

"But you will live. You will do something."

"You will leave a mark," said Issa. "I promise you that."

And Ailsbet would have to be content with that much. She could have no more.

Then came the sound of the footsteps once more, and Issa was forced to leave, while Ailsbet was left alone.

Chapter Thirty-six
Issa

WHEN ISSA RETURNED to the palace in the bright light of morning, it was abuzz. There were servants in every hallway, but they looked away when they saw her. At last, she heard voices and flattened herself around a corner to eavesdrop.

"Prince Edik. Yes, cold as stone this morning. He was to be gone, but the guard called and called for him. Finally, someone went to fetch him out of his bed to ask if he wanted to meet the executioner with his sister—"

With a sinking heart, Issa moved toward the

servants who were speaking and demanded more information. "Tell me what you know. Did you see him yourself or is this a rumor you are passing about?"

The man seemed affronted. "I didn't find him, if that's what you mean, but I saw him on his bed, still as death. His lips were closed, but his eyes were open. He looked like he'd been covered in ash." He did not seem to realize he was speaking to Princess Marlissa.

"Did you call the physician?" she asked.

He shrugged. "He came and said the same that we all knew. Dead hours ago. Poisoned."

Just as his mother had been poisoned. Edik was dead, not merely banished. Issa should have known it would happen this way, no matter what King Haikor had promised.

The man continued, "The only question now is—who did it? Duke Kellin, do you think? To show the king his loyalty? Or one of the other nobles?"

Issa was angry enough that her neweyr sprang up out of her. A vine grew from the edge of the palace through the cracks in the walls and up the floor beneath the servant's feet. It pressed him back and pinned him against the wall.

She was ashamed of herself, using the neweyr in

this way, and let him go. He and his companion fled silently down the hallway.

She went to Edik's rooms herself, realizing only then that she had never been to them before. She knocked, but no one answered and the door was not locked. She stepped inside, smelling something sweet and rank. She wrinkled her nose. She saw no sign of Edik's body in his inner chamber. The bed was stripped, but the room looked as if it had not otherwise been touched. There were metal soldiers on the floor, as if Edik were to return any moment to play with them. She noticed a piece of paper and bent down to see a crude drawing of a hound. It was Midnight, the black puppy she had given Edik. Had the king poisoned Midnight, as well? She would never be able to ask Edik what he thought now. Issa wiped away tears at the sight of this last memento of the prince.

"Good-bye, Edik," she said quietly, and stepped out of the room, returning swiftly to her own chambers.

Issa sat before her fire and thought what she might do while Ailsbet was still alive. There was only one choice that had any hope, but it felt wrong, a betrayal of all she had ever believed in, but she could not leave Rurik knowing that she had not done all she could for the other princess. The execution was set for the morning of the following day, so she did not have much time.

Issa put on her best gown, made of golden silk. She struggled without the help of maids, to do up the stays and put on the sleeves. At last, she put on her stockings and shoes.

When she was finished, she perfumed herself with rose water and rouged her cheeks. She tucked tiny wildflowers that she drew up out of the floor of the palace into her loose, unbraided hair and went to the Throne Room to appear before King Haikor. Lady Pippa was sitting in the queen's smaller throne, but Kellin was not there, and Issa felt relieved at his absence.

"I have come first to ask you of your own free will to release Princess Ailsbet from the Tower," said Issa to the king.

"Release her?" said King Haikor. "She is a princess no longer and therefore qualifies for no royal mercy. In addition, she is ekhono, and all my life, I have hunted and killed her kind. What reason is there for me to do differently with her?"

Issa raised her chin and spoke loudly enough that no one could mistake her words. "Because I am the woman with taweyr."

The effect on King Haikor's court was immediate. Lady Pippa shrieked and stood up, pretending to swoon. Her ladies cried out and hurried to her side. The men of the court drew back as if Issa had threatened them physically, raising their weapons.

King Haikor was the only one who remained calm. "Impossible," he said. "We all saw what she did."

"Did you? I was right there, on the horse directly behind her. And besides, with the taweyr, there is no need to be close enough to touch, is there? You have killed men a battlefield away, have you not?"

"I know what I saw," said King Haikor. "I was there. Many witnesses were there."

"Yes, but I purposely misled them, and you. I have both the taweyr and the neweyr, and I come to show them to you today."

"Impossible," said King Haikor.

"Ah, but it is not." Then Issa made sure that all in the room heard her clearly, for she wanted no mistake about the prophecy. "There is a prophecy that I learned of years ago, that the two islands will come together as one when the two weyrs are again joined in one person."

"The two islands come together? But the land itself has changed. Even the taweyr and the neweyr working together cannot alter that," said King Haikor.

"Can they not?" asked Issa. She thought of the servant she had trapped with her vines not long ago.

"Prove it, then," said King Haikor. "Prove that you have taweyr."

Closing her eyes briefly in order to focus, Issa pulled vines from the palace garden toward her, climbing them up the outer walls and into the mortared stone, keeping them hidden until they were underneath the marble floor directly beneath King Haikor's throne.

Issa made sure the vines did not grow spindly, but kept their full heft and strength. Then with a cry, she opened her eyes and pulled them violently up underneath the marble floor where the throne was. The heavy, ashen chair, carved with roses, was thrust suddenly into the air and came crashing down. The marble floor beneath it was cracked, though the vines themselves could not be seen. Issa was relieved, for she could not reveal that she was using only the neweyr, and making it appear to be the taweyr.

King Haikor stared at the throne. "You—you are ekhono."

"I am a woman with both weyrs," said Issa, holding her head high, thinking of the prophecy and how it might frighten King Haikor that she had begun to fulfill it.

"A throne destroyed—that is a simple thing. Easily done," said King Haikor. "It means nothing." But his voice trembled.

He might not feel the power she had used as his own familiar taweyr, but he could not believe it was anything else. As far as King Haikor wished to believe, the neweyr could not do something like this.

"Do you wish me to prove myself a second time?" asked Issa. She had expected this, had prepared for it as much as she could.

King Haikor looked around the Throne Room, into the eyes of his nobles. He could see that they were astonished and afraid, terrified of the ekhono in their midst. Only Haikor himself was defiant.

"Yes," he said. "And do it unmistakably."

All this time, Issa had assumed that the taweyr was stronger than the neweyr, at least when it came to brute force. But she had never tried to use neweyr as a weapon before. Perhaps no one ever had.

Issa poured all her energy into her neweyr, and into the vines that she had sent under the throne. Now she threaded them back to the gardens where their roots lay and then toward the Tower itself. The first half of the distance was easy because the vines had already lengthened that far. But once she had to go beyond that, her neweyr felt strained.

When she felt the first stone of the Tower begin to shake under the onslaught of her vines, she let out a little gasp, noticing that the nobles in the Throne Room were suddenly looking out the windows. It took another stone falling before one of them realized that it was the Tower she was targeting.

King Haikor strode forward. "You cannot do this," he challenged her. "I know you cannot."

But he was wrong. He did not understand the neweyr. How could he? He had spent all his life ignoring it. He had not wanted to see that there was any part of power that was not his own. And that would be his downfall.

Issa told herself the neweyr here had long been buried, but only needed some coaxing to return to its normal strength. The courtyard of the palace was empty of visible greenery, but that did not mean the lifelessness went into the soil itself. She could feel the female animals around the palace and in the city as distinct pulses of blood and life. They seemed to recognize her in return, and welcome her, as her own animals would have done in Weirland.

The vines grew as she wished them to, as if it were spring, and she were drawing them out of the earth. But the violence she intended them to be used for made them harder, stiffer. She had changed them to the very core in some deep way, and she did not know what the results would be, in those vines or in the neweyr itself. She did not know if this change would be permanent. She continued forward with it anyway.

Still hiding the thick vines from sight, Issa broke open the door to the Tower and felt the outraged cries of the guards within. The one who had laughed so nastily at Ailsbet was the first to flee, with one glance up at the palace where King Haikor watched him. Eight other guards were at his heels.

"No! Stop!" the king shouted. He made his hand into a fist, and the fleeing guards shot up into the air, screaming. Then he threw his fist forward, and the guards came crashing down into the dirt.

Issa heard a terrible crunching sound. She looked up and saw that all the men lay on the ground, dead, their necks broken.

Those men died because of her actions, she reminded herself. It was the first time she had felt so guilty. She had done it with the neweyr, and now her father could never tell her that she did not understand what it meant to make the difficult decisions necessary to rule. It was a weighty feeling, and for a moment, the vines stopped growing, and she had to breathe deeply while her vision cleared.

It was another chance for her to stop, but she did

not do it. She put herself into the vines again and began to feel that they were like her own fingers. She had them climb the stairs of the Tower, always hidden so that they were beneath the stone and no one watching could see that it was the neweyr doing this work. It would look like the taweyr was cracking the stones one by one.

A gray dust filled the air of the Tower. Issa could see the dim figure of Ailsbet standing and moving to the door, looking out. She did not call for help or show any sign of terror.

She waited.

She trusts me, thought Issa.

And so she went on, using her neweyr from a distance, up and up, until she reached the door of Ailsbet's cell. With the vines exerting pressure, the door popped open with a tiny sound.

Ailsbet let out a cry of surprise and hurried down the stairs.

Issa made sure that Ailsbet had enough time to get out. Then she sent the vines up to the top of the Tower, and instead of going in a straight line now, they went in circles, boring inside the outer walls, splitting them apart stone by stone. She began to speed up as she realized how easy it was. She had only to look inside the stones for the weakness, the bit of life that remained in each one. For even stones were not fully dead. She had always known that, but she had never used it before.

King Haikor stood open-mouthed, and the nobles of his court let out a combined, hushed sound of awe as the Tower's uppermost level toppled over and dropped in bits and pieces to the ground.

The dust settled, and now Issa could see for herself what was left of the Tower. The top half had fallen, like a tree whose top branches had been clipped, or a moose with its antlers sheared off, or a man who had been beheaded.

Issa stared at it to make sure that no sign of any vines was visible. Then she found herself smiling, for she could not imagine anything she could have done that would have brought her more satisfaction. It was so right, this end of King Haikor's Tower, where he had sent so many men to wait for death. The neweyr had defeated the taweyr in the end. And no one knew it was neweyr but Issa.

She thought suddenly of the prophecy, and wondered if this was what it meant, not that the two weyrs would be joined together in actuality, but that they would appear to be joined. Could it be that easy? Had she fulfilled it already, and would the two islands be joined back together?

But there was no feeling of moving ground, of momentous change. The skies were as blue as before, and the silence seemed to grow more profound. King Haikor, of course, was the one to break it.

"My daughter," he said.

"She lives," said Issa. Did he care about her, after all?

"She is condemned to death," said King Haikor. "She is mine to punish."

"She is yours no longer," said Issa. "You gave her life to me when you told me to show you my taweyr."

The king's face hardened. "I shall not have you here in my court. You must leave now, this minute. I shall not tolerate your presence here. I should have you killed," he said.

"I shall take your daughter with me. To Weirland," Issa said.

"Never," said King Haikor in a low, threatening tone.

"She will go to the continent," said Kellin, stepping forward. "And I shall make sure she can never return. For she has injured me as much as she has you." His voice sounded harsh, as if he truly hated Ailsbet.

Issa almost believed it herself.

"Make sure she is gone, then." King Haikor

snapped his fingers at his remaining guards and gestured toward Issa. "Make sure this one is gone, as well."

Issa followed the guards out of the Throne Room, but when she looked out into the courtyard, she could see a hint of green poking out of the gray dirt, and she knew that whatever King Haikor thought about her actions, what she had truly done was to bring the neweyr back to the palace grounds, where it belonged.

CHAPTER THIRTY-SEVEN
Ailsbet

KELLIN FOUND AILSBET near the crumbling walls on the west side of the palace. She was heading toward the docks. Toward Ambassador Belram's promise and the flag of the swan of Aristonne, if she could still depend upon on it.

She started at the touch of his hand on her arm, then turned and let out a small gasp of delight. Clutching tightly to his shoulder, she asked, "How?"

"Issa claimed she had the taweyr herself," said Kellin. "She used neweyr, disguised as taweyr, to destroy the Tower as proof."

"Truly?" Ailsbet did not understand how it had been done. She suspected she would never know. "And now?" she asked Kellin.

"She will return to Weirland and prepare for what comes next," he said. "But I came to tell you about Edik."

"What is it?" asked Ailsbet.

"Edik is dead," said Kellin. "Poisoned in the night."

Ailsbet swayed, her stomach twisting like hot metal. Her taweyr had suddenly come back to her with a vengeance, and she wished to use it for precisely that. "My father," she said.

"He seems ready to go to war against Weirland," said Kellin. "I must do what I can to stop him." He sounded bleak and hopeless.

Ailsbet replied, "He is bloodthirsty, selfish, full of moods and passions, and unpredictable. He does nothing but what suits him at the moment, and he is getting worse, Kellin. There is only one way to stop him. You must see that."

Kellin shrugged. "For now, I promised him to see you gone from Rurik."

"I could battle him with my taweyr. I could be queen in his place." Hadn't Kellin said exactly that?

"You are drained," said Kellin. "And newly come

to your taweyr. You do not know how to use it properly. Your father has years of experience, as well as hundreds of men he can call on to give him tawyer in taxes. I thought that in time, you might find allies, and prepare for the right moment. But now?"

Ailsbet knew he was right. By showing her taweyr when she had, she had made it impossible to have any future other than one in Aristonne, banished from Rurik forever. She had been planning to choose it anyway, but it was less sweet knowing there was no other choice.

"And if you were to lie to him, to tell him that you had seen me off?" she asked.

"Why would I do that?"

"To keep me safely hidden away, in a place where you could come and teach me about the taweyr, and find supporters against him. There are many of his nobles who hate him."

"There are," Kellin agreed.

Ailsbet felt a stir of eagerness at the thought of fighting her father. "And would you take the risk with me?"

"Is that what you want?" asked Kellin.

It was a heady sensation, to think that she could rise up against her father and perhaps defeat him. The scenes of the battles her father had won came to her, depicted on stained-glass windows and tapestries all through the palace. She could be the one fighting him, but she could win. It was a strong temptation.

"I brought you this," said Kellin, and handed her her flute.

She took it from its case and put it to her lips. It immediately soothed her senses and dampened her pleasure at the thought of death. Was that why Kellin had brought it to her?

She stared at him. "Would you be loyal to me instead of to my father, if I asked it?"

He held out his hand. "Give me the flute and all your music, and promise me that you will give your-self wholeheartedly to the kingdom of Rurik and its people, and I shall," he said.

But music was the one thing she could never give up, and she had never cared so fervently about the people of Rurik and the kingdom as Kellin did. "I will go to Aristonne," she said at last. She would have her music and give up being princess. It was what she had always wanted.

And so Kellin took her to the dock.

Ailsbet nodded at the unweyr who were working there. She had never seen more than one at a time, but here were dozens all together, the rarest people in the two islands. They did not look so very different on the outside, but they were different. She would be like them soon enough, once she was out on the ocean.

She watched their concentrated faces, their strong muscles. They needed no weyr to add to who they were.

Yes, that was what she wanted.

This was who she was.

With Kellin at her side, Ailsbet approached the boat that flew the Aristonne flag and thought of Prince William. Ambassador Belram was waiting for her on the deck.

"King Haikor sent you this to help speed your journey," said Kellin, offering her a small bag of gold.

Ailsbet suspected this was from Kellin himself, but she did not argue with him. She loosened the purse and let one coin fall out into her hands. Her father's head was there, standing out in relief, worn very little.

"Thank you," Ailsbet whispered. "Thank you so much." She would have sent him away then, but Kellin insisted he must wait until he had seen her board the ship.

"To report to the king?" said Ailsbet.

"He is still my king," said Kellin.

The ship was much larger than Ailsbet had

imagined it would be, but when she stepped on board and felt the tip of the ocean for the first time, she could feel the pressure of the taweyr begin to ease inside of her. It took some time for the sailors to pull in the anchor and prepare to leave, and all that time, Kellin stood on the docks, watching her.

At last, the wooden deck of the ship seemed to come to life, and Ailsbet had to put a hand out to keep herself steady. Then she stood on the deck and watched as Kellin and Rurik grew smaller in the distance, and the ocean tore at her taweyr until she took out her flute and began to play.

Chapter Thirty-eight

Issa

THE NIGHT AFTER THE TOWER had been destroyed, Issa was ready to leave for Weirland with her few remaining servants. She and Kellin met just outside the palace gates, but his hands were empty of belongings, as if he had decided to leave everything of this life behind him.

He smiled at her, and she ran toward him. It was dark and unusually cold for early autumn, and she wished that she were already long gone from here, safe with the man she loved.

Breathless, she reached him and flung herself into his arms. It felt so good at last to be able to be with him without guilt. Edik was dead. Ailsbet was gone. Neither she nor Kellin could be held to their old betrothals. Issa wished she could have saved Edik, but she would not throw away her chance at happiness because of that.

She leaned into Kellin and kissed him. This time it was a tender kiss, soft and deep. There was passion in it that grew as the kiss continued, and Kellin pulled her closer. He seemed intent on proving how much he loved her, all in this one moment. But they had time together, she thought. They would have the rest of their lives.

He let her go at last, and she leaned her head against his chest in companionable silence.

"I have to tell you something," he said.

"What is it?"

"I cannot come with you immediately."

"Why not? Of course, you can, Kellin. You cannot stay here, not after you spoke up for Ailsbet in open court after King Haikor denied her name as his daughter. King Haikor might have looked on you as a favorite before, but not any longer."

"Just for a little while," said Kellin. "There are a few last things I must do here."

"A few last things? What are they? I shall help you do them, then, and we shall go together." Issa did not want to go back to Weirland alone, did not want to wait for him there.

"You cannot help me. I must make sure Rurik does not immediately descend into civil war. Issa, you must go back to Weirland now, with your servants to protect you. You are no longer safe here, now that King Haikor realizes you are a threat. Whether or not he discerns that you used the neweyr instead of the taweyr, you showed power against him that no one else ever has, and that may embolden others."

"How long do you think he will believe that it was taweyr?" asked Issa.

"As long as it suits him, I suspect. But I swear I shall come soon. Unless you are tired of waiting for me and ready to find another man who would be better suited to Weirland?"

"Of course not," Issa said. "I will never love anyone else but you. You must know that."

He kissed her again. "I like to hear it even so. And Issa, I will never love anyone but you. Promise me that you will trust me."

"But it is dangerous here in Rurik,." she said. "Now more than ever, with King Haikor so angry and anxious to prove himself."

"You must trust me. I have the taweyr. I know how it must be wielded for the best of both kingdoms. Do you argue with me on that point, now that you claim to have the taweyr yourself?"

"No, Kellin," said Issa.

"Then do not argue with me now. Trust me. I shall come to you. Nothing can stop me from doing that. I have hoped for too long to give up my chance with you now."

"King Haikor will try to stop you," said Issa.

"Let him try," said Kellin, and he kissed her one last time. Issa would have been glad for it to go on forever. She did not need to breathe so long as she had Kellin in her arms.

But he pulled away and helped her on her horse, and she rode off with her servants, leaving Kellin behind to prove that their love would be stronger than King Haikor's hatred.

Over the next few weeks, the company made its way north through Rurik to the land bridge and then home to Weirland. The weather was cold and wet as autumn marched on, but to Issa, the journey home seemed shorter than the earlier one. Word traveled ahead of her, and she was greeted by many people who had gathered at the gates to see her return. It was such a relief to be home that she had only just passed through the gates when she slid off her horse and let her feet touch the ground.

She let her sense of the neweyr spread out to include the whole palace, and then the kingdom beyond. There were her forests. There were the fields of grain ready for harvest. There were the streams and the sun-drenched orchards. There was her sky, her clouds, her winds. Her world. She had not ruined it with her misuse of the neweyr, after all.

But the castle, when she turned to it, looked smaller than it had been. Her father, too, seemed smaller as she greeted him formally. They retired to his chambers later, and she told him all that had happened in Rurik with Haikor and Edik and Ailsbet. Only what had happened privately with Kellin she left out. He did not interrupt her once, nor ask her questions when she was finished. There was a new relationship between them. She was no longer merely his daughter and a princess. She was not a queen, either, perhaps, but she was something else. It would have to be seen how useful she would be to her people and her kingdom now, and if she would ever again use the neweyr as a weapon.

Lady Neca was waiting outside her father's chambers to take her to her own.

"I am glad you have come back," said Neca.

"Am I back?" Issa asked.

Neca looked at her. "I think you will be, when

I've put your hair into a proper braid," she said.

Issa laughed ruefully and put her hands to her hair, which she had worn loose since she left King Haikor's palace, all through the journey north. It had bothered her, but she had not wanted to braid it in case it gave away too much of her identity. She had told the female servants in the party to wear their hair loose, as well. Such a simple thing, but it mattered so much. She had missed the single plait down her back. "Oh, Neca. You know just what to say, don't you?"

Neca spent the next hour teasing Issa's hair gently out of its tangles, sometimes with neweyr, sometimes with her own hands. Then she plaited it tightly and handed Issa a mirror to look at herself. The sight of herself in the mirror only added to her sense of being at home and at peace, at least for now.

"Do you truly have the taweyr?" asked Neca in her blunt fashion, which only made Issa realize how she had forgotten this way of speaking while in Rurik.

"No," said Issa easily. It felt good to tell the truth again.

She told Neca about Kellin now. Every detail, from their first meeting to their last one, and his promise to come after her.

"Does your father know?" asked Neca.

"Not yet, but I will tell him." She hoped her father would not object. She would tell him, in time.

But in the morning, she took Neca first with her to see Kedor. The young man had grown several inches since Issa had seen him last and looked full-grown now. Certainly, Neca seemed to treat him so, and as a consequence, Kedor paid very little attention to Issa at all.

She told Kedor that Kellin had promised to come to Weirland to see them both, and that he loved her.

"Trust him, then," said Kedor. "He has never broken a promise in his life."

"I must trust him." He must come back to her. She would wait however long she had to, so long as she knew that he was coming, and that they would be together at last.